FOR CAUSE

FOR CAUSE

A
3J LEGAL
THRILLER

MARK SHAIKEN

1609 Press LLC
Denver, Colorado

Mark Shaiken

Copyright © 2025 by Mark Shaiken

Published by 1609 Press LLC

Denver, Colorado

ISBN (print) 979-8-9908537-2-0

ISBN (eBook) 979-8-9908537-3-7

LCCN: 2025923873

Cover Design and Interior Layout by *Damonza.com*

Editing by Debbie Burke, Queen Esther Publishing LLC,

https://queenestherpublishing.com

First Edition

Printed in the United States of America

*To all my family and friends. I am
eternally grateful you are in my life.*

Chapter 1

THE VIDEO

Turn on any television station after hours and you're likely to see a fast-talking, sometimes boisterous attorney broadcast right into your living room, telling you he'll win all your cases. There are former client testimonials. Call the number on the screen, operators are standing by 24/7. Hire him and you'll win big bucks. His smile is as sincere as any door-to-door salesman's.

But he's not selling you a product. He's selling himself. And like any salesman, he's puffing. Bending the truth just a little.

News flash. Attorneys lose cases. Even the ones on late-night television. After all, in a trial of two parties, someone will win and someone will lose. It's just math. It's a simple system. Often, there's no way to predict who will win. Skilled, prepared attorneys lose. Unskilled, unprepared attorneys win.

The good ones learn to be better, not bitter. They learn they can't save everyone, and sometimes you can't save anyone. They learn they can't always save a client from himself. Sometimes clients withhold critical facts until it's too late for the attorney to do damage control. Sometimes opposing counsel drops a bombshell at the beginning or in the middle of an emergency hearing and the losing attorney has no way to foresee the bomb or the resulting wreckage of what had been, only moments before, a promising case.

᪥

"Your Honor, the banks call Paul Elkin to the stand."

Elkin took four minutes on the stand to explain his tech expertise. He said he had examined a video, and in his expert opinion, it was genuine. Opposing counsel played the video, and Elkin confirmed its authenticity. Opposing counsel then said to the court, "We offer this video into evidence as the Banks Exhibit 1."

That video changed everything.

᪥

The good ones learn to rationalize the losses and move on to the next case. And in the end, every attorney knows it's a wins and losses business. Winners get hired. It pays the bills. Hence, attorneys keep track of the wins and losses. It's their record, one of their metrics, just like a baseball pitcher's win-loss record.

And some attorneys take late-night television ads and puff up their metrics.

Most lawyers are aware of all this. She was. Yet, back at her desk, sitting alone after the hearing, she still pondered.

It wasn't perfect-posture sitting. It was rumination-sitting, and it looked like this: she hung her head down, her chin touching the top of her pressed white shirt. Elbows on the desk. Thumbs on her cheekbones. Pointer and middle fingers at the top of her forehead near her hairline. She was oblivious to the circular motions her fingers were tracing on her temples.

Josephina Jillian Jones, "3J" to her friends. The renowned Midwestern business bankruptcy attorney and partner at the famous Greene Madison law firm with offices high atop downtown Kansas City, Missouri. In solitary, silent defeat. Her mind raced, but despite working in overdrive, it gave her no discernible thoughts. Nothing apart from the knowledge that she was on the path to losing an important hearing and that her client was now sliding down the slippery slope to financial ruin courtesy of her failure to see the loss coming.

What happened?

∽

At first glance, it was uncomplicated. She filed a Chapter 11 bankruptcy case for her clients. The bankruptcy code requires all debtors to refrain from fraudulent conduct, act honestly, and have a modicum of managerial competence. Bankruptcy law frowns on gross mismanagement.

Seemed like Congress got that one right: it was a small price for bankruptcy protection.

If management behaves, they can keep the business running in bankruptcy as before. The default is that management remains in place. They call it a debtor-in-possession.

Most debtors obey the rules. Most want to be in the good favor of the bankruptcy judge overseeing the case, with the power of financial life and death over the debtor if the debtor makes a misstep.

But if they don't, it is cause to appoint someone else to run the business.

Here, the banks, armed with a video, asked the court to remove management on an emergency basis and put a third party—a trustee—in place to run the business and, if the trustee saw fit, to sell the business, possibly at a fire-sale price. Or even close it down with no sale.

What was the debtor's misstep? The video showed the debtor's current management committed fraud, dishonesty, incompetence, and gross mismanagement. How was that conveyed in the video? Remarkably clearly. It was a video of the debtor's chief executive officer speaking at a gathering, apparently recorded by someone in the crowd.

Based on the video, the judge had the power to remove the debtor "for cause."

Judges seldom grant this kind of motion early in a case, particularly a major one. But when there's a video where the debtor's chief executive officer looks right into the camera and says, "I've been running a scheme now for several years where the books and records of the company aren't accurate. I put them in the oven and cooked them. I overstated the value of the assets. You've heard of Enron? There were lessons to be learned. Some I learned, and… let's say… *applied*. Plain and simple, my accountants failed to understand it and signed off on the books and records each quarter. The same for the banks' auditors."

With a smile, he raised his glass while the crowd laughed. It looked like a party. Someone in the crowd called him by his name—Remmy. One even offered a toast: "Long live Paxton Energy."

The video was thin on detail, but it was rich in "for cause."

Somehow, the banks managed to get the video. It was unclear how that ever happened. But what was clear was that the opposing attorney moved to fire management and hire a third-party trustee.

What about 3J? She and her mentor, William Pascale, failed to foresee her opponent's attempt to introduce into evidence a video showing her client revealing the plot to cook the books for all the world to see and hear. In all fairness, how could they have foreseen something like that?

Hey, no attorney wins all of his or her cases. Right?

Clients come to lawyers with problems, but solutions aren't always easy to find. Debtors don't always play the game fairly. And if they're not playing fairly, they aren't telling their attorneys about it.

When the trial had started, there was a fix for what the banks' attorney sought, and 3J and Pascale had a plan. What to do in response to what the banks might try to prove.

If he testified, her client's CEO would sell well to the court. A choirboy on the stand. Articulate. Knowledgeable and businesslike. Starched shirt, dark suit, red tie. Great education and business pedigree.

No fraud. No mismanagement. No dishonesty.

That was the plan. Put the client on the stand, look straight at the judge, and say, "It ain't so, Judge."

But then someone hit the play icon and the video started. No choirboy there.

3J replayed in her mind what had transpired so far in court.

Right there on her legal pad, she had written the plan to counter the banks. It wouldn't be hard. On the stand, her client would allay any concerns about his company and himself. She had a plan; at least she thought she did. Until she and her mentor watched the video in court for the first time, along with Judge Daniel Robertson, a United States Bankruptcy judge. She watched the video and then realized her case was over.

After the video ended, 3J and her mentor leaned in and whispered to each other. The judge withheld a ruling on the admissibility of the video until the lawyers finished conferring. Then she stood up and asked the judge to withhold admitting the video into evidence pending her investigation of it.

The opposing lawyer reached over and gave her a copy of the video. In the moment, she didn't thank him, but he wasn't being sarcastic. He was just doing what needed to be done. Sharing the detonator for the bomb that could ruin the business. No special code needed to detonate. Just hit the play button.

Judge Robertson knew 3J very well. She was a regular in his court. She was a trusted member of the bankruptcy bar, bringing clients to his court who were down on their luck to reorganize their financial affairs. She excelled at it.

She was honest. She tried to pick clients who were honest as well and to do it as expertly as any debtor's lawyer could.

But the video spoke for itself.

Judge Robertson was astute and fair-minded. He showed empathy when needed and no leniency when the situation called for it. He had practiced bankruptcy law for many decades before taking the bench. He had seen it all in his practice, but no one knew how he would handle transition-ing from presenting cases to deciding them. The consensus among the lawyers who appeared in front of him: he handled the change with poise and wisdom. He had a perfect judicial temperament.

But this case was different. If the judge admitted the video, he would have no choice. There could be no leniency. The bankruptcy code overrode any temptation the judge might have to give the debtor and its management a second chance.

The judge took a brief break after 3J's request, returned to the courtroom, and told 3J she had twenty days to figure it all out.

"I will postpone ruling on the admissibility of the video until we reconvene this hearing twenty days from now. The clerk will send out the notice resetting this hearing. When we reconvene, we will count on staying as late as it takes to finish up that day."

The judge had complete control over how things were done. But then an assistant at the Office of the United States Trustee, the guardian of the bankruptcy system in the United States Justice Department, rose. She asked the judge to appoint an examiner in the interim to nose around the company and try to keep the CEO and management honest, and, well… examine the company and its management. The judge agreed without even hearing from 3J. Appointing an examiner was mandatory under the bankruptcy code if requested by a party in interest or the U.S. Trustee. The judge had no discretion. While it was highly unusual to rule without hearing from 3J and all the evidence was not in yet, there was nothing 3J could say.

3J slumped down. The examiner was the first step down the slope to ruin.

She asked the judge to make Paul Elkin come back for questioning at the next hearing. The judge agreed and directed Elkin to reappear. Elkin nodded that he understood. He seemed to enjoy being at the center of attention—all eyes on him as he rendered his expert opinion. He seemed to like his role in detonating the bomb.

How was a trustee appointed? It was within the judge's power to do it "for cause," which included things like fraud, dishonesty, and gross mismanagement. That's what the statute said. That's what the video showed.

If it were real. In the world we live in, one can never tell.

We live in a world where lawyers can lose cases based on evidence that might be real or fake. No one really knew for certain anymore.

There's a room off the courtroom where attorneys take their clients to debrief behind closed doors after a trial. When they got there, the client told 3J and Pascale it wasn't him in the video. Did she believe him? It looked like him. It sounded like him. It moved like him. His friends in the video called out his name and his company's name. Was it something he might say? She didn't know him well enough yet to decide. Was the scene in the video something he or someone else might record? Everyone has a phone to record movies these days. People record and post all kinds of wild things without filters or restraints. No permission needed. Just hold up the little rectangular device, point, and start recording.

The lawyers said little, so the client filled the void. He pounded the table and called it a fake video. Isn't that the fad? If you don't like the facts, call them fake. He was mad. If the video was a fake, who wouldn't be mad?

They teach law students that if you have the law on your side, pound away at the law. If you don't, pound away at the facts. If you don't have the law or the facts on your side, pound the table.

Here was her client pounding the table. Not a good look. No good facts. No good law. Except that despite what they teach law students, sometimes people pound the table because someone screwed them.

≈

She was back at her desk, slumping, shaking her head, lost in thought. The pain of defeat for an attorney cuts deep. 3J knew this firsthand. Even before she had handled a case on her own and lost, Pascale had mentored her well and schooled her in the art of winning and, yes, losing. She got an A in Pascale's winning and losing classes. Even so, when she lost, she felt pain. It was a selfish feeling, but unavoidable. She won most of the cases she took to trial, but the sting of a loss and the horror of watching the client's financial ruin unfold were sometimes too much to bear.

Like this time.

She had to find someone to definitively say whether the video was genuine or not. Not her expertise.

Chapter 2

THREE WEEKS EARLIER

IT WAS THEIR usual late Friday afternoon get-together at O'Brien's in Westport, the Kansas City drinking district south of downtown. Pascale and 3J usually met there for a drink to talk and put a period, and occasionally an exclamation point, on another week in the bankruptcy trenches.

They sat in an old oak booth just past the end of the bar. O'Brien's called it the "drinking rail," where customers often stood to order and drink their poison.

It was more private in the booth and quieter than at the drinking rail or the tables scattered throughout the bar, although, on a Friday evening in O'Brien's, quieter was relative. But at least they could hear each other in their booth. Kansas wheat beer for him. Irish whiskey, neat, for her. No one knew why 3J's ritual was drinking Irish whiskey straight up; she often acknowledged she could have the whiskey over ice, then would ask with a smile, "But why would I?"

A very Midleton, Ireland, view. No ice in Midleton to water down the man-made amber liquor that was Ireland's gift to the world. And no ice for 3J.

Usually, 3J carried the conversation with Pascale, the aging bankruptcy mentor, listening, nodding, agreeing, supporting, and providing course correction when rarely needed. This time, however, it was Pascale doing the talking.

"I met someone last week at a Saturday function. The CEO of an oil and gas company. Paxton Energy. They have offices in Wichita, Ulysses, Kansas, and on the Plaza here in Kansas City. He goes by 'Remmy.'" Pascale paused, surveyed the bar, picked up his glass, and sipped his beer.

"Pretty good-sized company. The Ulysses office is in the heart of the Hugoton Gas Field. High-tech, as he explained it, always exploring new ways to identify and extract oil and natural gas. He came across as smart, but like anyone in the oil and gas business, he's a risk-taker, and he had that look that risk-takers have. Just a little wild-eyed. Part genius. Part irrational. Part hopped-up on discovery, drilling, and production endorphins."

"I don't know of him or his company, Bill."

"Me neither. Then on Sunday, he called me. Thought it might be a good time to get together and talk. Bankruptcy talk, he reported. Made me wonder if meeting him at the party was happenstance."

3J listened as she swirled the whiskey in the glass bearing the etched O'Brien's logo.

"I met him on Monday morning, while you were in court on the Loden Company matter. Paxton Energy was Remmy's great-grandfather's company, and his family's been in the business ever since. Privately held. Not traded on any stock exchange. Back then, the only office was in Ulysses. Now it's grown, and so have its locations.

"Like many energy companies, it has a big line of credit

11

from a bank group headed up by a bank in Hays, Kansas." As he spoke, 3J noticed that he looked tired. A worn-around-the-edges kind of tired that would not fade after the upcoming weekend. The effects of getting older were showing. She smiled at him while he spoke.

"Right now, I forget the name of the bank. I have it written down back at the office. But the line is something like $60 million.

"Anyway, the banks are getting nervous. They don't like some of Paxton's latest drilling proposals and claim that the drilling would be too risky. He and the banks are at real loggerheads."

"Sounds like a battle over who'll control the drilling decisions," 3J observed.

"Exactly. And Paxton's none too happy about having to share the decision-making process. He's soft-spoken, but he got animated describing what he called the banks' 'invasion' of his province about where to drill. I think he even described it as a 'trespass.'

"As he explained it, he has a staff of engineers and geologists and a world-class number cruncher, and as far as he's concerned, they've always made the drilling decisions and always will."

"Has the company ever defaulted?" 3J probed.

"Never. Paid the banks every dime when due. Even during the downturn in the industry in the 1980s."

"Bill, why does he need to talk to a bankruptcy lawyer?"

"Exactly my question. Why? He was a little reluctant to explain much of what was on his mind when I asked, 'How can I help you?'"

"Other than a bit of education on the Kansas oil and gas industry, it sounds like a big waste of your time, Bill."

"Ahh, patience, my friend. Patience. We shook hands, and the Monday meeting ended. Monday night, he called again. 'Can we meet again on Tuesday?' he asked.

"'Sure,' I told him. Tuesday morning, bright and early, there he was with a cup of coffee waiting for me in our reception area. We met, and this time he revealed the problem. He needs to draw on the line to pay ongoing expenses and to drill. The banks told him they officially disapproved of the new drilling plan, and unless he backed off that plan, they would freeze the line, and they wouldn't fund the draw to pay the expenses either."

"Oh. Wow. That's an instant mess," 3J said, shaking her head.

"Exactly. Since you've mostly wrapped up the Loden case, I was hoping you could dive in with me on our new client's problems—Paxton Energy."

"Fine. Great. Where do we begin?"

"Paxton sent over a bunch of paperwork already. I've sifted through some of it. If you have time, let's meet tomorrow at the shop and start figuring out what we know and what we need to know."

"Of course. See you at nine."

Pascale paid the bill, and they rose to leave the bar. Normally, 3J's boyfriend, Ronnie Steele, would be behind the busy drinking rail pouring drinks for patrons and would wave to her as she exited. He'd have the "I'll see you later" look in his eye. But Steele had left the bar's employ two months before to start up his own private investigation firm, Sterling & Steele, a partnership he formed with Monica "Moe" Sterling, his former vice squad partner from his years on the Kansas City, Missouri, police force.

It seemed strange to leave O'Brien's without Steele behind the rail on a busy Friday night. But he would be back home at her condo high above downtown Kansas City, so it wouldn't be long before they were together for more than a wave and a brief look as he scurried to keep patrons happy.

3J and Pascale navigated through the crowd, snaking a path to the door where the three-hundred-pound, six-foot-eight bouncer, Eugene Martin, "Bitty" to his friends, relaxed on a large stool as he surveyed the crowd, ready to keep order when necessary.

"Hey, Bitty. Great crowd tonight. You doing okay?"

"The usual denizens. Heard that word recently, and I like it. Some drunk and some not. All happy, or on the road to happiness, one drink at a time. And, you know me. I'm always more than okay. And you?"

"No complaints, man. Take care."

3J and Bitty had worked together on a case a little more than a year ago. Bitty and a few others had saved 3J from imminent harm, and she hoped she could repay him someday. She appreciated the soft-spoken giant sitting at O'Brien's entrance.

As they got to the sidewalk, Pascale said, "I'll walk you to your car, 3J."

She always felt Pascale's regular Friday evening, post-drink escort to her car was unnecessary. She could handle herself. She could run faster than the aging Pascale. She might even be stronger. She got looks and even the occasional catcall or whistle, which she ignored, but Pascale's presence would keep the horny, college-aged drunks at bay. It was chivalrous of him to protect her, and when she was being honest with herself, it probably was safer for her to have a tall White man walking with her than to return to her car alone, an attractive Black woman with lots of drunk, White twenty-somethings milling around.

❧

3J turned the key in the door and entered her home away from the law firm, a high-rise condo at the south end of downtown filled with glass from floor to ceiling overlooking the Kansas City skyline to the north. Music played in the background. Count Basie. What else? It was Kansas City on a Friday night. "Jumpin' at the Woodside," named after the Woodside Hotel in Kansas City, where he and the band would stay. Classic Swing Era music. She loved Basie—the leader of the "Barons of Rhythm"—who played at Kansas City's Reno Club and other clubs before departing to New York City and greater fame.

Ronnie Steele met her at the door. They kissed. He handed her a glass of red wine, a Gifford Hirlinger red blend from Walla Walla, Washington, where 3J went to college. Her favorite. She put her wine down, and they began dancing even before she dropped her briefcase. She laughed. It came from deep within.

He loved her laugh. Most did.

She loved any music from the swing era, especially with a Kansas City connection, and he knew that.

For a few minutes, they were swing dancing like two teenagers in the 1940s. But they weren't dancing at a 1940s Lindy Hop Night get-together designed for them to let loose and show off their Lindy, Big Apple, and Balboa skills. They were two adults in love, together in the 2020s, dancing a private who-knows-what version of swing dancing. Slow, rhythmic, in unison. Perfect harmony music. No 1940s acrobatics. Perfect 2025 harmony dancing.

When the song ended, their mood slowly changed from the swing dance music kind of fun to the other kind of fun. They made their way to the bedroom, her arms around his neck and his around her waist. Once in the bedroom, she shed her clothes, revealing her athletic frame, curves, and her breasts, which Steele called the best breasts in the world. "Perfect in every way, just like the rest of you," he would say.

"Oh, have you surveyed all the breasts in the world before you made that statement?" she would playfully ask.

"I have not," he would answer, grinning.

He had a habit of talking about her body in the bedroom. She didn't mind; she liked it. She had a habit of watching his, too, and he didn't mind either.

Their relationship had grown from acquaintances to friends to occasional lovers to him moving in with her as their full-blown love for each other grew.

As they approached the bed, Ronnie pulled her close to his lean, muscular frame and told her that Fridays were now the best night of the week. "I don't have to work at the bar late on Fridays anymore, 3J. I can just be here at home, meet you at the door, and escort you into our little lair where I can express my love and affection for you."

"Well, sir, stop talking and please start expressing away."

"Yes, ma'am." He picked her up as they got to the bed and laid her down on her back. He then slipped next to her for the preliminaries.

They were a quiet couple in bed. But quiet didn't mean they weren't active and passionate. There was still plenty of pleasure to go around. Like their dancing, they moved in unison in bed. Two becoming one. No one took the lead. No one rushed. They acted together. No matter how stressful her week was, Steele had a way of making it all go away on Friday night, when they took slow rides to the top floor where the magic happened.

Later, when she put on her terry robe and walked to the couch in the living room, she was the most relaxed bankruptcy attorney on the planet.

Saturday morning in Greene Madison's small interior conference room on the twenty-seventh floor—the bankruptcy floor. The attorneys nicknamed it the "War Room."

"Wow, this is big, Bill," 3J said as she surveyed the papers. "A $60 million line of credit. Paxton wanted $3 million to pay ordinary course of business bills. Utilities. Service companies. Payroll. Nothing crazy. It also looks like the company has stockpiled quite a bit of cash to begin the new drilling projects. It will obviously need more. Compared to some debtors who limp in here with a shoebox full of disorganized records and no cash, Paxton Energy is quite a different creature."

"Agreed. I'm not sure that Paxton would win the battle right away to get money to drill the new wells, but it has enough of a war chest to survive just fine in bankruptcy without help from the banks."

"What's this guy Paxton like?" 3J asked.

"Smart. Quick. Business degree from the Tuck School of Business at Dartmouth. There's also the Paxton Scholarship Fund the family established to help needy kids access Tuck."

"Impressive pedigree. He'll make a good impression on the bankruptcy judge right out of the gate."

"He also told me he's of Native American descent. One-eighth Kiowa," Pascale said.

They read some more of the papers, and 3J asked, "What about the banks' collateral?"

"The energy assets, which are substantial. Drilling contract rights, oil and gas in the ground, and oilfield equipment. And, of course, gas extracted into storage before transport and sale and oil extracted for sale. Lots of accounts receivable as well—what the oil and gas buyers owe Paxton. Valuable stuff."

"How did Paxton value the assets?"

"Looks like the company did most of the work internally. The banks never required Paxton to hire a third-party appraiser."

"How did the banks value the assets?"

Pascale paused, flipped through some papers, and shook his head. "I'm not sure if they did. For a while, they had a small firm in rural Kansas that they used for energy valuation work, but it looks like that guy retired, and anyway, as far as I can tell, that firm just kicked the tires for the work done by the Paxton team and signed off on it. I guess the banks decided against finding a new firm and just had their auditors review Paxton's numbers and sign off on them."

"Really? For this size loan?"

"Looks like it," Pascale confirmed.

"That's pretty unusual, Bill. Paxton's not publicly traded. Are the banks?"

"I don't think so. Most are family-owned local community banks throughout western Kansas. I guess they think they understand oil and gas well enough. They've banked Paxton

Energy for forever. They must also think they have a good enough grasp of the company."

They worked in silence, going through all the papers, and after a few hours, 3J looked up, stretched, and asked, "What do you think, Bill?"

"Best case I can see here is we file Chapter 11 papers for Paxton Energy and Remmy Paxton personally because he's the guarantor of the debt. It looks like the Paxton family incorporated Paxton Energy in Missouri way back when. It has a small office here, and it looks like it has some active Kansas City, Missouri, bank accounts with cash. Therefore, it looks like we'll be able to file the bankruptcy cases here in the Western District of Missouri."

"Agreed," 3J said. "At the outset of the case, the company should have full access to the cash to pay its bills. And as it sells oil and gas, it ought to be able to use that cash in operations. Maybe offer a nominal payment to the banks, but maybe not for a while. I have to believe that the energy reserves, the land, and the cash aren't going down in value, so for a while, the banks won't be in a good bankruptcy position."

Pascale smiled. "No, they won't."

3J returned the smile. It often made attorneys for the debtors happy when they had the upper hand against a group of banks, at least at the beginning of a case.

"What next?" Pascale asked.

"I'd like to meet Paxton and maybe whoever heads up the company's valuation team."

"Good idea. I'll set it up."

Chapter 3

REQUEST DENIED

THEY GATHERED AROUND a large conference room table at The Central Bank on Vine Street in Hays, Kansas. Viewers of *Gunsmoke* or the original *Wyatt Earp* television programs might recognize scenes portraying a typical western Kansas town. Hollywood got much of it right, like the fields, the horses, the tumbleweed blowing across the street, the gunfights, the boozing at the saloon, the ladies of the evening, the local two-story hotel, and the dusty main drag. Much of it, but not the mountains in the background that Wyatt Earp or Matt Dillon rode by on their horses heading out of town. Then and now, Hays sits on the High Plains, flat, with crops, ranches, oil and gas, and now some solar and wind farms as far as the eye can see. No mountains. Just flatland.

It was a rough-and-tumble railroad town with an Army fort during the Wild West days that had morphed into a farming community when thousands of German-speaking Russians left Russia, some of whom found their way to Hays by the late 1870s and took up dryland farming.

It's the largest city in western Kansas, population about

21,000, with the nearest larger city, Salina, population 47,000, one hundred miles away. Hays was no longer a rough-and-tumble prairie town. Just golden wheat and sunflowers in the late summer, soybeans, cattle grazing, horses dotted around, the occasional tornado on the horizon, and snow—lots of drifting snow in the winter.

Now, after the summer wheat harvest, they met. All the banks in the bank group, except for the newest—Franklin Trust of Wichita, Kansas—were old-school, family-owned Western Kansas banks that had been around since the days when Wyatt Earp used his Buntline Special, a Colt Single Action Army revolver with a custom extra-long barrel, to keep the peace. Hays was one of the first towns where he wore a badge. The Central Bank logo was a badge, much like the one Earp wore.

Over the years, the Paxton Energy loan had grown as the company had grown. But a year ago, the five banks—Liberal Community Bank in Liberal, Kansas; Dodge City Trust in Dodge City, Kansas; People's Bank in McPherson, Kansas; WaKeeney Bank in WaKeeney, Kansas; and Central—thought their share of the loan had grown too large for them to handle. It had made up too much of each of their overall portfolios. To shrink down their exposure, the banks sold a share of the $60 million loan to Franklin Trust. Now Franklin owned 47 percent of the loan—$28 million. The rest now each owned $6.4 million of the loan, a substantial reduction of exposure for each bank.

Franklin was much larger than the others. No longer family-owned, it had a diverse group of owners, although it wasn't publicly traded. It had offered to buy over 47 percent of the loan, but the other banks were unwilling to cede total control to Franklin. None of the other banks had ever been in a bank group with Franklin, nor had they ever dealt with Franklin's oil and gas lending department.

The newcomer had capital to burn and a reputation for snap decisions and lighting brushfires. Franklin liked to control their loans and their bank groups. Its lenders had a swagger that some banks found offensive. Franklin's management didn't care what other banks thought of it. If others thought its reputation was being tough, that rugged look was good for business.

Remmy Paxton had asked to draw on the line to buy land where Paxton Energy could drill. Franklin didn't waste a moment in saying "no" and had pressured the other banks to reject the request as well.

They came together in Hays to discuss Paxton, Remmy, Franklin's view, and the overall situation. It was the first time Franklin attended the bank group's meeting.

The banks had scheduled the meeting for 2 p.m. Wayne Shumaker, executive vice president of Franklin, entered the room last, placed a small envelope in the middle of the Central Bank conference room table, and sat.

He was a handsome, rugged-looking, middle-aged man. Gray hair. Square jaw. Thin eyebrows. Sideburns to the middle of his ear. Broad nose, as if he boxed as a teenager, but he hadn't. Banker's suit and tie: expensive. Wingtip shoes: expensive. Maybe five foot eleven. Gray eyes. At some point in his life, he probably looked athletic. Now he had the beginnings of a belly.

"Whaddaya got there, Wayne?" Chet Drucker, Central's president, asked.

The two only knew of each other in passing.

"It's a DVD, Chet. Go ahead. Play it. I think it'll shorten this meeting considerably."

Shumaker sat at the table as he talked, hands clasped across his belly, and he smiled. He twirled his thumbs absentmindedly twice while waiting to see the group's reaction to the video. He was excited to play it for the other bankers and couldn't control what some might think was fiendish delight.

Drucker opened the envelope, removed the disc, and fiddled with the DVD player connected to a television in the room's corner. Finally, he hit the play button on the remote.

After a few moments, the file on the DVD loaded, and on the screen was Remmy Paxton, looking into the camera, boasting that he had, for years, inflated the values of Paxton Energy's oil and gas assets. What he said next was unintelligible. There was too much background noise. It looked like someone had recorded the video on a mobile phone at some kind of cocktail party or get-together.

The bankers in the room were silent. Not much can shock an experienced banker, but the video left the bankers in the room dumbstruck.

"Jesus, Wayne. What are we looking at here?"

"Jesus right back at ya. Exactly what it appears to be, Chet."

"Where the hell did you get that?" Drucker asked.

"Showed up on my desk one morning a couple of days ago. I thought you boys said you audited Paxton Energy's books and records twice a year and never had a problem with the records or the values assigned."

"We have without fail over the years. We've complied with every state and federal regulation governing this loan and how we service it."

"Damn the regulators," Shumaker responded, raising his voice. "They ain't got a dime in this loan. We've now got $28 million in it, and you still have over $6 million each. That's what matters. Not the government bean counters and box checkers. I'm not asking what you did to comply with some starched-shirt ledger spy in a state or federal currency office. I'm asking what you did to protect your asset—this loan—and your bank and your owners from fraud."

"Fraud's a damn serious allegation, Wayne. Damn serious," Drucker said. "I'm not there yet."

"Yeah, that video is damn serious too. Fraud's the only word that fits."

"How do you know it's real?" Drucker demanded.

"How do you know it's not?" Shumaker retorted. "Right now, it's as real as it needs to be for me to know that the answer to the request to draw on the line to buy land to drill is a hard no. It has to be. There's no other choice."

"We started banking Paxton Energy back when Remmy's grandpa ran the company. And we've banked them ever since," Drucker said. "It's a solid family. It's a solid company. We've never—repeat, NEVER—declined a draw request. Paxton Energy has NEVER failed to pay us when due." Drucker paused each time he said "never." He was no longer speaking in an even-keeled business tone. He was one notch below screaming and straining to keep from shouting. But he was having trouble controlling himself, and he was getting louder with each word.

"Remmy Paxton has never taken advantage of this bank!"

"The past means little to us at Franklin because we weren't in this loan in the past. We're here today with a sizable chunk of this loan. It undeniably looks like he's been pulling the wool over your eyes for some time now. Boys, it's time. I want to put it to a vote. I move to deny the request."

The vote was swift. The only bank voting in favor of advancing more money to Paxton Energy was Central.

There would be no advance.

Drucker shook his head. What he billed as a perfunctory bank meeting had turned into an unexpected lending dumpster fire. "Now what?" Drucker asked, visibly upset.

"Paxton wants money to buy land and drill. Answer? No," Shumaker summarized. "Paxton also wants money to pay ordinary course bills. I say the answer on that one is also a hard no until Paxton withdraws the request to buy the Oklahoma land so he can drill on it. The company needs to pull out of the deal it has to purchase the land. Period. Just tell him the project is too risky for our taste."

Chet Drucker frowned. The meeting had gotten away from him. He was no longer the lead bank in charge. He was just reacting to Shumaker's agenda. "I'm not comfortable telling him that, Wayne," Drucker said. "It's no riskier than many of the loans we've approved in the past. We made good money on every one of those loans. They were excellent investments for the banks."

"Again, Chet, that's the past. The past is on you guys. Not Franklin. Franklin is the here and now. And now, the answer should be no. What do the rest of you say?"

Again, all the banks agreed with Shumaker except Central.

The meeting ended on a cordial note. Even Chet Drucker shook everyone's hands as anyone would expect a banker to do, and as Chet's father and grandfather before him had taught every banker who ever worked at Central.

Etiquette mattered even in the face of critical disagreements, even disagreements that could signal the end of a borrower.

❧

After the meeting, Chet Drucker called Paxton to tell him that the banks had rejected the request to draw on the line. He had decided not to share the video with Paxton. Instead, he told Paxton the new drilling project in Oklahoma was just too risky for their taste.

"Too risky? How? It's the same kind of project you and your fellow banks have approved for decades. Dammit, Chet. What can I do to make this right with you guys?" Paxton asked.

"There's nothing you can do, Remmy. We've decided."

"Based on what?"

"I would rather not share the details, Remmy. The banks have just decided to decline this lending opportunity."

"It's got to be that new bank, Franklin Trust, isn't it?"

"Like I said, I won't be able to comment on the banks' deliberations, Remmy. I think the decision is final. And unless you abandon efforts to buy the Oklahoma land, the banks also decided not to fund the draw request to pay the bills."

"Jesus, Chet. What the hell's going on? I've got to keep the lights on, don't I? Shit. Any other good news for me?" Paxton asked, unable to hide his sarcasm.

"Remmy. I'm truly sorry," Chet said. "But that's all I can say to you."

❧

It was a two-hour and forty-five-minute drive back to Franklin Trust from Hays, east on I-70 to Salina, then south on I-135 to Wichita. For the first forty-five minutes, Shumaker drove his Ford F-150 pickup truck in silence. Then, he dialed his colleague at the bank, Greg McCoy. "The deed is done," Shumaker declared.

McCoy wanted the details.

"Yeah, what could they do?"

McCoy wanted to know if the banks were unified.

"Only Central Bank voted to allow the draw."

"What about the video?" McCoy probed.

"Sure, I showed the video. Jesus, man. Just like we discussed."

"How did the bankers' take it?"

"They were shocked," Shumaker said. "What banker wouldn't be?"

Shumaker listened to McCoy's concerns. "I know. I know. If Paxton's lawyers figure this out, we'll all be screwed. But they won't."

McCoy was worried, maybe even wavering. "Dammit, Greg. Get your head out of your ass. Now that we've blocked Paxton's draw request, your brother-in-law damn well better nail down the right to drill on this land."

He listened as McCoy assured him that he thought his brother-in-law had everything lined up.

"You think? Jesus, man. You think so, but you don't know so. Shit. You and he need to know so."

He shook his head as he listened in silence. "I'm in the worry business, my friend," Shumaker hissed. "It's what I do. No need to tell me not to."

He waited, but McCoy said nothing.

"You just remember this, Greg. I need to get my share of the bonus and that override oil and gas interest when your brother-in-law gets his loan to buy this land. Dammit man, let's get this done."

He listened.

"Well, good. Don't you forget that. Y'hear?"

The call ended.

Shumaker turned on his radio and tried to listen to music for the rest of the trip but couldn't. No matter how loudly he played the music, his thoughts drowned it out.

He took another call. It was Chet Drucker.

"Wayne, I think you should get an expert to look at that video and make sure it's real. Someone to confirm it's Paxton talking. It's the prudent thing to do. We can't be too careful in this day and age."

"I'm pretty darn sure it's real, Chet. I've got my reputation to protect as well. I wouldn't have brought it to the bank group if I had thought it was fake. But look. I don't have a problem with that, Chet. I'll let you know."

Shumaker had figured someone would ask to verify the video was authentic. Greg McCoy and he had already worked this angle out. He wasn't worried about the authenticity. They already had somebody lined up who would verify the video.

But he was worried… in general. He just talked most of a bank group into freezing a line of credit for one of the best and most respected oil and gas companies in the Midwest. Why? To clear the way for Greg McCoy's brother-in-law to borrow money from Franklin at a higher rate than the Paxton loan paid and buy the same land Paxton wanted to. The prize—he and McCoy would get a bonus. And they'd get an interest in the oil pumped by the brother-in-law.

He'd played outside the edges before. Taking money from a borrower under the table to push a loan through the loan committee for approval. No invoices. Just a payment to an account controlled by Shumaker. Taking an ownership stake in a borrower like a venture capital firm might. Only Shumaker didn't pay for his interest. It was his upside for pushing the loan through the loan committee for approval. Taking an interest in a borrower's oil and gas production.

He had strayed off the banking reservation on more than one occasion. Never a problem. Always a win-win for him and his borrowers. He got what he needed, and the borrower got what they wanted—the loan, minus Shumaker's take. No one at Franklin had caught up with him and uncovered his schemes yet. He was careful.

And now Paxton. Not a bad piece of maneuvering, but without a doubt, much more complicated and much further outside the line.

He wrote it all down in his personal ledger to keep track of the deals he had manipulated at the bank. He needed the ledger to keep the bonuses and his wheeling and dealing straight in his mind. But there were plenty of moving pieces in this deal, and even writing it down in his ledger didn't simplify matters. He called McCoy back.

"We need to get that expert to say the video is genuine, just like we figured. We talked about this before. You've got the guy, right? He'll deliver the opinion we want?"

He listened.

"Great. Just what I like to hear. Get it off to him and have him tell us it's real. Let's get this done posthaste, please."

Shumaker returned to not hearing the music playing. McCoy was a greenhorn when it came to banking risk in the oil patch and playing outside the edges. He had potential, but he didn't know what he was doing, and he knew little about oil and gas loans. All he knew was that he had a brother-in-law he wanted to help. He came to Shumaker because he knew

Shumaker headed up the oil and gas lending division. McCoy was a potential complication. He was too nervous. Shumaker had never had a partner in his shady deals at the bank before. But McCoy had the brother-in-law connection, so he was a necessary complication. More journal entries in the ledger to keep it all straight.

Shumaker was worried about McCoy, but his bank colleague would have to hold it together. No panicking.

Greg, play it cool, man, Shumaker implored as he drove alone with his thoughts. *We got this.* A new oil and gas loan is on the horizon. And more money for Shumaker.

It was always about money. That was Banking 101. "Them's that got it decide who else will have it and who will not," Shumaker's father, a banker in the old days, had told him. Shumaker remembered it as he pursued his own lending career.

Words to live by, he figured.

After the call to Shumaker, Drucker arranged a call with the other owners of the bank. He explained the video. The other owners were uncomfortable with Drucker's vote and directed him to change Central's vote to "no" on both issues. Drucker reported to the other banks that Central was changing its vote.

And with that, the vote against Paxton Energy was unanimous.

Chapter 4

REMMY AND BREE

PASCALE LED REMMY Paxton and his wife, Bree, to the Greene Madison main conference room on the twenty-eighth floor, where 3J sat. Paxton did not bring the head of his valuation team.

It was a large, elegant room with muted colors, expensive appointments, an unmatched view of downtown, and the place where new clients came to meet their attorneys and form the impression that they had hired the best attorneys in the Midwest.

3J rose from behind a stack of Paxton Energy papers, introduced herself, shook hands with the Paxtons, and gestured for the couple to sit.

Paxton explained who he was. He grew up in a small town near Ulysses, Kansas, a town of fewer than five thousand. A town of farmers tending to the surface land, except his family, which was in the oil and gas business and focused on what hid below. He had Kiowa tribe ancestors. He was a hair shy of six feet tall, trim, with brown eyes and short gray and silver hair. He looked to be in his sixties. He wore a dark sports coat, a white shirt, and, eschewing current fashion mores, a narrow, solid blue tie. He said he was a third-generation graduate of the Tuck School of Business at Dartmouth. He had married Bree, his high school sweetheart, and they had been together for most of their lives.

She was five foot six with icy blue eyes, wavy, dirty-blonde hair that came down to her shoulders, and no makeup. She didn't need it. Bree Paxton's eyes went well beyond sparkling. They pierced and caught your attention and held it. Right now, they were shimmering in the conference room lights.

She wore a dark green pantsuit and a white shirt. She could have been in her fifties. The truth was, she could have been in her forties. She was one of those rare people whose appearance gave nothing away about her age. She also went to Dartmouth around when Remmy was there. 3J figured that meant Bree was in her late fifties or early sixties. *Everyone should look that good at that age.*

Paxton explained that Bree had limited involvement in the business, but he wanted her to listen to the lawyers explain the bankruptcy option and give him her best advice.

Paxton gave the history of Paxton Energy and emphasized how successful it had been. "I'm fourth-generation oil and natural gas through and through," he proudly explained.

"Give us an overview of what's going on with your bank group and the company," Pascale said. This was Pascale's client. It was his show. Even though she would handle the lion's share of the work, 3J let him take the point position in the meeting.

"Sure thing. Grandpa, Dad, and now me, we've used the same small bank group for many decades. All Kansas banks. All knowledgeable about oil and gas."

He described the original five banks and how Wichita's Franklin Trust had just joined the group.

"Franklin is the largest of the six banks, and, as I understand it, now holds 47 percent of the loan. $28 million. The other banks divide the remaining balance between them—over $6 million each. Most of our contact is with Central as the lead bank. Chet Drucker is there."

"What's the dispute?" 3J asked.

"We have the chance to drill for oil in a new field in Oklahoma. Land owned by the Stockton family in Kiowa County. Bearfoot Stockton isn't selling only the drilling rights. To raise money, he's outright selling the land and the rights to drill.

"I've talked to him. He's known our family from way back. Like us, his family comes from Kiowa ancestors. We've made him a fair offer—cash—and a small override interest in production if we're successful in our drilling project, which, of course, we expect to be. We've agreed in principle and have a memorandum of understanding we've both signed. We were about to have the lawyers start on the definitive documents. It's how our two families have conducted business in the past. To pay for this, we need to draw on our line to make the deal happen."

Paxton paused, smiled at Bree, and continued, "As always in my business, it could be a dry hole. Could be black gold. That's the nature of the energy business, right?"

"I assume you've done your engineering homework?" Pascale asked.

"Of course. We've got the best engineers and geologists in the business. When we go out looking for oil, we don't use a witching stick and wander around fields waiting for the rod to dip or twist."

Paxton smiled when he mentioned the witching stick.

"I'm not familiar with the stick. What is it?" 3J asked.

"Ahh. A romantic symbol of the old wildcatting days at the dawn of the oil and gas industry," Paxton explained. "It was a Y-shaped stick. Folks would hire a guy to walk around a field with it, and it was supposed to dip, twist, or move when oil was near. Kinda like a Ouija board for oil and gas. Communicating with the spirits through the witching stick to find oil and gas. Smart folks paid con artists with a stick from a willow tree branch who said they could speak with the energy spirits from the great beyond. Crazy damn part of the history of the energy business. Rest assured, we use science, not voodoo, to find our next drilling prospect."

"Ahh, got it," 3J said.

"What kind of reserves are you talking about?" Pascale asked. He had handled oil and gas bankruptcies before and had more than a passing familiarity with oil to be developed.

"We classified 20 percent of the likely oil to be drilled as 'possible reserves,'" Remmy explained. "We think the oil is down there, but we concede it's more of a long shot. Maybe a 20 percent chance of success. About 40 percent are 'probable reserves.' Maybe a 60 percent chance of success. The rest we categorized as 'proven undeveloped.' We expect to recover those barrels with certainty."

Pascale rubbed his chin as he thought. Bree and 3J listened quietly.

"I can see you know something about the business," Remmy continued. "And you look concerned about the reserves. You're thinking 'dry hole.' Big drill but no Texas tea."

"The thought was crossing my mind as you spoke," Pascale conceded. "Only 40 percent is proven undeveloped."

"I like to say I'm not in the oil and gas business, Bill. I'm in the risk business. I'm a gambler of sorts. Perils, pitfalls, and imminent failure everywhere. All these monikers we give to the reserves. Well, they're no more than labels we assign. My grandfather told me, 'It ain't oil and gas until it's extracted. Before we bring it up to the surface, it's just a bet. A risk. A wager.' Look, we wager a good chunk of our money, and the banks' money too. That's the partnership we've always had with them. Most of the time, we make good money because we're good at what we do. And all of the time, the banks make great money because… Well, because they're the banks, and we've always paid them back with interest."

"But they said no this time. Perhaps too big of a wager for them?" Pascale responded.

3J's eyes moved from Pascale to Paxton and back like it was a tennis match.

Bree looked down at her hands folded on the table. She was the embodiment of calm and patience. She must have witnessed these discussions many times before; it would be difficult to be a Paxton and not have heard this. She seemed unfazed by the nature of what Paxton Energy actually did. After all, she had married into the risk business, and she trusted her spouse. He might not have had a witching stick, but he had an outstanding gut to gauge a project's success.

"I hear ya, Bill," Remmy replied. "But we've done nothing differently this time from any other drilling project. We presented the banks with our facts and the opinions of our expert engineers and geologists. We've told the banks how many barrels we can extract. And we've asked the banks to let us draw on the line to get started with the drilling. Same as we've done with them over the decades. Truthfully, this project is less risky than some of the other ones we've had success with that the banks approved."

3J watched Paxton as he spoke. He seemed thoughtful and convincing; he obviously knew his business inside and out. Over the years, she had learned about microexpressions, tiny involuntary facial twitches that gave away whether someone was lying or hiding something. Professional gamblers, psychiatrists, and law enforcement had used the observation technique for years. She saw no tells on Paxton's face.

"For decades, they said yes," Paxton continued, "and now, this time, they said no."

"Did they say why?" Pascale asked.

"No explanation. One word: 'No,'" Remmy said shaking his head. "We had also submitted a pretty standard draw request having nothing to do with the new drilling project to pay bills, payroll, and the like. We use the line of credit to smooth out the flow of our cash. The banks said they'd honor the draw request but only if we abandoned the drilling project. Again, no explanation."

"Do you have any sense of what's going on with the banks?" Pascale asked.

"It's gotta be the new Wichita bank, Franklin Trust," Remmy answered. It's big. It's the new player. The folks there know the oil and gas world well. They should know how this works. It has a reputation as a tough-nosed bank. I also wonder if the banks are getting squeezed by the regulators. I'm at a loss. I don't know."

Pascale explained how Paxton Energy could use the bankruptcy code to operate and avoid paying the banks for a while. As in other cases, the strategy was that the lack of payments might bring the banks to the bargaining table and reconsider the denial of the draw request. If not, Paxton might find a new bank group to replace the existing one.

Paxton said he was familiar with oil and gas bankruptcies. "Back in the mid-eighties, oil and gas companies were falling like flies," Remmy explained. "I was young and learning the business. My dad sent me down to Texas to oversee some of Paxton Energy's oil well operations. While I was there, I watched other companies file for bankruptcy to try to survive while they waited for the price of oil to rise again. Some survived. We did; many didn't. The names of the dearly departed read like a who's who directory of once-famous oil and gas companies." He paused and shook his head. "Maybe someday, someone will design a granite monolith with the names of those companies etched into it, rising out of a Texas oil field. A new tourist attraction for anyone willing to drive hours into the middle of nowhere."

Pascale nodded. He knew that reliving the 1980s was an emotional process for anyone connected to the oil and gas industry. "Okay, we'll need a list of all of Paxton Energy's assets and liabilities, names and addresses of creditors, contacts at the creditors, cash in the bank, and cash flow from your producing properties. Also, we'll need to understand how Paxton values its assets."

"Sure thing."

"Outside appraisers?" Pascale asked.

"We do it in-house."

"And the banks?"

"They audit us with their internal folks and sign off on our books and records, including the valuations."

"Got it. We both have some work to do. Let me see you both to the lobby."

Chapter 5

VALUATIONS

WHEN PASCALE RETURNED to the conference room, he sat across from 3J and asked her, "What do you think?"

"Sounds like a good case and a good client. Why did you ask about the valuations?"

"There are plenty of ways to value oil and gas assets. Some aren't as legitimate as others. Remember Enron? The 'Crooked E?' Back when Enron was a thing, it would use a technique called 'mark to market.' Sounds complicated. But in its basic form, it wasn't. A company should report profits as it earns them, like when it sells oil and gas and deposits the cash. Not Enron. When it signed a long-term deal, it estimated—some said *guessed* or *fabricated*—what it would make over the lifetime of the deal and booked the aggregate lifetime profit as if it had all come into its bank account at once.

"Before my time, Bill," 3J reminded him. "But like most bankruptcy lawyers, I've read a little about Enron and its escapades."

Pascale continued, "It also hid bad debt in separate entities, but I don't have the sense that Paxton has numerous companies. But I'm just curious what it does to value some of its riskier reserves, like the 'possible' reserves and whether the banks have lost their appetite for risk."

"But it sounds like the banks regularly audit Paxton."

"Indeed. After Enron, the regs and laws tightened up. Banks are now required to. And to be certain, it's harder to take the banks for a ride after Enron. Harder, but not impossible. It can still happen. Energy markets are pretty complicated. Oil and gas companies use trading contracts, derivatives, and futures prices. There are still gray areas that management can exploit to 'polish' the books if management is of such a mind. Executives can still pressure subordinates to create false data. It's always a guess—albeit educated—what's in the ground, and as Remmy told us, the banks' auditors rely on the information that management presents. Maybe they'll catch a falsehood, but maybe they won't."

"Are you saying you think Paxton is a bad actor?" 3J chose her words as she processed the Enron story.

"Not at all. I didn't get that impression from speaking with him, and I don't mean to leave you with that impression either. Just something to watch for and keep in the back of your mind," Pascale instructed. "What did you think of him?"

"My read, for what it's worth, is that Paxton is kind of a 'what you see is what you get' guy. He wants to drill for oil like his daddy and his granddaddy. He didn't seem like a books-and-records cooker or a mark-to-market type. Or what did you call it? A gray-area book polisher." She smiled at the notion. "Or he could just be a great liar. You never know in our business, right?"

"Agreed." Pascale replied. "For now, we'll assume he's on the up-and-up." He gathered the papers to bring them back to the War Room. He had accomplished his purpose. 3J would keep an eye out for anything unusual.

Chapter 6

OKAY THEN—SEE YOU IN COURT

3J WANTED TO arrange for the banks and Paxton to meet to see if she could restart a discussion about the banks financing Paxton's drilling plans. She learned that Frank Davis, a bankruptcy attorney at one of the other large firms in town she had worked with before, just started representing the banks. Davis was a regular on the "Best Lawyers" list in Kansas City. *Solid lawyer, decent guy,* she reflected. It would be a good case to work on with him.

She called him up and floated the idea of a meeting. He thought it sounded like a wise course of action and said he needed time to reach out to the banks and confirm that a meeting was in order.

A few hours later, he called 3J back. "3J, Frank here. Listen, I spoke to my banks, and the answer was a hard 'no.' They wanted me to tell you there's nothing to talk about. They don't like the idea of financing these particular wells at this particular time. They don't see any middle ground, so a meeting wouldn't be a good use of anyone's time."

3J sighed. "Not the answer I was expecting, Frank. What's the harm in meeting?"

"In my world, none. In the banks' world, it's a waste. I'm living in their world right now. Look, I don't know them well. They came to me through a referral from a lawyer friend in western Kansas who doesn't practice bankruptcy. All that's to say I don't have a lot of influence over my clients right now. I just have to do their bidding."

"Okay. Next stop—the Western District of Missouri Bankruptcy Court," 3J replied. "See you there."

3J wrote Pascale an email telling him about the banks' position and asked him to secure a retainer and an engagement letter from Paxton and the company. For her part, she'd start preparing the bankruptcy papers as she had for so many companies before them. Based on Paxton's recollection of the bankruptcies of so many oil and gas companies in the 1980s, the process should all come back to him in no time.

For 3J, it was nothing new. It's what she did. A great deal of any law practice was repetition. Lots of "been there, done that."

Only this time, it wouldn't be anyplace she had been or anything she had done.

Chapter 7

THE SCHEME

3J HAD FILED the Paxton Energy and Remmy Paxton bankruptcy papers a week ago, but things were quiet. Frank Davis had gone radio silent. It was a little unusual that the bank group attorney wouldn't reach out to her after the bankruptcy cases were on file. But not unheard of.

Davis certainly wasn't known for a lack of diligence. Maybe he was still living in the banks' world, or they directed him not to reach out to her, or they would rather not pay a lot of money to a big-city attorney.

The clerks of the court assigned the cases to Judge Daniel Robertson. 3J was a regular before him. She was in court the next day to secure orders allowing the company to operate in the ordinary course of business. At the initial hearings, the court had approved her first-day motions, allowing the company to continue to operate under a budget she presented that the court approved. The banks didn't object. The budget included payment of bills (like payroll) and funding work needed for some existing drilling projects. But no new drilling. The court also permitted Paxton to use its cash on hand and cash from the sale of oil and gas as it was extracted from the company's existing production.

The budget excluded any payments to the banks, at least for the moment. Again, the banks raised no objection. Indeed, while Frank Davis attended the first day hearing to consider the debtors' motions, he said nothing more than to introduce himself to the court as the banks' attorney and rattle off each of their names. No bank representative was in attendance. Davis didn't ask for a role in drafting the orders approving the use of the cash.

Paxton Energy owed the banks a ton of money. 3J had never seen such a passive reaction to a Chapter 11 bankruptcy filing. Several days later, however, her laptop dinged with an email from the court's electronic filing system letting her know the banks had just filed a pleading in the Paxton Energy case.

It was their first, but it was a consequential one. It was a "Motion to Appoint a Chapter 11 Trustee," signed and filed by Davis. He had not contacted 3J beforehand to give her a heads-up about filing the motion for such a serious matter, which surprised her.

If successful, the motion would signal the beginning of the end for Paxton Energy. A first-round knockout in a heavyweight fight with the banks dancing around the ring, their still-gloved hands celebrating above their heads while the debtor lay on the mat out cold as the referee, here the bankruptcy judge, counted to ten and then called the fight.

The motion alleged that Remmy Paxton, CEO of Paxton Energy, had engaged in fraud, dishonesty, incompetence, and gross mismanagement. It wasn't as long a motion as she would have expected, given the gravity of the allegations. The bankruptcy rules required the banks to plead fraud "with particularity" for circumstances that amounted to fraud. While it wasn't a long filing, it said enough. It alleged that for years, Paxton Energy had overstated the value of its assets in a complicated "scheme" to borrow more money from the banks than it was entitled to. It alleged that the banks had only recently discovered the fraud and decided to shut down any additional funding for drilling while they tried to figure out what to do next.

They alleged a trustee could be appointed "for cause," and Paxton's conduct was more than enough "cause."

3J forwarded the email to Pascale and headed to his office to discuss it. When she arrived, he was reading the motion and frowning. She entered and sat while he finished.

"First things first," Pascale said. "We need to get Paxton in here as soon as possible. This time, let's make sure he brings whoever heads up the company's valuation group."

They called Paxton from Pascale's desk phone, and as they talked, 3J's cell dinged. It was another email alert from the court filing system. Judge Robertson had set the motion for an evidentiary hearing in two days. 3J groaned. There would be no time to take discovery to determine the evidence the banks relied on to support their motion. It looked like it was sizing up to be one of those Wild West trials by ambush—the banks could now spring evidence and witnesses on Paxton with no meaningful chance for the lawyers to investigate, prepare, and respond.

Not her favorite way to have a trial. But it sometimes happened in bankruptcy cases on emergency motions, and all a debtor's counsel could do was play the cards they were dealt the best they could.

Chapter 8

WHAT'S IN THE BANKS' EVIDENCE BAG?

FIVE OF THEM took their seats around the War Room conference table. 3J, Pascale, Remmy Paxton, Bree Paxton, and Linda Knoll, introduced as the vice president in charge of valuation at Paxton, who officed in Wichita. She was tall—almost six feet—slender, with brown eyes, light gray hair, and oil and gas exploration wrinkles around her eyes and across her forehead from decades of worrying about the success of every Paxton drilling project. She had been with Paxton for over thirty years and seemed to have crow's feet around her eyes for every one of them. She was Remmy's second cousin.

Knoll was an engineer by training with a degree from Houston's prestigious Rice University, known for churning out top-notch, sought-after oil and gas engineers and geologists.

"If there's something wrong with the way we value our oil and gas holdings, it would be my fault. All I can tell you is that we use industry-standard methods," Knoll explained in a slight Texas accent. "Tried and true methods. Nothing from the

Enron script. We analyze the extent of the oil and gas under-ground—the reserves—then we forecast the timing and extent of production, look at a twelve-month trailing average of prices, consider the risk of production, apply a discount to account for the receipt of money in the future, and arrive at a value." She scanned everyone's face and smiled. "That's the simple version."

"Any valuation disputes with the banks over the years?" 3J asked.

"Look, there's always a disagreement followed by an exchange of ideas," Paxton replied.

"We're talking about hydrocarbons underground," Knoll continued. "Deep in the earth. Hiding. Evading analysis. We *think* we know what's there. We *think* we know how and when we'll pull them out. We *think* we know what the price will be when we project pulling them out of the ground." She looked at the attorneys again. "But it's a lot more certain to value a cubic foot of gas or a barrel of oil we've extracted and sold. Valuing what's in the ground is as much an art as a science.

"My team runs our numbers, I review and sign off on the calculations, and I send them to Remmy for final approval," Knoll finished.

"Who interacts with the banks on the numbers?" 3J asked.

"Remmy," Knoll explained.

"Not you?"

"No. That's Remmy's gig. Always has been. It's his name in the logo."

"Do the numbers ever change after you give them to Remmy?" 3J probed.

"They can. Remmy knows what he's doing. He can correct and adjust the numbers. That's within his purview. Again, it's his company."

As Knoll explained the process, Remmy and Bree watched her closely. If the Paxtons' stare bothered Knoll, she didn't let on.

"Do you ever go back to compare Remmy's final numbers to the ones you submitted?" 3J asked.

"Not really. I've been with Remmy for my entire career. If I thought for a second there was any reason to distrust him, I'd turn in my key card and leave at once."

Knoll made her point; she was beyond reproach and had a fully operational moral compass.

As 3J reflected on what Knoll explained, Pascale asked, "Linda, you never interacted with the banks?"

"Y'know, Mr. Pascale, not really. My job is to give Remmy the best numbers I can. I crunch the data and deliver my valuations to him. After that, I'm on a new project, the next field, and well, new data. I'm not a relationship kind of person. Remmy is. The banks are his to manage."

"Pascale and I need to talk," 3J said. "Remmy, we'll call you later tonight if that works for you."

"No problem. Talk to you soon."

After Knoll and the Paxtons left, 3J and Pascale sat in silence, trying to develop a strategy to deal with an emergency motion in a bankruptcy case where the ink on the filing papers didn't have a chance to dry.

"Bill, I'm worried that Knoll won't make much of a witness. If Paxton had submitted her numbers to the banks over the years, she would be golden on the stand. If she knew which numbers Paxton had submitted, she'd be platinum. But she doesn't know either. All she can say is that she produces good values, hands them off to Paxton, trusts him to do the right thing, and moves to her next project."

"Right. The allegation isn't that no one at Paxton Energy created good valuations. The allegation is that the company distributed inflated valuations to the banks. And 'company' is a misnomer. In the motion, it's all Paxton, of course."

3J squeezed her eyes shut as she spoke. "If Paxton did this, how can I put him on the stand to testify? This kind of fraud on a bank is a federal felony." She opened her eyes and looked at Pascale as she shook her head. "If he testifies, and he has done something fraudulent, he'll have waived his Fifth Amendment right against self-incrimination."

Most attorneys counsel their clients against taking the witness stand and testifying if there's a chance they will incriminate themselves. Most clients listen to their attorney's advice.

Pascale rubbed the back of his neck to ward off the instant headache he had and the terrible set of facts they were faced with. "This is pretty fucked-up, 3J. Pardon my French. We have no time to hire an expert. Knoll's a 'no-go,' and Paxton may be a 'no-way' to testify."

By 10 p.m., 3J and Pascale were still in the office, trying to come up with a strategy to save Paxton Energy and keep Remmy Paxton out of jail. They phoned Remmy, and Bree joined the call. Remmy vehemently said he would testify and explain everything.

"I didn't cook any books, folks," Remmy said emphatically. "I think the banks are talking about adjustments to the final numbers. Whatever adjustments I made to Linda's numbers were minimal, inconsequential, and had no meaningful effect on the values. Linda's the expert, but there's always a range. I might make an adjustment using a different part of the range than Linda chose. But my adjustments, such as they were, had no impact on the banks at all.

"And in case you're wondering, we're not a mark-to-market outfit. We take in cash and report cash when we take it in, not when we sign a long-term supply agreement."

Pascale explained the Fifth Amendment and the right against self-incrimination. He told Remmy that he would waive that right if he testified about his adjustments and they turned out to be fraudulent. "You do not want Judge Robertson ruling that you submitted fraudulent numbers to the banks after you've testified."

Remmy said nothing.

"Remmy, we're going to have to make the call about you testifying during the hearing. We don't know what evidence the banks have. After we hear it, we'll have to evaluate it and huddle up in real time—"

"They have nothing," Remmy interrupted.

"The three of us will make the call at the hearing. Okay? It's our job to protect you from things like jail time for fraud," Pascale advised him.

For the first time in any of the meetings, Bree Paxton spoke up. "Remmy... listen to them. Jail. My Lord. We have a family. We have friends. We have a life. We've built something apart from Paxton Energy together. Let them do their jobs."

"Bree, I did nothing wrong. I can explain the minor adjustments I made to the valuations, like changing the discount rate from 8 percent to 7.9 percent, because that's what other oil and gas companies were using at the time. Sure, did a marginally lower discount rate increase the overall value? Of course. A lower rate means a higher value. Fraudulent? Not in the least. There's always a range. Always. And at every turn, the banks had the right and power to disagree with me and use their own discount rate. They never did."

3J and Pascale listened to the debate between the spouses. The level of detail Remmy used showed that Bree Paxton was much savvier about the business than either had let on.

"Remmy, you're in the risk business. But... jail? Jail, Remmy?" Bree's voice faded out, barely audible.

The call went silent.

Pascale said, "3J and I have some more thinking to do on a strategy. We have tonight and tomorrow. We'll call you both back."

When the call ended, 3J said, "We all have debtor clients who don't make it. Some months into the bankruptcy case, the business implodes. But I've never lost one in a matter of a week or so."

"Boy, I'd like to see what the banks have for evidence, 3J."

"You and me both, Bill."

Chapter 9

TRIAL BY AMBUSH COMING

3J WENT HOME. She couldn't share the day's events with Steele. Cupid's arrow couldn't pierce the attorney-client privilege. Even though it was Steele, revealing what was going on in the case would be unethical.

Steele had cooked dinner, as he often did. His years at O'Brien's had made him quite skilled around a skillet and an oven. They ate at her kitchen island in silence. "Nickel for your thoughts, 3J?"

"Sorry." She gave a closed-mouth smile. "Can't tell you. Attorney-client privilege."

"Even for me?"

"Even for you, *amore mio*." She twirled her pasta. "Tell me, how was your day?"

"I'm sure not as eventful as yours and not privileged. Tailed a guy for our client, his wife, soon to be his ex. Sat in a car all day with a camera in my lap, hoping for conjugal indiscretions I could capture on a small SD card. I hate that kind of assignment, but it's a good-paying gig. The thing is, I saw nothing. If he's breaking his vows, I didn't see it."

He took a sip of wine and continued, "In my vice years, stakeouts were long and tedious. And then something happened, and the whole thing went from zero to sixty in a nanosecond. It doesn't look like there's going to be any sixty on this assignment. One big zero. The wife will be disappointed."

Later, they sat on the couch and listened to The Prez, Lester Young, who settled in Kansas City and played sax with Count Basie for six years. Rumor was that he left the Basie band over a dispute that he wouldn't play on Friday the 13th. Others in the band said Count Basie had been considering his dismissal for months. Either way, while he played and recorded with Basie, they made jazz history. After Young, they teed up the 1939 album, *Count Basie and the Kansas City 7*.

"I Want A Little Girl" played on the turntable. Slow, smooth, soft-spoken jazz. 3J tucked her feet under her body, put her head down on Steele's shoulder, and as she closed her eyes, she tugged on his hand and pulled it around her shoulder to hug her.

Every so often, the best way to find a solution to a problem was to stop thinking about the problem. That's what 3J hoped for as the couch swallowed her up. At least for one song, she didn't think about Remmy Paxton. She drifted as the music coaxed her into peace.

Music can also help the mind subconsciously reorder things. Get them organized. Help your mind point you to an answer that you didn't or couldn't see sitting at your work desk.

3J opened her eyes and said, "I may have the plan for my new case."

"The case you can't tell me about?"

"That's the one. I need to call Pascale."

It was late, but Pascale answered the phone. 3J had moved

to the bedroom and closed the door behind her so Steele couldn't hear. She wasn't worried about his eavesdropping. He would never do that. She was just being thorough.

"Bill, here's what I suggest we do. The banks will go first since it's their motion. They'll put on their evidence, whatever it is. I assume a person to testify. At that point, we'll ask for a break and huddle. If the evidence points to fraud and we can only counter it with Paxton's testimony and a waiver of his Fifth Amendment rights, we'll tell the court we need a continuance to depose whoever testified and to gather the necessary records to show the banks' evidence is BS.

"There may not be enough time, even with a continuance, to hire an expert. We may need to go back to Linda Knoll to examine what the banks' witness said on the stand and the records used. Then, she can testify that the records are perfectly appropriate, even with Paxton's minor tweaks."

Pascale listened, considering what 3J proposed.

She continued, "I'm sure, given the quick hearing the judge set, he'll be inclined to grant us time to put together our case. He's not one for a trial by ambush."

"It's risky, 3J, but there's nothing better for us. We see what's on the banks' collective minds and react in the moment. I agree the odds are in our favor to get more time to respond. By getting such a quick hearing, the banks may have overplayed their hand."

"How so?"

"We see what they have for evidence, and then we get time to respond. Maybe depose whoever testifies. Maybe hire an expert ready to go a couple of weeks later."

"Sounds good under the circumstances, Bill."

"I'll call Paxton and read him into the plan. I'll email you right after my call if he has any pushback."

Paxton had no pushback.

They didn't know it yet, but Paxton would not need to prepare to testify. There would be no immediate response to the video. The banks were armed and would soon drop their video bomb on Remmy Paxton and Paxton Energy intending it to be a financial kill shot.

If the bomb took out Paxton's attorneys as well, so be it. Just some necessary casualties in the bankruptcy world.

Chapter 10

THE WALK BACK

AFTER THE SHORT hearing on the motion to appoint a trustee, 3J and Pascale had one of those wordless walks from the courthouse back to the Greene Madison offices at the corner of Twelfth and Walnut Street. It was the last downtown skyscraper built by financier and real estate developer Mory Robinson before he turned his attention to a Justice Department investigation, which he avoided by tragically dying of cancer and staying out of the Fed's line of fire from six feet under.

They entered the grand marble and granite lobby and summoned an elevator to take them to the twenty-seventh floor. Once they got in, they remained nonvocal. As they exited, 3J turned left for her office, and Pascale headed to the right.

They weren't morose or rude. They usually talked. Just this time, they didn't. Such was the fallout from watching a video for the first time that could tank their clients.

Ironically, their emergency hearing strategy had worked, and now they saw what the banks had in their evidence lockers. A short video in 1080p. The question was, how would the Greene Madison team counter it? In their silence, they

55

had come to the same conclusion: they had to counter the evidence on two fronts. First, they needed an expert to scan the books and records and form an opinion that the numbers were fair and the method used by Paxton Energy was well within industry standards.

There wasn't time to find an outside expert, familiarize the expert with Paxton Energy, review everything, and generate an opinion. No. It had to be Linda Knoll.

Second, and most importantly, they needed another expert to examine the video and opine about its authenticity. Was it real or fake? She wondered if they could prove it was fake with sufficient certainty, or would something less, something only calling into question the video's veracity, be enough to counter the appointment of a trustee? Would it be enough to show there was no cause?

They had twenty days to put the case together before they were back in court for the rest of the trustee hearing. Not enough time, but they had no choice and would have to make it work.

3J recognized that society had blurred the line between truth and fiction in the 2000s. Any time spent on Facebook or Instagram reading posts confirmed this. It was the reason she didn't spend her time reading them. But she realized the posts were there, many not even generated by a human but by artificial intelligence and a bot to promote one nefarious agenda or another, and she worried that we now seemed to live in a world that valued deception over truth.

Someone had said to her recently, "The truth is the lie, and the lie is the truth." They were making a joke, but it wasn't funny. It was an alarming reality. It could be the Paxton video.

Nothing is as it seems anymore. Her confidence in what might be real was fading quickly.

Suddenly, that became the mantra of the Paxton Energy bankruptcy case.

Chapter 11

DEEPFAKES

PASCALE AND 3J had agreed that he would work with Linda Knoll to develop their retort to the allegation of books and records improprieties. 3J would find the video expert and develop testimony to show the video was fake—if it really was. The more definitive the opinion, the better.

3J phoned a private investigator in New York City whom she'd worked with on several cases—Moses Aaronson. He was quirky but the best private eye she had ever known in her career.

He always picked up on the second ring. To her surprise, the call rolled over immediately to a recording and the voice message said, "I am taking a temporary sabbatical. Emily, the dog, and I have hired a driver, and we're off to see America." The message ended, and the call did as well.

Now what? 3J wondered. All she could think to do was to phone Belita Davies, nicknamed "Rome." Rome was Aaronson's tech-savvy colleague who worked on every matter with 3J when she hired Aaronson. Rome was the Bryn Mawr College liberal arts degree graduate, now living in London, who was legendary in the tech universe and had helped save several of 3J's clients.

Rome picked up on the first ring.

"Wonderful to hear your voice, 3J," Rome said in her British accent.

"Yours too. I need your help, Rome, and we're on a very short timeline." 3J explained the problem and asked, "Is Moses okay?

"Yes, Moses has taken a vacation—he likes to call it a sabbatical—to see America. He and his rat terrier, Emily, are off to who knows where in the lower forty-eight.

"Do you think you can maybe help me?"

"I'm here in the States, staying with friends on the Philadelphia Main Line while Moses is off. 3J, forgive me. I know a little about deepfakes but there are many others who live in that world 24/7. I think the best I can do is give you a little fake video background and a name of one of those who are immersed in the area. I have to warn you. The individual I'm acquainted with is not working on Wall Street in a high-rise building. He lives and works in the shadows. In his earlier days, he showered and shaved every once in a while and made Red Bull a very profitable company."

"Rome, I've got nothing right now, so I appreciate any help you can offer."

"Okay. First, a crash course. Deepfakes are the work of humans, but not exactly. They are really a form of artificial intelligence. Some think they are the grandest of deceptions. They epitomize valuing deception over truth.

"They combine doctored images and sounds, and then they stitch them together with machine learning algorithms. At the beginning of the use of deepfakes, they were funny, even playful. A claymation video where the clay creature looked and sounded like a real Hollywood celebrity goofing around. A scene where a cartoon character with the head of an actual person makes a joke or does a funny dance. One that comes to mind is a deepfake of Tom Cruise doing magic tricks. All relatively harmless. And in the beginning, the technology lagged, so it was usually obvious when a video was fake.

"But deepfakes have really grown in sophistication; they look and sound real. And their use has taken a dark turn. Real nefarious stuff. Sometimes, the deepfake might be the creation of an image of a person who does not exist but who is spewing propaganda. Sometimes, it is fabricating the image and voice of a person who exists. One historical line of thinking is that deepfakes started in 2017 when a Reddit user who called himself 'deepfakes' shared pornographic videos he doctored. I believe he took celebrity faces and swapped them onto other porn stars' bodies, supposedly by manipulating Google's open-source, deep-learning technology. To create the fake voices, AI and synthesizing technology generate voice skins or clones that sound like a real person."

"Okay, Rome. Hang on a second. I'm taking notes here, and I need to catch up," 3J said. Rome paused and waited for 3J. "Okay. Whew. Lots of great info. Please continue," 3J said as she took a sip of her Earl Grey tea.

"There are so many examples," Rome continued. "Some porn. Some not. A deepfake pornographic video of Taylor Swift in 2024. A deepfake video of Scarlett Johansson denouncing Kanye West's antisemitic remarks. A recent deepfake video of Rafael Nadal giving financial advice. A new AI actress named Tilly Norwood created by Eline Van der Velden.

"There is also AI and other tech out there to identify a

deepfake video, but as the identification process gets more sophisticated, so does the tech to create a deepfake. It is a cat-and-mouse game where the deepfake mouse creating the video is always a step or two ahead of the identification cat."

3J heard a siren in the background from wherever Rome was speaking. Rome paused and resumed when the siren passed.

"The identification tech looks at patterns: how a person speaks and moves. Things like eye movement, facial expressions, positioning, emotion or a lack of it, unnatural and awkward body movements, skin tone, odd hair characteristics like frizzy or flyaway hair, teeth abnormalities, and some more obvious ones: blurring and misalignment," Rome explained. "It analyzes voices and patterns. To catch all of this, the tech may slow down the image, zoom in, and employ other playback manipulations. The tech will examine the video pixel by pixel and sound bite by sound bite."

3J took more notes and said nothing. She was out of her league when it came to the technology. She only knew about the subject from a continuing legal education seminar she took last year when the speaker warned of deepfakes infiltrating the courtroom.

"Rome. Help me. What do I do here?" 3J pondered.

"Here is the gentleman you want," Rome offered. "The last I heard, he was in St. Louis, but he has worked as a freelancer for many outfits. Some are legitimate and some are not. He has created these videos, and he has also developed ways to detect them. I understand his detection methods are state-of-the-art. As you might imagine, the detection end of things can be quite lucrative. Imagine how much a rich celebrity like Taylor Swift might pay to prove the pornographic video of her was a fake.

I heard the deepfake of her had over forty-seven million views before someone took it down."

"Okay, I'm sold. Name and number?"

"Darius Wilson. DW to some of his friends. I will text you the number," Rome replied.

3J thanked Rome and wished her a good downtime in Philly. She then immediately phoned Wilson.

"Mr. Wilson, Josephina Jillian Jones. I got your name and number from a mutual friend, Belita Davies—Rome. I've worked closely with her over the years. I think I need your services."

"Which services?" Wilson asked in a professional tone.

"I am a courtroom attorney. The other side has introduced a video that we believe may be fake. We need you to examine the video, tell us your opinion, draft a brief report, and testify."

"When?"

"Well, now. That's the thing. We need to be back in court in twenty days with you on the stand."

"Ms. Jones, Rome and I go way back. When she was at Bryn Mawr, I was a fledgling American studies major at Haverford College just down the road. I'd do most anything for her and any of her friends. But I work for Robbie McFadden these days. Not sure if you know him."

"Oh, my," she said, startled. Then, in a hushed voice, she added, "Yes, I do."

Wilson continued, "Do I create videos for his clients? Sometimes. Do I look at videos and determine if they are fake to help clients out? I haven't since I've been in Mr. McFadden's employ, but I am equipped to do so. Do I freelance? I do not. Not anymore. Strictly a member of the McFadden team these days. You need to talk to Mr. McFadden. That would be best for both of us. Good day."

3J leaned back slowly in her desk chair. She needed an expert, and now she'd have to talk to Robbie McFadden? She didn't see that coming in a month of Sundays.

She was aware of Robbie McFadden. He was the head of a modern-day mob organization in Kansas City. The Irish mob. He was slick, handsome, and a renowned business executive, albeit not the CEO of your run-of-the-mill business ventures, nor were many of his methods taught at the business schools. Of course, unlike a typical business, he had to address his heightened need for secrecy, law enforcement, and violence that went hand in hand with a criminal organization. As a result, many decisions had to be made differently than in legal businesses.

And he had divisions. Not the typical divisions found in legal businesses. Murder for hire. Drug trade. Kidnapping, which she learned about in a case she handled last year. Gambling, the numbers, prostitution. Pretty much the traditional set of divisions you might expect to see in a 1940s black-and-white film noir starring James Cagney.

And now, apparently, he had a new division. One not seen in the film noir days of good guys and bad guys and shoot-'em-up endings. This was Robbie McFadden at his best. Spotting an opportunity and seizing it. His new deepfake video division.

He was legendary at police headquarters. The KCPD had never made charges stick. McFadden would enter the police headquarters with his entourage of criminal lawyers and stride out a free man. No shackles. No concern on his face. Grinning for the cameras. Offering a sound bite for the evening news as his lawyers worked behind the scenes and beat the overworked and outmatched Jackson County District Attorney's office at every turn. He was just the latest example of what historically made Kansas City a rough Missouri River town. Grift and graft, Kansas City style.

And something else about McFadden. He was the scourge of Ronnie Steele's existence. Steele and his vice partner, Moe Sterling, had tried and failed for decades to shut down McFadden's operations and put him behind bars. McFadden was always just a little smarter, a little better, and a little slicker than the vice squad and Ronnie Steele in particular.

3J was now conflicted. She desperately needed an expert. She only had one name from Rome. Would she actually reach out to McFadden, whom the love of her life considered to be Lucifer? If she did, would she be able to keep her new expert hire a secret from Ronnie Steele?

3J called Wilson back and asked how she should go about contacting Robbie McFadden. He told her to go down to a bar in the Bottoms district of Kansas City—the Bottoms Bar—and she could try to speak with McFadden. The Bottoms Bar? She had never heard of it. Wilson would call McFadden and tell him she might stop by.

As she thanked Wilson, he hung up. He was all business, not much personality. But as a fresh addition to the McFadden team, he was probably just being careful and trying to keep the boss happy. Not ideal for her, but he was all she had.

Her mind was racing. And now, she identified another dilemma: should she just go down to the Bottoms or should she first consult Pascale? It would be reckless to keep Pascale in the dark, but she would have to, at least until she had something substantive to report. She was also concerned that Pascale would say, "Absolutely not" to working with McFadden. 3J decided she would adopt Rear Admiral Grace Hopper's view: "It's easier to ask forgiveness than it is to get permission."

She grabbed her backpack and headed to the Greene Madison garage for a quick trip to the Kansas City Bottoms to meet with famed mobster Robbie McFadden.

In her car, she turned on KCUR radio for some jazz and the next song up was "Danger in the Dark," by Eddy Duchin and His Orchestra, from 1939.

How apropos.

Chapter 12

MR. MCFADDEN

ONCE IN HER car, 3J asked the guidance system for directions to the "Bottoms Bar." Surprisingly, the navigation system had the bar in its database. She drove west and descended hundreds of feet from downtown's perch above the confluence of the Missouri and Kansas Rivers to the area of Kansas City called "the Bottoms." Cattle and stockyards in the old days. Flamboyant hotels. Jazz at all hours. Betting. Numbers. Women. Booze. Drugs. It had it all. In those days, the Bottoms fed America's insatiable love of steak and Kansas City's need for fun before, during, and after work.

No cattle in the modern era. No more flamboyant hotels. No more music. Just some gentrification. Lofts, restaurants, bars, and businesses. It was tame compared to the wild cattle days. She had been down in the Bottoms many times and in many bars, but not in one named the "Bottoms Bar."

She located the bar. It sat in the shadow of the interstate overpass. Homeless men and women with their dogs camped out under the highway in makeshift tents, which protected them from the elements. It had taken a while, but the unhoused urban disease had found its way to Kansas City, and like other cities, it was there to stay with an ever-growing population.

The bar was one of those blink-once-and-you'll-miss-it establishments. And she almost drove past the entrance. She pulled up to a gravel parking area on the side of a rundown building. It had been a while since anyone had pulled the weeds growing in between the gravel. On the wall was a sign that warned, "Private Parking," which she could barely read behind the graffiti sprayed on the wall. In a window, an old blue and yellow neon sign strained to flash "The Bottoms Bar" on and off. A black Cadillac Escalade, polished and detailed, was parked near the entrance. There were no other cars in the parking area.

The homeless encampment was 120 feet away, and the homeless had the good sense to keep their distance. Perhaps it was McFadden's sinister aura.

The moment she entered, two large White men with bulging muscles and what appeared to be bulging holsters grabbed her, spun her around, and were about to frisk her. This was her first frisking, and she didn't much care for it.

She grunted and struggled to break free to no avail. *Look at these big White gangster roughnecks frisking an attractive Black female attorney! Only in America. Where are the cameras?*

"Boys, boys. Where are your manners?" A redheaded man with a trim red beard, dressed in a black suit, white shirt, and red power tie, sat in a booth near the back of the establishment. He posed the question to the large bodyguards, who still had 3J by the arms but were unsure what they were supposed to do next. 3J squirmed, but the men had immobilized her arms. McFadden had trained the boys well. They weren't letting go until ordered to do so by the man in the booth.

"Boys, let Ms. Jones pass through. I don't think we need to worry about patting down such a famous attorney-at-law here today, now do we?" He chuckled. "We don't want her to sue us on our first date."

Instantly, McFadden's hired hands released 3J, and the man in the booth waved to her to approach. The bodyguards returned to their places at the end of the bar, which they leaned on while surveying the scene. At this moment, there was little to survey, as the only people in the bar were McFadden, 3J, the bodyguards, and the bartender.

McFadden stood, straightened his coat, and gestured for 3J to slide into the booth. Suddenly, she wished she hadn't come to see him. The words "terrible mistake" flashed through her brain over and over like the gigantic, hi-def ticker tape news messaging in Times Square that no one could miss. 3J saw the warning in her head. She ignored it.

"Mr. Wilson contacted me and said you might be coming here for an unscheduled meeting. Welcome to my office. It's not much to look at, but it serves my purpose, and they stock my favorite Icelandic vodka." He smiled at her.

She felt a shiver of fear coming on and fought it. "You impressed DW, you know, with what's-her-name? Sicily?"

"Rome," she corrected him. She resisted shaking her head at the notion that here she was sitting across from the biggest hood in Kansas City. But she had come on a mission. She was an attorney. She had a client in need. She had a job to do. It was that simple. She closed her eyes, breathed deeply, and got on with it.

"I would have set up an appointment, Mr. McFadden, but I was unsure how to do that with you. I apologize for coming over unannounced."

"Yeah. I don't exactly keep my calendar online where potential clients can just schedule an appointment." He smiled more at his own subtle humor than to ease 3J's concerns. "Not a worry. That's why I have the boys. Can I get you a drink?"

"No, thanks."

McFadden waved, and in short order, the bartender brought over a vodka on the rocks. He twirled the drink.

"So... ? You're not here for small talk, I'm guessing."

3J explained her problem. She needed to hire Darius Wilson. He needed to perform his analysis quickly and then testify. She needed to hire Robbie McFadden's guy.

"I'm intrigued. Y'know, a business needs to keep up with the times or it immediately falls behind. You can't get too comfortable. Complacency can be dangerous. In my line of work, you quickly learn to be comfortable being uncomfortable. You learn to keep your antennae up. Helps you stay alive. An important goal for me. But here I am talking to a barrister—an officer of the court—about deepfake videos. These videos are illegal in some parts. Makes me a little uncomfortable to talk to a court officer about them."

He shook his head, smiled, and sipped his vodka.

McFadden continued, "But you came all this way. Let's agree on this. We'll consider our conversation—shall we say, hypothetical—at least for now." He nodded and raised his eyebrows. She nodded in return.

"All right, deepfakes," McFadden began. "Turns out, there was a real demand around the Midwest for people to create fake videos. I myself am not on social media, and I'm not as high-tech savvy as I should be. As a result, this demand was news to me. But it's there, and while there were freelancers filling the need here and there, I saw an opportunity to offer the videos. Highest quality. For a price, of course. I am an entrepreneur, after all."

He smiled at 3J and sipped his vodka again, slowly rubbing the condensation on the glass with his thumb.

"Now, why do these folks want a deepfake video? Not really my concern. I hear tell they can be a funny birthday present. Or they can be quite effective in ruining someone's career. Discrediting a politician. Placing an entrepreneur in a compromising situation. Or maybe as a way to make some money. You know, blackmail. Raising money by coercion."

He paused as if to give 3J an opportunity to speak. McFadden was silky smooth and even polished, articulate, compelling, and yes... engaging. Everything Steele had told 3J, he was. At no time, however, did 3J forget he was also dangerous, and at times, lethal, and she was sitting in his lair with his armed muscle just feet away.

3J had nothing to say, so she just nodded, and McFadden continued.

"Back in the day, this was quite a town for that last item on the list: let's call it alternative fundraising. Here, allow me to explain. Ever hear the story of Bobby Greenlease? He was the kid of a Cadillac dealer here in town. Lived in Mission Hills. The kid went to school at Notre Dame de Sion."

McFadden fiddled with his glass. He looked at the glass, not 3J. "Same school as my kids. Someone snatched the kid from the school right under the noses of the nuns. Tricked one nun into handing over the kid. He was just a six-year-old.

"Then came the ransom demands. I read it was $5 million in today's dollars. Old man Greenlease went to his bank's executive, Arthur Eisenhower, who, by the way, was the brother of President Eisenhower, to arrange to pay the ransom. Next thing you know, there are fake ransom demands out the wazoo. Hard to separate the real one from the fakes. Kinda like these deepfake videos today."

3J had heard that McFadden counted himself a student of Kansas City history and was in the habit of telling parables. Occasionally, they were relevant. Occasionally, they were not. At all times, however, he expected his audience to listen. 3J complied with the protocol.

"It was a botched job from the start. A rich car dealer driving around from location to location carrying a duffel bag stuffed with money. The kidnappers and the impostors gave conflicting instructions. Eventually, the money got to the actual kidnappers. In days, the police caught a woman who confessed, and then the cops found the body of the boy buried. Carl Austin Hall and Bonnie Brown Heady were the drunk, drugged-up kidnappers. Like I said, I've got kids. Damn shame about little Bobby, not to mention the parents. No parent should ever have to get the call that someone snatched their kid. Hall and Heady didn't make it to the old age home. Missouri executed them in the gas chamber. Good riddance." He swirled and sipped.

"My point is this whole extraction of money from rich folks thing has been around Kansas City long before the internet showed up in our living rooms. Now it's high-tech. If somebody wants a video, we'll assist in its creation. If they use it to extract money—something like, 'You pay me and I'll take down the video'—it's their business, not mine."

"I don't need a video, Mr. McFadden. Unfortunately, a group of banks has already provided me with a short one, and the banks say it's my client in the video admitting to bank fraud, so I already have one. If it's real, my client is done for.

What I need is for Darius Wilson to examine the video and opine whether it's real or fake. Rome says that Mr. Wilson is the best."

McFadden listened and stroked his red beard. "Up to now, we haven't been in the business of examining videos created by others. Strikes me as more like detective work than the kinds of things my organization does. In fact, not too long ago, a banker came in here and told me someone posted a porno video of him and said they would take it down for a price. Kinda like what happens to celebrities. The banker didn't want to pay the blackmailer. He wanted proof that he wasn't in the video to force the deepfaker to remove it from the internet. I turned him down."

"Why?"

"He was a banker. I've had some bad experiences working for bankers in the not-so-distant past. I think you were even involved in one of those matters."

McFadden was referring to Jordan Browne and a case 3J handled that involved the kidnapping of Browne's brother, Amadi, a bank president.

He smiled. He knew 3J handled the Browne kidnapping matter. 3J knew McFadden had arranged the kidnapping. There was that ticker tape again. Undulating around the ABC building and across 3J's mind. But she ignored the ticker and just sat there, motionless, across from McFadden.

3J and McFadden should have been like two magnets with like poles repelling each other. But the magnets weren't working, and there she was, asking for his help.

"You're going out with Ronnie Steele, aren't you?"

"Yes. I don't see what that has to do with my request."

"Stand down, Ms. Jones. Nothing threatening intended.

Give him my regards. Decent guy notwithstanding his career obsession with taking me out of commission. I'm sure he wouldn't use the words 'decent guy' about me. I get it. I understand he's in the private detective business these days. With his vice partner, Moe Sterling. Why not use them?"

"I can't. He's not a deepfake expert, and neither is Moe."

"Moe. Damn good cop in the day. Does Ronnie realize you're here, talking to me?"

"Pass," 3J answered.

"Pardon?"

"We need to focus on my client and the video, Mr. McFadden. Not Ronnie Steele."

"All right. All right. You've got some kinda spunk." McFadden looked up at the ceiling and rolled his head to relieve tension in his neck. "I guess I'm willing to cross over to the dark side here, and we'll see what happens."

"Dark side?" 3J asked. "I thought that was your side."

Ignoring her comment, he said, "Tell you what, Ms. Jones. For fifty grand, you can have Darius Wilson. A flat fee. Analysis, report, and testimony. The whole works."

"Fifty grand? Jesus!"

"He won't help you, my friend. It's just you and me."

They sat in silence. McFadden continued, "Fifty. That's it, and that's all. I'm willing to help, but I'm not in this for my health. This is a business I'm running. What's it worth to save a company these days?"

He paused to see if 3J had a response. She didn't.

"By the way," he continued, "that's the discounted price. Because I like you. Call it a friends and family discount."

There was that McFadden smile again. Disarming.

"Experts are expensive, right? Every lawyer I ever hired is

expensive. Crazy expensive sometimes. The monthly bills are like a tome. I'm guessing you're expensive too, right?"

"I need to talk to my client."

"Sure thing. It's a free country."

"Not really," 3J said as she stood to leave.

McFadden smiled. "Fair point."

"If they want to hire Mr. Wilson, how do I communicate with you, and how do I get you the money?"

"I'll call you tonight. Leave your mobile number with the boys."

3J stood to leave. She handed the musclemen her card. She extended her hand and offered to shake McFadden's hand. She wasn't sure whether he would shake her hand or turn her palm downward and kiss the top of her hand as if they were having the conversation in Paris. But he was all business and shook her hand.

On the drive back to the office, 3J realized that there was a huge problem. She didn't want to tell Pascale about McFadden. And she needed to speak with Remmy Paxton. She would have to talk to Paxton without Pascale on the line, even though the latter was his client. But she was already going to get significant blowback, so in for a penny, in for a pound. It was just a matter of timing, and she had no time at the moment to deal with Pascale and his likely response.

She phoned Remmy from the car, explained the McFadden and Darius Wilson situation, and asked if there was a way to raise fifty thousand dollars quickly, perhaps from Bree Paxton's personal wealth, which was outside the bankruptcy cases, to pay McFadden for his service. She explained that there wasn't enough time to come up with another option. This was the only hope.

Not half a second went by and Remmy said, "Yes. Do it."

And with that, the payment to the demon who officed in the Bottoms for the hope of saving Paxton Energy became the prevailing plan—the only plan at the moment. Darius Wilson would examine the Paxton video and determine whether it was a fake or genuine. And if he determined it was genuine? Then what? Then, Paxton Energy would go down, and Remmy Paxton would go away—in handcuffs.

❧

On the car ride back to her office, 3J thought about her meeting with McFadden. He had gravitas. She would expect that from a mob boss. But he also seemed like a deep thinker. Then she remembered something Katie Couric had said in a speech she gave once in Kansas City: gravitas is just the Latin word for testicles. True about McFadden. He certainly had a set of those.

3J would need a bit of that to explain this situation to Pascale and Steele. At some point... not yet.

When she returned to the office, she found Pascale and related the conversation with Rome and Rome's recommendation. Like 3J, Pascale had also worked closely with Rome and had developed both a high level of trust in Rome and admired her skill set and knowledge.

3J omitted the part of the story that Wilson worked for Robbie McFadden. Without it, Pascale, thinking that hiring Wilson was just the normal engagement of an expert, told 3J to proceed quickly and set up a meeting.

"Bill, have you made any progress with Linda Knoll?" 3J asked.

"Just getting started," Pascale explained. "She needs to take a deep dive into the books and records as Paxton presented them to the banks. I tasked her with making a spreadsheet to compare the final valuations presented to the banks. She's thorough. I'm just holding my breath for the conclusion."

"How far back did you ask her to go? Paxton Energy has been at this a long time, and Knoll has been there a long time too."

"I asked her to start with a five-year look back. That would cover five renewals of the bank loans and at least ten presentations of value by Paxton to the banks. Seems fair?"

"I think so, depending on what she finds."

"Agreed. When Wilson comes over here, I want to meet him."

Chapter 13

AUTHENTICATION

JUDGE ROBERTSON WAS back in his chambers the day after the trustee hearing. His law clerk, Jennifer Cuello, sat in the easy chair facing the judge's desk, pad in her lap. It was their standard morning routine. It gave them a chance to discuss any upcoming and recently completed hearings. It also gave the judge a chance to assign research projects to her.

She had thought about applying to Greene Madison as her two-year clerkship was ending. It would be an opportunity to work for 3J and Pascale, whom she admired. The judge thought it would be a great fit. But her parents' health was failing, which took up more of her time. She wasn't sure it was the ideal time in her life to change jobs. She had asked Judge Robertson to extend her law clerkship, which he was pleased to do.

She was reliable, they made a great team, and he enjoyed working with her. Her law firm life would have to wait.

Cuello knew the Paxton Energy case and the issues well because she had attended the first trustee hearing.

"That hearing yesterday was one of the shortest I've had,

especially considering the gravity of the request to appoint a trustee," the judge said. "It was quite dramatic. Mr. Davis did what he had to do. Even so, something about the trustee issue doesn't feel right. Off-kilter. What was your reaction, Jennifer?"

"Good lawyers. New debtor. Crazy video. Examiner appointed. Bang-bang. Obviously, it took Ms. Jones and Mr. Pascale by surprise. A lot went down in such a short time," Cuello replied.

The back-and-forth between the judge and his law clerk was normal. The job of being a judge is a solitary affair. The process of deciding cases can be lonely. A judge talks, throws out ideas, and sorts out issues only with their law clerk.

A federal clerkship was the job of a lifetime for any law student who had just graduated. There were very few of these positions in the country and even fewer in bankruptcy. Cuello felt lucky every day she drove to the courthouse to work.

"The statute says I have to appoint an examiner if the US Trustee asks for one," the judge told her. "I had little choice. But this video presents a real conundrum, to say the least. I agree with you. Ms. Jones had no idea about the video. It was reasonable to give her a short amount of time to put together a response and a defense. In the end, her client might deserve a trustee, but she deserves a chance to see if she can figure this all out. A brief chance."

Jennifer nodded.

"But I'm worried about where this is all heading. Is Mr. Paxton going to say the video is a fake? Doesn't everyone these days? If he does, who should I believe? Will Ms. Jones bring in her own expert? I'm betting she will. Then I'll have dueling experts. How will I break the tie?"

He walked to his window and looked out past the edge of downtown to the confluence of the Missouri and Kansas Rivers beyond. The spit of land where Lewis and Clark made camp at Kaw Point in 1804 on their epic journey to the Pacific. The window with the view was where he liked to contemplate.

"I heard a radio interview on KCUR some years ago where an art student was trying to put the two rivers in better context. The radio piece said something like, 'The confluence is why Kansas City exists today.' That's so true. Remembering how we got here should be high on our list of what's important."

He turned and smiled at Jennifer. "But I'll be damned if I can understand how we got to a world of fake videos and judges who are ill-equipped to decide what's real and what's not. Not just judges. Most people can't tell the difference and assume everything they read is true and everything they see is genuine, unless they don't agree with it. Then they assume it's fake."

Cuello nodded. "But I'm sure it will become clear. It almost always does."

"We can hope, right? In the not-so-distant past, a witness would come into court, present a photo, identify the people in the photo, state who took the photo and that it was genuine, and the photo came into evidence. People could later argue about the significance, but it came into evidence.

"Fast-forward to the wonderful social media time we live in. How does a lawyer authenticate a video and have it admitted into evidence now that we have fake videos floating around?"

"Well, Judge, Frank Davis did it one way. The video identifies the debtor's CEO. He's well known. The expert says it's real, and the person speaking is Paxton. He says he examined the video using his state-of-the-art techniques and determined the video was genuine. Other people in the video call the star of the video 'Remmy.' The CEO's real name. Someone mentions the company's name as well."

"Excellent summary. That's the precise spot we're in. Maybe that's the end of the story, and maybe not. My guess is, for Ms. Jones to survive this scuffle, she'll have to find someone to say it's a fake. Then it'll be up to me to figure out what to do.

"Meanwhile, I seem to recall an article or two I read about the process of authentication. Please find those for us to read. Maybe it muddies the waters even further, but I'm hoping it will light a path for us."

"Will do, Judge."

Chapter 14

1859 EVERGREEN PLANTATION AND PAPA

HER EYES WERE closed as she lay on the hard bed in one of the twenty-two slaves' cabins made of narrow slats of wood. The cabins lined part of the plantation and housed the more than one hundred slaves who lived and worked there. In the distance, she could hear the whooshing sound of a belt snapping and slashing the back of James, a slave she knew well. She didn't know what James had done. Slaves didn't need to have done anything to take an evening beating.

It was the threat of a beating that weighed on every slave's mind. Just the knowledge that they might be next. That and a complete lack of freedom.

The Civil War was about to break out. It was 1859 on the quiet Evergreen Plantation, between New Orleans and Baton Rouge on the Mississippi's west bank, forty miles upriver from New Orleans. A wealthy aristocratic family owned the sugar plantation with a mill that belched out the smell of burnt refined sugar. It smelled like a dessert chef in New Orleans's French Quarter was caramelizing sugar with a flame.

Her name was Bessie. Even with her eyes closed, she could still see everything. Maybe too much. With her ears covered by the crook of her arm, she could still hear everything and maybe more. She had seen and heard it before. She knew all too well. There was no way to block out the knowledge.

The beating took place near the quarters where she tried to sleep. It was a typical Louisiana evening—hot and humid. She shared the quarters with other slaves and the Louisiana bugs as large as the live oak trees that majestically lined the entry to the plantation grounds and whose limbs formed the canopy that shaded the entry path from the relentless Louisiana sun. The same trees that masked what really went on at Evergreen.

Bessie was pregnant. The teenage boy from the family that owned the plantation had raped her. The teenager with the hazel eyes. No one committed a crime when the victim was a slave. No crimes against slaves. They were property, not humans. No Family Leave Act. No employment law rights. Not for slaves in the pre-Civil War South. She worked by day in the kitchen, cooking the food that fed the family; her meals helped the teenage boy who raped her turn into a full-grown man.

The Evergreen Plantation. 1859.

Bessie was 3J's ancestor, and the child she would deliver was the source of 3J's eyes. The slave child ancestor with hazel-colored eyes. Passed down to 3J through generations of Creole DNA and a constant reminder of her roots.

Papa liked to use the family history to make a point to his young daughter who he always called Jo. "Jo, near the end of the Civil War and extending to after emancipation, Blacks on the Evergreen Plantation stopped working to demand better conditions and wages. The slaves used something named the Freedmen's Bureau to relocate slaves and help them transition to post-Civil War life. Slaves boycotted for better wages and conditions as they continued to work on the plantations after emancipation."

A young 3J listened intently to her father's history lesson.

"The plantation owners opposed the Bureau and called in federal troops to force the former slaves back to work," Papa continued. "Sometimes these troops shot at the former slaves. Bessie was one of the boycotters. All she wanted was a chance at a better life, and she lost her life during a boycott. Shot down. It orphaned her young son."

Sometimes after the story, Papa would offer a lesson.

"We can't right every wrong, Jo," Papa explained. 3J nodded. Not every crime has a remedy. The South wronged every slave. Bessie, even more so. There was no remedy for that, just more work every day for the plantation man until they shot her down. But that wrong turned into you. Here you are with those eyes, Jo. You're Bessie's reward."

"What does it all mean, Papa?"

"Think about your Bessie, Jo. You gotta do what you need to do to make things right. You can't give up. You gotta keep trying. And sometimes you gotta do something that The Man will think is wrong to make things right. Do you understand?"

"I think so, Papa."

Chapter 15

WARD PARKWAY

"**An interesting day** indeed, gentlemen," Robbie McFadden said to the two bodyguards driving him to his home on Ward Parkway, where the Kansas City money lived. Old school and nouveau money mingling together like an Old Fashioned's sugar and whiskey instead of oil and water.

It was where the legitimate businessmen bumped elbows with the likes of McFadden, separated only by large plots of land, tall wrought iron fences, and only subtle differences in business philosophies and the way to the top.

Kansas City: smack-dab in the middle of the country. Center cut, like a fine-aged steak. Ward Parkway: the medium-rare center of that steak cooked to perfection.

"I don't think I've ever had a Greene Madison partner walk into the bar and hire me before. Come to think of it, I don't think I've had any partner at a law firm hire me, at least not in the recent past."

"I don't remember it happening before, Mr. McFadden," one of the front seat occupants agreed.

"Took a lot of gumption for her to walk into the bar and

then stay. I'll give her that. She walked in and didn't hesitate. She's got some kinda testicles."

"Do you like her, boss?"

"I don't know her. And given what she does and what I do for a living, I don't see us getting all cozy, professionally. I don't see us getting together and laughing it up at a cocktail party soon. But, at this point, I can say is I like what I see. She's got a brain. I could see myself respecting her. I could see her tolerating me. She's got balls. And... She's easy on the eyes. But I'm a happily married entrepreneur, so I'll just focus on the brain. Another client in need of my services."

He looked out his window as the large SUV made its way near The Country Club Plaza and its Italian-tiled buildings, where old and new money Kansas Citians shopped.

"Now that I have her card, I guess I'll have to add her to my little Rolodex." He chuckled. "I have no doubt she'll be the only bankruptcy lawyer in it. I need lawyers in my business, just not with her expertise. But then again, it's a big, tangled world and ya never know, right?"

The vehicle went past the Plaza and neared the entrance to Ward Parkway, the wide, winding, tree-lined boulevard named after Hugh Campbell Ward, a Kansas City attorney and land-owner who worked with J.C. Nichols, the fabled Kansas City real estate developer, to conceive a majestic winding thorough-fare. Ward conveyed ninety acres to the city, which added it to the parks and boulevard system, and the city's landscape architect, George Kessler, designed it.

"God, I love this street. Nothing like it anywhere in the Midwest," McFadden said. "We all owe old J.C. Nichols and that Ward guy a debt of gratitude. Y'know, old Ward and J.C. also developed Sunset Hills."

Sunset Hills was the neighborhood overlooking Ward Parkway that was built on bluffs rising over the Plaza. Elevated terrain hosted grand homes built at the turn of the previous century. Many of the homes had little to no backyards, and the backs of the homes perched precipitously on the edge of a bluff.

"Many's the time I've toyed with the idea of moving to Sunset Hills if the right house came on the market. I love Ward Parkway, but the Sunset Hills views, damn, they're good. But navigating its windy, hilly streets in the winter? Nah. Not for the faint of heart."

"You want me to detour through Sunset Hills?" the driver asked.

"Sure, why not?"

After they meandered through the steep Sunset Hills, they headed for McFadden's Ward Parkway home.

"I wonder if old Ronnie Steele knows that his woman hired me. The world is full of cruel jokes. I'd pay big bucks to see the look on his face if she tells him who I hired. But if I were her, I'd figure out a way to keep him in the dark."

His bodyguards in the front seat smiled. They also found the image of Ronnie Steele learning that his girlfriend hired Robbie McFadden amusing. Irony can be amusing and also a sweet revenge.

"I may just look a little deeper into this case that Wilson will work on with her. Maybe I can help Ms. Jones. You know, no charge. Just being a good Samaritan. God, that'd really piss off Steele. Just like in the old days. That would make my week for sure, and I might enjoy a diversion into some investigatory work."

McFadden paused and smiled.

"Not my usual hustle, but who knows?"

Chapter 16

MEET DARIUS WILSON

Darius Wilson sat in the War Room, scrutinizing the Paxton video with 3J, Pascale, and Remmy. Also at the table was Greene Madison's head of IT, Millie Brownstein.

Wilson was a notch over six feet tall, slender, with long fingers and a scraggly mustache. He looked to be in his thirties, although he was balding, so his precise age was not clear. His eyes were dark and brooding. Everything about him oozed intensity. 3J had found out he went to Yale for a master's in computer science after undergrad. So he was pale, Yale, and male, as she once heard someone describe an attorney who had graduated from there. Most importantly, according to Rome, he was a leading authority on identifying deepfakes.

He had neither pen nor pad to take notes as he examined the video for the first time. He belonged to that generation. He nodded, a deliberate movement, as he watched the video.

After several plays, Wilson said, "If this is a fake, it's not a bad one. Not perfect, but not bad." Looking at Brownstein, he continued, "I'll need a copy of the video file. I assume it's an MP4?"

"Correct. Looks to be an MP4 file in 1080p resolution at twenty frames per second," Brownstein responded.

"Wish it were more frames per second, but I can make that work."

"What happens next?" 3J asked.

"I have some proprietary software back at the shop that I've developed. It not only helps me make videos for clients, but I can also use it to do a rigorous assessment to identify tells in the videos that will inform me if it's fake. The world uses artificial intelligence to make these things. I can use AI to determine if they're fake. Pitting AI against AI, if you will. My detection module is like Sensity.ai, Deepware Scanner, and Microsoft's Video Authenticator put together, only more so.

"I can blow up frames. I can slow the video down. I can look at the pixels. Examine the voice and any background sounds. Look for anomalies. Things in the video that don't move right. Things that don't look quite right. People that don't sound quite right.

"What would be helpful, indeed, is if there were a video of Mr. Paxton that we knew was real. Maybe something filmed by Paxton Energy. High-quality. Something to establish a baseline of Mr. Paxton's mannerisms, body language, speaking style, and pace."

"We have several videos of me I can provide to you," Paxton offered.

"I'm sure there may be more that I'll need, but this will be a good place to jump off," Wilson said.

"What kind of timeline are we looking at?" 3J asked.

"I'm finishing up a couple of projects, and then I'll have time to turn my attention to this right away. I'd ballpark it at about a week to ten days for me to provide you with my conclusion and explain how I arrived at it. From there, you can let me know what you will expect from me in court." Wilson smiled. "Y'know, I've never been to court before. Always managed to avoid it. Better for my health to steer clear. I've got some friends, though, who one task force or another caught up with and who ended up seeing the inside of a courtroom. And worse. I visit them occasionally in their new federal home.

"But Mr. McFadden says he can help protect me from that kind of unfortunate outcome while still serving his clients' needs."

There it was. Wilson had uttered the name.

Everything had gone so well until Wilson said it. Pascale's demeanor changed instantly. A flicker of disbelief, a slackened jaw, his eyes widened, a flash of anger, and then his face froze.

"McFadden?" Pascale asked. "Did you say *McFadden?*"

"Yes, Robbie McFadden. He's my boss. You could say I'm on his staff. Head of the Tech Creation and Investigation Department. I'm thinking of calling it the TCID. Ms. Jones and he worked out the terms of my engagement."

"They did? I see," Pascale said deliberately. His features slowly returned to normal, and now he looked calm. But he was struggling—fighting the urge to lash out at 3J. He stood, shook Wilson's hand, and thanked him for coming.

Wilson and Paxton left. Pascale collected his papers and pad and went to his office. 3J followed him like a new associate might follow the partner to whom they reported. Deferential. A step or two behind to stay out of his line of sight, but trying to keep pace.

3J had a feeling this would not end well. She was concerned that one meeting with the mobster had torched her working relationship and friendship with Pascale. This might be the worst meeting they had since he had recruited her out of Washburn Law School to work in *his* bankruptcy department. The one *he* built. The one *he* staked his reputation on. The one who was now working *with* Robbie McFadden. The one she would inherit someday.

At least the one everyone thought she'd inherit before the Wilson meeting. After the meeting? Maybe not.

Chapter 17

A DAMN MOBSTER?

PASCALE ENTERED HIS office, famous for its clutter, sat down, and began to straighten the files and papers strewn across his desk. It was a hopeless task. He never cleaned. This was out of character. He said nothing. He ignored her.

"Aren't you going to speak to me?" 3J asked.

Without looking at her, he said, "What should I say? You chose not to tell me. I guess you thought maybe I'd never find out. Considering that, what would you have me say now that I know?"

"I want you to do what you always do… Speak your mind."

"Contrary to popular belief, I don't express my opinion on every topic," Pascale replied not making eye contact with 3J. "On this one, I have nothing to say. My mind is a blank canvas. Whatever I might offer for you to consider is already in the past. Yesterday's news. We shouldn't be here, but we are. And now, there's nothing I could say and nothing I wish to say."

This was worse than getting chewed out by Pascale. She wanted to explain, both about why she hired McFadden's man,

Wilson, and why she did it without consulting Pascale first. But Pascale had no interest in hearing the whys and wherefores.

"You made the mess. Now we'll have to deal with it," Pascale muttered.

She had done things like this before, and she would do things like this again. It was part of the way she was built. Danger attracted her in uncontrolled ways. There was a line. Occasionally, she stepped over it and back. But this was a long leap over the line that divided what a lawyer should and shouldn't do. And she knew it.

Her track record was well known. When 3J was at the helm, things tended to work out, even if what she did was wrong. Good results. Questionable methods. They had discussed the methods. He had even lectured her. He knew that someday she would go too far. Someday had now arrived. Hiring Robbie McFadden could never work out.

"I have to get with Knoll and start looking over her shoulder as she develops her analysis. I'll let you know… if there's something to let you know."

And that was it. No raised voices. No "How could you?" No "You've let me down." No "Are you insane?" No "Who the hell do you think you are?"

If she were a child, she would be told to go to her room because Papa had nothing more to say to her. A personal timeout to give her time and space to think about what she had done and contemplate the error of her ways. As a kid, it happened too often. Now, she told herself, Pascale had just done the same as Papa: told her to go to her office, her room at work, because he had nothing to say to her. A business timeout because Pascale wanted her to think about her actions, not talk to him about them.

She inched her way out of Pascale's easy chair and breached the doorjamb, almost shuffling on her way back to her office to be alone with her thoughts.

∽

That evening, she arrived home at 7. Even though it had only been a few blocks, it seemed like a much longer walk down Walnut Street as she pondered if, when, and how to tell Steele about Robbie McFadden. She opened her door, but there was no one there to greet her. Instead, as she entered her living room, she saw a side view of a solemn and bleak-looking Ronnie Steele sitting in one of the club chairs he had turned ninety degrees so he could stare out the windows.

Something was wrong. Every fiber in her body told her he already knew. She didn't know how, but he did.

She filled her lungs and held her breath. She knew what was coming. Steele had spent his entire career in vice trying to put Robbie McFadden behind bars. In Steele's binary world of good and evil, McFadden was evil. She hoped she could find a way to talk him out of feeling the way he did. She was sure this wouldn't be a Pascale-like meeting with little or nothing said. Silence wasn't Ronnie Steele's style.

Steele turned to face her, and the argument began. As expected, he took a very different approach from Pascale's.

He spoke. She listened. His voice was rigid and uncompromising. It was clear he wasn't seeking an exchange of ideas.

"Robbie Fuckin' McFadden? A damn mobster! Are you serious?"

"I had no other options, Ronnie. It was my only choice. We have less than three weeks. The client is circling the drain.

We need to prove a video is fake. I called Rome. She gave me one name: Darius Wilson. Turns out, he works for McFadden. It's the only solution, or the client is done for."

But Steele was having no part of it. He kept shaking his head. He mumbled "I can't believe this" over and over.

"3J, I chased this man for my entire career. He is bad. Plain and simple—bad. Some things you do, I've learned to understand and accept. Some of your methodologies I've come to live with. Not this one. This isn't a gray area. If you get in bed with this guy, it won't end there. I promise it won't. It's like signing the contract for your soul with the devil at the crossroads. You went down to the Bottoms. That's his cross-roads, dammit!"

"How did you find out?" She had to know.

"You mean why didn't your subterfuge work?"

"No. I meant what I said. How did you find out?"

"Someone on the force was watching McFadden's bar in the Bottoms. Par for the course. Just like Moe and I used to do. The cop saw you walk in. He told Moe. Moe told me."

3J put her hand on her forehead in disbelief. "Ronnie, what do you think is going to happen? McFadden and I will become the next Bonnie and Clyde, and I'll run around the countryside with him robbing banks and shooting cops with a machine gun and driving the getaway car? I've done what I had to do to try to save a client. The rest of this is just a big kerfuffle that will pass. It'll have to."

"Not a kerfuffle. It's an epic fucking mistake, 3J. Epic!"

They went to their respective corners in between rounds. After a few minutes, the silent bell rang and a new round began. 3J tried to strike a conciliatory note. "Ronnie, we're just going to disagree about things from time to time. Sometimes on big-deal things. Can't we just learn to disagree better?"

"Sure. Of course. On most things. But not on this particular big-deal thing."

"I'm sorry, Ronnie. Occasionally, the attorney gig challenges relationships."

"I've heard that said before. I think the way you operate, the attorney gig can get in the way more than just once in a while."

She felt the verbal punches like a boxer feels body blows when he's on the ropes.

They both dragged in deep breaths and said nothing for one of those moments that seemed like an eternity.

"You're saying it's me?" 3J asked.

Steele took a few moments to answer. "I guess so." More silence. Then, in a moment of resignation, he said, "But I guess there's always tomorrow."

"People assume there's always a tomorrow. And there is until there isn't. There's no guarantee a new day will bring us opportunities to work this out."

"What does that mean?"

"It means I'm committed to working this out now. I can't wait to see what tomorrow may bring."

Steele shook his head in disgust. "Sorry. Not going to happen. Not tonight. I'm too upset. Let's table it and see about tomorrow. I'm sure there'll be at least one or two more tomorrows for us. We're still almost young."

3J went to the bedroom, dejected, and as she changed her clothes, she heard Steele close the front door by easing it shut. She knew without looking. He left. For now. At least she hoped it was just for now. No note. No goodbye. He just slipped out the front door.

She dragged herself into the kitchen, her slippers scuffing against the hardwood floors. No keys on the kitchen counter. *At least he took his keys.*

She ran her hands over her hair. What a mess.

Steele had left for a motel not too far from 3J's condo. After checking in, he called Pascale. He didn't share the details, just that he needed to talk. They agreed to have coffee in the morning at the Oddly Correct Cafe on 41st and Troost, an edgy roastery that reveled in the slow-pour, meticulous creation of dark brews for its laptop-centric customers.

The next morning, they met, ordered pour-overs, and grabbed a small table near the front window.

After explaining the fight, Steele said, "Bill, I just don't know what she's thinking. Or maybe she's not."

"Oh, she's thinking for sure. She never stops thinking. I'm sure you know that. Nine thousand things going on in her mind all the time. A tornado of thoughts swirling around. I don't know how she keeps it all straight."

"Well, if this decision came after a thoughtful session considering options, it was a terrifyingly poor decision."

"I hear you." Pascale waited a moment and sighed. "Look, I just work with her. My role differs from yours. I'm her colleague and friend, even when she veers off course. I declined to speak with her about this yesterday because I wouldn't have said anything useful, and had we talked, I might have said something damaging. Now you want to talk, and I'm inclined not to, just like with 3J yesterday. And I will not pick sides. You're both my friends."

Steele watched Pascale over the rim of his coffee cup. They each played baseball at Kansas State University, Steele fifteen years after Pascale. They first met at an Alumni vs. Varsity fundraiser softball game when Steele was a junior roaming the left side of the K-State infield as the team's shortstop and captain. They stayed in touch and struck up a close friendship when Steele left the vice squad and took up residence behind O'Brien's bar.

Pascale continued, "But if I go down the path of talking to you, this is what I'm saying. From the purely professional side of things, is it a crime to work with McFadden, or more properly his guy, to save a client? It is not. No guns, whores, threats, gambling, porn, numbers, drugs, or other assorted criminal activities were involved in this engagement. In my mind, someone's already committed the crime if the video is fake. And in a true twist of irony, we're asking McFadden, Mr. KC Crime himself, to help us save our client from the consequences of that crime. Most important to me, is the analysis of the video a crime? It is not."

Steele's face contorted when Pascale suggested that hiring McFadden was the right thing to do and that McFadden might be a force for good in the project and look like a hero for once. It was a painful revelation after Steele had spent decades chasing the crime boss. He didn't expect it from Pascale, but he said nothing. He came to listen, not to fight. He'd done all his fighting the night before.

Pascale continued, "Do we have to like McFadden? Of course not. Do we have to respect him? I don't think so. Do we condone what he does for a living? I think you know my answer to that."

Pascale stopped for emphasis and swirled his black coffee in his cup. The crema melted into the sea of black gold beneath it.

"But do we need him? Right now, you bet we do. There are no other options besides letting our client lose. I also hate it, but I don't see any other way to go. Unless you have a better solution for our client, I'm afraid that as to the matter of Mr. McFadden, it is case closed."

"Bill, he'll end up hurting her. He won't hit her, but he will hurt her in other ways. That's what he does. I don't know what he'll do or how, but it will be a painful experience for 3J."

Pascale said nothing. He was also worried whether it was possible to work with McFadden and escape his tentacles. He had no solution. He was just going to have to rely on 3J to steer clear of that outcome.

Steele closed his eyes. He let his lungs fill, held it for several seconds, and exhaled. "Y'know, she's a full-time project, but it didn't go well last night. Now this morning, I feel like I jumped off a cliff and tried to buy a parachute on the way down. Not ideal."

"Nothing is, my friend. Just tell her how you feel. That should work."

৯

Steele had all day to let Pascale's short speech sink in. He reran the speech over and over in his mind. He wanted to limit his motel stay to one night. He wanted to return to the condo. He just couldn't.

Not that night. He needed more time.

৯

3J got home later that night. She opened her door with care, hoping Steele would be there but not knowing what to expect. She peered in before entering. The lights were off. No Ronnie.

The empty chair still faced the windows. She felt conflicted. It would have been nice to have him back the day after they fought, but she worried that would be too soon. Ronnie seemed to have resolved that dilemma for her. It wouldn't be a one-day separation, and there would be no commissioner she could appeal to.

She sighed, but there was no one there to hear it. No one to hug her or offer comfort. *Maybe it's for the best,* she reasoned.

She didn't hear from Ronnie and stayed up most of the night tossing and turning, mind racing.

The next day, Ronnie checked out at the front desk and headed back to the condo. He let himself in, moved the easy chair back to face the couch, sat in it, and waited. He had the rest of the day to think in solitude. Even as the sun set over downtown and the stars and the buildings shimmered in the evening light, he wasn't sure whether this would be a reconciliation, a truce, or the next round of the world championship fight.

At 8, the door opened and 3J entered. She looked at Steele, smiled, and walked into the bedroom to drop off her backpack and change into jeans.

When she emerged, Steele was still there. She was grateful and spoke first. "I've had a lot of time to think, Ronnie."

"Me too."

"Love should be more than the second-to-last word in a text. You know, 'blah blah blah, Love 3J.' And I think for us, it is more. But I gotta do what I think I gotta do when I put that stupid lawyer costume on in the morning. It's what I signed on to do when I passed the bar and the Supreme Court gave me that sheepskin license to practice law."

She paused to see if Steele had anything to say. Like over the morning coffee with Pascale, he was in a listening mode but couldn't hide the pain in his face.

"Ronnie, goddamn it. If I thought for a second I had an alternative to Robbie Fuckin' McFadden, I'd pursue the alternative and wave goodbye to the organized crime leader. But I'd pursue it because *I* decided to pursue it."

It came out with a bitchy tone, and it was time for Steele to speak.

"Look, 3J, we can be bitchy like we were the other day. But I don't think it's useful, and I don't want that kind of back and forth."

He was right. The minute she uttered the words she regretted them and the tone she had used.

Steele had nothing more to say. He walked over to her and they hugged. Not the kind of embrace that would be followed by the bedroom and the jettisoning of their clothing. The kind of hug that two adults engage in when nonverbal communication is at its most powerful. A two-souls-as-one hug.

Nothing lasts forever, and some things last for never. At least for the moment, whatever Steele and 3J had would make it through the night. One moment at a time. There was time to deal with forever later. Maybe that was all any couple was entitled to.

Chapter 18

THERE IT WAS

PASCALE AND 3J had decided they needed to depose someone from the banks, as well as Paul Elkin. It had to be a representative of Central Bank to start, the Hays lead bank in the group. 3J sent out the notice to take the deposition in three days and directed the bank to designate a knowledgeable representative to testify about the Paxton loan and the video and to bring to the deposition all documents relevant to the video. They scheduled the deposition to start at 9 a.m. in a conference room at Greene Madison.

3J figured someone would object to the deposition taking place in Kansas City and would make her go to Hays to take it. But no one objected. It was much easier for Frank Davis to defend the deposition in Kansas City than in Hays. Three days' notice bordered on an unreasonably short period of time, but the hearing was coming up and she and Pascale didn't think they could wait any longer. Frank Davis, the banks' lawyer, would probably push back at such short notice. But he continued to surprise her and said nothing.

In addition, Pascale and 3J decided to take a flier and

depose a knowledgeable Franklin Trust representative as soon as the Central Bank deposition ended and also to bring documents related to the video. They were fishing on both fronts, but as the biggest and newest player in the bank group, maybe someone at Franklin knew something.

Again, she scheduled it for Kansas City, not Wichita, where the bank was, and again it was scheduled for only three days out, and again no one objected.

She also sent a subpoena for Paul Elkin to appear at her offices and testify the day after the bankers.

◆

"Swear the witness in," 3J directed the court reporter.

"Raise your right hand," the court reporter instructed the witness. "Do you swear or affirm to tell the truth, the whole truth, and nothing but the truth?"

"I do."

The witness lowered his hand and sat next to Davis.

3J began. "State your name for the record."

"Chet Drucker."

"Where do you work?"

"Central Bank of Hays, Kansas."

"In what capacity?"

"I'm the president and chief executive officer. I'm also a shareholder."

"Did you bring any documents with you today?"

"I have not."

"Why not?"

"I don't think Central Bank has any documents about the video."

"Are you familiar with Paxton Energy and Remmy Paxton?"

"I am. The company is a large borrower at the bank, and Remmy is the guarantor of the loan."

"Are you familiar with the video played in court last week in the Paxton Energy bankruptcy case? I believe you were present at that hearing."

"Yes."

"Tell me what you know about it."

"Honestly, very little, Ms. Jones."

3J hated it when a witness testifying under oath began a sentence with "honestly" or "truthfully." She knew it was usually a nervous tick that some witnesses had, but all the answers needed to be truthful and honest, not just the ones where the preamble to the answer began with the word "honestly." All she wanted was for the witness to be faithful to the facts and answer her questions. If they were telling the truth, they didn't need to waste time convincing her they were truthful.

"Just tell me what you know."

"We had a bank meeting in Hays at Central Bank before you filed the bankruptcy cases. That would make it some weeks ago. All the banks were present. We were there to vote on Remmy's request to borrow on the line of credit to pay bills and acquire land in Oklahoma to drill. Or at least I thought that's why we were there. We had reviewed Remmy's proposal. It was risky. In my view, however, it was worth the risk. Remmy's record of success on these kinds of drilling projects has always been first-rate."

Drucker paused.

"Go on. What happened at the meeting?"

"Our newest bank group member brought an envelope. A Franklin officer placed it at the center of our conference room table."

"Who was that?"

"Wayne Shumaker, executive vice president of Franklin Trust. He's handling Franklin's interest in the Paxton loan. He had driven from Wichita to attend the meeting and brought the envelope with him."

"What was in the envelope?"

"A DVD. It was the video you saw in court. I played it at the meeting before we got started talking about the line of credit request. It was the first time I'd ever seen it. It preempted any discussion about the details of the line of credit request."

"Who filmed it?"

"I don't know."

"Where was it filmed?"

"I don't know. If I were to guess, it looked like a cocktail party to me. Everyone seemed to have a drink, and they were smiling and drinking as they talked."

3J continued to ask Drucker questions about the video, but Drucker knew very little. He didn't know how Franklin and Shumaker possessed it. He didn't know when someone had filmed it.

"Is it genuine, Mr. Drucker?"

"You mean, is it a fake video like you hear about these days?"

"Correct."

"I'm not an expert at all. I asked that question at the meeting. I said something like, 'How do we know it's real?' You can't be too careful in the modern era."

"What was the response?"

"Franklin ignored me and called for a vote on the draw request. Everyone voted to reject Remmy's request except for me. I voted to proceed with the loan and his proposed project."

"Had the bank group ever rejected a Paxton Energy request to borrow money before this meeting?"

"No."

"Never?"

"Never."

"Did the group vote to call the loan and demand full payment at this meeting?"

"No."

"Didn't you find that odd? Franklin thought the video was real and used it to block the proposed project but wasn't asking for all their money back?"

"It seemed odd to me. All Franklin seemed to be focused on was blocking Paxton's new project."

"Did you do anything to satisfy yourself that the video wasn't a fake?"

"Yes. After the meeting, I called Shumaker and caught him in his pickup on the way back to Wichita. I demanded his bank hire an expert to look at the video and determine if it was real or fake."

"Did he?"

"Yes. No pushback."

"Who did he hire?"

"The man you saw in court at the hearing. I forgot his name. Give me a moment... Paul Elkin. That's his name."

"Have you ever spoken with Paul Elkin?"

"No. I left the expert thing to Shumaker."

"Are you satisfied with Elkin's conclusion that the video is genuine and shows Remmy Paxton speaking into the camera?"

"Honestly, I don't know what to make of the whole mess. I've known Remmy his whole life. His family and mine were friendly. We saw each other growing up from time to time at family and friends' parties. I just don't know what to make of it, Ms. Jones."

"Do you believe Paul Elkin?"

"Like I said, I'm not sure what to make of all of this. I've not met with him. I'm not a tech expert either."

3J paused to review her notes.

Drucker volunteered, "I should add something, so there's no confusion. After the bank group meeting, I called the other owners of my bank, and they were uncomfortable with the video and decided Central should join the other banks and oppose the Paxton requests. I advised the other banks of the decision, and therefore the banks voted unanimously to deny the Paxton requests. I let the other banks know of our decision."

3J nodded. She continued with more questions but concluded she had gotten everything out of Drucker that he knew. She didn't think he was lying, the "honestly" tic notwithstanding. Up next was Wayne Shumaker. *That might yield better results*, she thought.

᷍

Drucker stayed. Shumaker, who had been waiting outside the conference room, entered, took the oath, and sat down next to Davis.

In preliminary questioning, 3J learned Shumaker was an executive vice president at Franklin Trust and had been with Franklin for fifteen years. His specialty was oil and gas loans. He had been instrumental in Franklin's purchase of a large portion of the Paxton Energy loan, so he was familiar with it.

He seemed nervous. Some witnesses were nervous at depositions. Most bankers were not. Testifying was part of their job.

"Where did you get the video you brought to the bank group meeting several weeks before the bankruptcy filing?" 3J probed.

"One of the other bankers at my bank brought it to me the other day."

"Which banker?"

"Greg McCoy. He's an executive vice president at Franklin."

"Do you work for Mr. McCoy?"

"No."

"Does he work for you?"

"No. I specialize in oil and gas loans. He specializes in commercial real estate. Two distinct lines of work at the bank. We both report up the management chain," Shumaker explained.

"Chet Drucker demanded that you hire an expert to determine if the video was genuine or a fake?"

"I don't know that he demanded it. I'd say he asked me to hire someone, and I said, 'Fine.' I didn't see the expert thing as a big deal."

"You hired Paul Elkin?"

"Yes. Well, Greg McCoy hired him."

"How did Greg McCoy come to hire him?"

"I don't have much experience with fake videos. What do they call them—deepfakes? I emailed around the bank, and it turns out Greg McCoy had a loan a while ago at his prior bank involving a tech issue, and he had used Paul Elkin. My short answer—I asked McCoy to hire Elkin."

"What did you tell him to do?"

"McCoy interacted with Elkin. But it was a simple assignment: review the video and advise the banks whether it was genuine or a fake."

"Did he?"

"Yes."

"As he testified in court, in his opinion, the video is not a deepfake?"

"Correct."

"What time did you deliver the video to him?"

"I didn't deliver it to him. Since McCoy knew this guy Elkin, I asked McCoy to give it to Elkin. He was local in Wichita, where I office at the bank. I think McCoy had a runner deliver it to him late in the afternoon on a Wednesday."

"How long was it before he gave you his opinion?

"The next day at noon."

"How long did he spend examining the video?"

"Now, when I hire an expert, the norm is I pay a flat fee, so I might not know how long the expert spent because he didn't give me his time records."

"Or she."

"What? Yeah, right. Or she. But this guy, Elkin, charged us by the hour, and his bill was for two hours of work. According to Elkin, he spent two hours."

"Did that seem like a long time or a short time for this project?"

"Honestly, I don't know. I don't know how long a techie type would need to figure this out."

There was that word again—honestly. But unlike Drucker, when Shumaker said it, 3J's antennae went up. Shumaker's "honestly" sounded like what would follow was anything but.

She continued, "Did you ask Elkin anything about how he analyzed the video? Or how long he took?"

"No. never spoke with him. I just worked with McCoy."

"Did you ask McCoy anything about Elkin?"

"No. I didn't want it to seem as if I were questioning him,

like you're doing with me here today." He flashed a smile but only for a moment. "We trust each other at Franklin Trust. It's part of our name."

He smiled again. To 3J, it seemed like he was covering up a lie.

"Did you bring any documents with you today about the video?"

"No."

"Why not?"

"Other than the video itself, I'm not aware of any documents."

"Did you look?"

"I don't have any. I asked Greg if he did, and he said 'No.'"

"What did your bank do for due diligence before it bought into the Paxton Energy loan?"

"We talked to each of the bankers already in the loan. We looked at the bank groups' annual audits of Paxton Energy."

"Did you hire an appraiser?"

"No."

"Did Franklin send its auditors in to examine the Paxton books?"

"No. We relied on the audits conducted by the other banks."

"When you were at the bank group meeting, why didn't you put it to a vote to have the loan called and demand made on Paxton to repay it?"

"We just wanted to block the land acquisition and drilling. By doing so, we protected our bank from a large draw on the line of credit. I figured we could circle back to the rest of the loan later."

"Even knowing that Remmy Paxton was an alleged fraud?"

"Is there a question there?"

Shumaker was getting testy. He looked over to Davis for help. Davis offered none.

"You said you're in the oil and gas department at Franklin?"

"Correct."

"And I imagine Franklin has a pretty large portfolio of these kinds of loans?"

"We do."

"This land that Paxton wanted to acquire. Does it have a name?"

"I believe it's called the Stockton land."

"It's in Kiowa County, Oklahoma?"

"That sounds right. Some county named after a Native American tribe."

Shumaker's gratuitous mention of a Native American tribe seemed improper. But she decided not to pursue it. She filed it away for future reference when dealing with Shumaker.

"Mr. Shumaker, does Franklin have any loans secured by the Stockton land or the oil and gas beneath the land?"

"No."

"You're sure?"

"Yes, I'm sure. If we did, I'd know."

"Does Franklin have any bank customers who want to borrow money to acquire any of the Stockton land?"

Shumaker paused. He and 3J had a rhythm going until that question. Davis had experience; he was a seasoned attorney. Standard deposition advice was to school the witness to listen to each question and take time before answering. Shumaker wasn't doing that. He was answering questions in rapid-fire, succumbing to 3J's pace. Now he ground to a halt. He said nothing. He blinked.

3J saw concern flash across his face for an instant—an acknowledgment of trouble ahead. He looked like he was trying to think ahead to the next question and the next. He was taking too long now.

"Do you need me to repeat the question, Mr. Shumaker?"

"Yes."

"Does Franklin have any bank customers who want to borrow money to acquire any of the Stockton land?" 3J asked again, this time emphasizing each word.

They were at that moment where the witness knew 3J had him cornered. There was McCoy's brother-in-law, Martin Fillmore. He wanted a loan to buy the same land and drilling rights as Paxton and was willing to pay a goodly sum more for the loan than Paxton Energy. Franklin wouldn't have to share the loan with other banks. And Shumaker would profit from the Fillmore loan. A win-win for the bank and... for Shumaker.

But in the deposition, there was so much for Shumaker to process in such a short amount of time. He froze as he tried to figure out the lie he would tell. *Now this damn lawyer's asking me a question that'll identify McCoy's brother-in-law. McCoy should have to testify and clean this up.*

But McCoy wasn't there. Only Shumaker. Shumaker wondered whether he should tell the truth or protect himself, the bank, and McCoy. Only a lie would protect everyone, but should he? Would he? Most witnesses in this situation opted to tell the truth.

"Not that I am aware of," Shumaker said, his voice catching in his throat.

"You sure of that?" 3J pressed him.

"I am. No such bank customer."

There it was. Shumaker had done the dirty deed. Davis looked up for a moment but showed no emotion or reaction. Did Davis know, did he just suspect, or was he just stretching his neck? 3J knew he had a stellar reputation in Kansas City. It seemed unlikely he would risk it on a new client.

"Did you get a bonus when the bank bought into the Paxton loan?"

"I did. That's how I get paid. A bonus when the bank makes a loan, and in this case, when the bank bought into the existing loan."

"If the loan turns into a bad loan, do you have to reverse your bonus and give money back?"

"That's not how it works at Franklin."

"Is that true for all loans you make at the bank? If you make the loan, you get a bonus?"

"Yes, that's the Franklin way. I believe that's the way in most banks. No clawback of the bonus if the loan goes bad."

3J reached the end of her questions based on what she knew. But she didn't really reach the "end." There was more Shumaker knew. She knew it, and he knew she knew it. Instead of ending the deposition, she said, "That's all the questions I have at this time, but I'm continuing the deposition subject to reconvening if I discover anything new, and… I'm betting I will."

Shumaker had lied before. Many times. He could always look cool and collected. But not this time. Not this lie. As he got himself together to leave the Greene Madison conference room, he couldn't control his emotions. He looked worried.

3J gathered her papers to return to her office. Her thoughts were jumbled, and she needed to organize them.

༄

Back at the bar, McFadden was busy doing phone work. He put out feelers to his Wichita connections to gather information about Franklin Trust. He learned it had a mixed reputation. Quick to make a loan. Quick to call a loan. Quick to tell a borrower "No more money." Quick to foreclose. And, McFadden learned, quick to take a borrower to court. Most banks had a respectable win-loss record in court proceedings. They figured out a way not to lose, at least not too often, when a borrower and the bank got crosswise with each other. Franklin seemed to be in court more often with more losses on its win-loss sheet than one might expect.

He learned that the officer in charge of the Paxton Energy loan was Wayne Shumaker. A fifty-something banker who was in banking most of his life. At Franklin, he made only oil and gas loans, his specialty. But his reputation was to do as little work as he could get away with, and sometimes, not even that much. He favored buying into bank group loans where the other banks did all the work and all he had to do was review, approve, and collect his bank's share of the payments.

McFadden also learned that another officer at the bank, Greg McCoy, was a real estate lender who dabbled in oil and gas loans. At least oil and gas loans to his brother-in-law, Martin Fillmore, who borrowed money from Franklin to buy oil and gas interests and drilling rights. Fillmore had married McCoy's sister some years ago. Not much of a marriage. They had an arrangement, and they saw as much of Wichita's Hinge dating app crowd as they saw of each other.

As McFadden gathered this information, he wondered what he would do with it. The web was so tangled, however, that he found it fascinating, so he continued to dig. "What a tangled web we weave," he muttered to himself.

Then he stumbled on the one piece of connective tissue that made the hunt for the facts all the more satisfying. He found a document that had been recorded on the Stockton land. The document was titled *Lis Pendens,* a legal term meaning that the document was notice to the world. In this case, it let the world know Fillmore claimed some sort of interest in the same land Paxton Energy was trying to buy. Right there in front of him. A document stamped by the Kiowa County Clerk and filed in the real estate records with a recording number, date, and time.

But Stockton's signature did not appear on the document, only Fillmore's. As a result, McFadden assumed Fillmore wrote it. The document stated that Fillmore had applied for a loan from Franklin Trust to buy the Stockton land and that Stockton had already agreed to sell it to him. It was a warning to the world.

"Applied for a loan?" McFadden half-said, half-thought. "What a fuckin' world."

Chapter 19

THE CHERRY BLOSSOM

IT HAD BEEN quite the last few days for 3J. Ronnie Steele, McFadden, Wilson, Paxton, and an examiner. And the video. Paul Elkin's deposition was coming up. Maybe others too. Time was slipping away. Quickly. It wasn't surprising that she was having difficulty arranging the pieces of this case in her mind.

Too much information that had led nowhere so far.

She needed a walk to clear her head. Her usual custom was to go on these walks with Pascale. They called them their "walks and talks." The walks always seemed to help focus her thinking on a case she handled. But Pascale hadn't been in a talkative mood since the McFadden revelation. She understood why. She needed to give him space right now and let the McFadden hire blow over.

No companion this time. It would be a solo walk, alone with her thoughts.

She drove a short distance to Kansas City's 18th and Vine district and parked near Vine, intending to walk a few blocks to the place where a famous jazz club, the Cherry Blossom, had once operated. Maybe her walk would help her figure things out in the Paxton Energy case.

Vine was the once-thriving Black district in Kansas City, famed for a standalone Black economy and burgeoning social life, and it was the local Black population's answer to segregation. Over and over, Kansas City's Black population took something appalling—here, segregation—and turned it into a positive. In those days, the positive was Vine Street.

The breeze blew the season's first falling leaves and the ever-present litter across her path. She was on Vine to imagine walking there in the 1920s and '30s during the district's heyday. But before nostalgia could take hold for a few brief blocks, she couldn't avoid the reality. Today, Vine was almost desolate, trying hard to hide its history except for panels painted with images of the former façades, recreating the 1930s Vine Street for Robert Altman's 1996 film *Kansas City*.

The fake façades didn't do justice to the history. To some, they demeaned it. Down the block, the joint American Jazz Museum and the Negro Leagues Baseball Museum tried valiantly to cling to the history, but the museums alone weren't enough.

She began her walk as she tried to let the present fade away and reach for the history that had always steadied her.

Vine Street had been home to the nation's first Black-owned auto dealership, barbershops, doctors, dentists, and insurance offices. Grocers, tailors, billiard parlors, shoe shops, and cleaners. It had been a bustling place of commerce, with shopkeepers out front sweeping their front entrances and stoop areas, shoppers hustling, and kids playing.

Music would be in the air later in the day, as the sun set and the streetlights came on, when Kansas City jazz came alive. The façades were, of course, silent.

3J headed to 18th and Vine. Near the corner, the famous Booker T. Hotel welcomed visitors. It was a renowned Black hotel serving travelers and musicians who stayed there for convenience when they had a gig to play at night in the building across the street at 1822 Vine—her destination—where the Cherry Blossom Club thrived. It had a Japanese-inspired motif, right there in the Heartland. First Bennie Moten, and later Count Basie, held forth each night at the club, and finally Jay McShann in the 40s, when the club changed its name to Chez Paree.

It all closed down as the Swing Era declined. The Cherry Blossom building fell into disrepair, like the rest of the district. The club later burned to the ground in a two-alarm fire.

She paused in front of the fake Cherry Blossom front, closed her eyes, and heard a musical montage of Benny Moten, Count Basie playing in the club as he emerged as a bandleader, and Jay McShann. She heard solos by Coleman Hawkins, Jo Jones, and Ben "Bean" Webster, playing well past midnight and into the early hours of the morning.

She imagined hearing the famous saxophone battle, called a "cutting contest," between newcomer Lester Young and the established Coleman Hawkins with his muscular tone, where players improvised on the same tune to see who could outplay the other.

One night, egged on by someone in the audience, Hawkins crossed the street to the Booker T. Hotel, retrieved his horn, and joined the jam session. It went on for hours. People felt that Young won because he played a smoother variety of jazz, not trying to outpower Hawkins, and it made for spirited debate.

She knew that jazz was born in New Orleans, but she also advocated that after its birth, it grew up in Kansas City.

And then she opened her eyes. There was no music, only the sound of the wind blowing leaves and trash around, and the distant sound of someone loudly proclaiming that God was great on a corner to an audience of none. Just like the empty corner of the street preacher, there was no one on Vine to wonder why this well-dressed, attractive Black woman stood smiling with her eyes closed in front of a fake building front.

The Black economy and the Vine Street Black community—almost all gone.

3J sighed in resignation that she couldn't bring back the past, and right now, she had no more time to spend trying to make sure she never forgot it. She retraced her steps and reached her car and then looked back at the three blocks she had traveled. She had hoped that the ghosts of Vine Street would help her make sense of the Paxton case, a substitute for speaking with Pascale as they walked. But the ghosts had not. This time, a solo walk didn't help her figure out how to preserve Paxton Energy.

What had Louis Armstrong said about music? It was something like, "If it sounds good, you don't worry. Why? You just love it." Every so often, a bankruptcy case is good. It plays out well, according to the plan. As the lawyer, you just love it.

Not Paxton Energy. Not the players in the case. Nothing to love, and it just didn't feel right. The video started it all. Now the players: Wayne Shumaker, a teller of lies; Chet Drucker, a head-in-the-sand banker. Remmy Paxton. Was he a good guy or a dark-side guy with secrets he hadn't shared? Now a new banker named Greg McCoy had surfaced, about whom she knew almost nothing. And of course, Robbie McFadden. Enough said.

Not music to her ears at all, nothing to love so far, and her trip along Vine didn't help her gain any clarity.

As she drove back to the office, her thoughts turned to the Shumaker deposition. *Did Franklin Trust have an interest in the Stockton land? Shumaker said no. He was less than convincing in his answer. She needed to figure that out. Would Ronnie help? Time to talk to Pascale.*

And she still needed to prepare for Paul Elkin's deposition the next day.

Chapter 20
NO BOOK POLISHING

3J FOUND PASCALE at his desk on a call, going over books and records with Linda Knoll. He was wrapping up the call, so 3J took a seat in the easy chair, where she had sat over the years as they had solved so many of their cases together.

They hadn't talked much since the McFadden revelation, and she wasn't sure what to expect. But Pascale seemed to have moved on. When the call ended, he told her that he'd made some progress, and the five-year look-back revealed little in the way of meaningful adjustments between her reports to Remmy and his presentations to the bank group.

She still had work to do, but Knoll was at ease with the alterations Remmy had implemented; none were major changes. They were supportable and justified. And the changes did little to alter the overall value of the banks' collateral.

He also found Linda Knoll's numbers trustworthy. No book polishing. She just ran the numbers, and her conclusions were solid and justified.

"Bill, what if Franklin had an ulterior motive in voting against the Paxton draw request?" 3J asked.

"Like what?"

"Don't know. I'm trying out different ideas. What if someone else wanted to buy the same land and proposed borrowing that money from Franklin on better terms for the bank than Paxton was paying?"

"That would create a significant conflict of interest for Franklin Trust in the bank group," Pascale observed as he considered the possibility.

"Shumaker said 'no' when I asked him this question," 3J continued, "But I don't believe him. Everything about his demeanor begged to differ from his answer. He lied. No question."

"A conflict and a cover-up?" Pascale wondered.

"Indeed. I looked at the credit agreement that governs each bank's relationship with the others in the bank group. I found no duty set out in the agreement that each bank owes the other. But the banks are required to report to the lead bank any conflicts and, if necessary, recuse themselves from voting."

"Intriguing. But it looks like there are no bank police. The banks trust each other to self-report?"

"Correct."

"All right. What's next?" Pascale asked.

"I think I'll have to prove Franklin has some other motive. Some other economic interests. I'll ask Ronnie if he can take a look at real estate records and see if Franklin Trust has a recorded mortgage on the Stockton land."

Pascale shook his head as he pondered. "Look, 3J. Our window of time is shrinking fast," he said. "If Ronnie can't help, we'll need to find someone who can. If Shumaker is lying, he won't change his story, so we'll need to figure this out on our own and make our own luck."

❧

3J called Steele and found him still on a stakeout, hoping to make his divorcing client happy and rich by finding compromising images, but found none. 3J explained the assignment. Steele told her he was ready to jump in. Anything would be better than what he was doing: staking out a guy who made watching paint dry seem exciting. He reminded her that scouring real estate records was not his specialty, but he would figure out a way to get it done and give her an answer.

Next, 3J called Darius Wilson for an update.

"Ms. Jones, I've spent many hours examining the video. I am close to finishing the analysis. It looks like my conclusion will be that it's a fake. Definitely. Created by AI or some other image creation software."

"Call me 3J. And that's wonderful news."

"I need to run some additional tests, and then I can come to your office to show you how I reached my conclusions. I assume you will have me testify about my methods of analysis."

"Absolutely. I have another question. Apparently, this Paul Elkin guy concluded the video was genuine after only an hour or two of examination. Is that possible?"

"I suppose anything is possible, but my reaction is that it would be highly improbable someone could perform the proper examinations and run the tests I'm referring to in an hour. Sounds like an MAI opinion."

"MAI?"

"Yes, 'Made As Instructed.' A derogatory term of art in the world of expert opinions. If he formed an opinion in line with someone's instructions, his conclusion would be suspect and would take him very little time."

"You mean when McCoy at Franklin Trust hired Elkin, he told Elkin to render an opinion that the video was genuine?"

"Indeed. And lo and behold, a couple of hours later, Elkin did. MAI."

Chapter 21

3J'S CRIB

THE NEXT MORNING, 3J was at her desk bright and early, getting ready for Paul Elkin at 10 a.m., and sipping her Earl Grey tea. Her phone rang, and it was the Greene Madison receptionist. "Ms. Jones? I have a Mr. Robert McFadden... What's that? Oh... correction. A Mr. Robbie McFadden is here to see you. With two other gentlemen whose names I didn't get. He says he doesn't have an appointment."

For a second, 3J froze, unsure about what she should do. It was too early for Pascale to be at work. She decided to take the meeting and told the receptionist she'd be right up to get McFadden and his associates. They could meet in the War Room.

She found McFadden standing with his hands behind him, left hand holding right wrist, looking out the floor-to-ceiling windows on the firm's top floor, the twenty-ninth floor, to admire the panoramic view of Kansas City.

As she approached him, his two guards nodded as if to say they had instructions not to frisk her. Good thing for them. She was sure the firm should have a rule that there was no frisking of Greene Madison attorneys inside the secure Greene Madison hallways.

"Mr. McFadden?" she called out.

He turned to face her and extended his hand to greet her. She shook his hand, and the four of them headed for the twenty-seventh floor and the War Room.

"My receptionist's call surprised me. What can I do for you? Shall we consider this a social call?"

"Not a social call, but I don't intend it to be antisocial either. Wilson has been reading me into this little project and what he knows about the case. The other expert—Paul Elkin—has caught my attention. Obviously, it's a BS opinion. I'm confident that Wilson can discredit it. And I'm confident your team will get its money's worth out of Wilson. But I got to wondering: why is all of this even happening? Why would a bank group that could afford to hire the very best hire a flimflam man to render a flaky opinion?"

3J put her elbows on the small conference table and leaned in to listen. She had many questions for McFadden but held them until the end of the presentation. He was in her office of his own volition. This was his show.

Without warning, Pascale opened the door and entered the room.

One of McFadden's musclemen grabbed Pascale's arm. It was the usual vice grip with which 3J was now acquainted, but it was new for Pascale. Rather than struggle, Pascale maintained his composure and said, "Not in here, friend. Big mistake. Your boss there has a perfect record of avoiding the police. Let's keep it that way, at least for today. Let go."

McFadden nodded his head, and the guard let Pascale's

arm go free. It seemed that even Robbie McFadden had some measure of respect for the sanctity of a law office.

"As I was saying, why would a bank group hire a flimflam man and blow up this guy Paxton's plan? Paxton Energy is pretty successful, meaning it's made money, and it's made good money for the banks that have lent to the company.

"What motivates the world, Ms. Jones? Money. Remember what Warren Buffett said: 'Rule number one: never lose money. Rule number two: don't forget rule number one.' Banks live by those rules. Me too, of course. They're good rules. My point is, if money is the number one rule, then you've found the motive. Money."

3J stopped wondering why McFadden was in her office. He was making sense, and it was all organized as he explained his thought process. More organized than she was both before and after her visit to Vine.

"If money is the motive and the banks already make money off Paxton, then the only logical conclusion is that the banks, or some of them, or one of them, have found a way to make more money. But to do so, Paxton has to go.

"My limited experience with banks—they replace loyalty with Rules One and Two."

McFadden stopped. 3J wondered if he was done, looking for a pat on the back, seeking information, or something else. He was the performer. He seemed to pause to milk his crowd.

"There's one bank," 3J said. "I have doubts about Franklin Trust. New to the bank group. It now owns 47 percent of the loan. I deposed Franklin's executive vice president. To get to a money motive, like you say, I asked if Franklin had any interest in the Stockton land. That's the land that Paxton wants to buy in Kiowa County, Oklahoma, so he can drill."

McFadden seemed to study 3J as she talked. He was a student of people and human nature.

"I asked him if there were any Franklin customers with a loan secured by that land or any loans planned," 3J continued. "Before this line of questioning, he answered each question quickly. Too quickly. Very sure of himself. Almost dismissive of me and the process. But on this question, his facial expression, his body language, and his demeanor all changed. They all changed in an instant, and he got nervous. He froze up. I had to repeat the question. It took him a few moments, but he answered 'no.' It was an unconvincing 'no.' I think he lied."

"Lied? A banker? Well, color me shocked. That's something new for you, is it?" McFadden asked, showing a sneer of astonishment. "For me, it's the way of the world. Wouldn't shock me at all."

Pascale had been sitting at the table as the back-and-forth between 3J and McFadden unfolded. He said nothing.

"I'm trying to find out if Franklin has any loans around the Stockton land or on any portion of it. I'm afraid that'll be slow going. Rural county out-of-state and all."

McFadden smiled and folded his arms across his custom-tailored, plaid gray suit, blue button-down shirt, and floral tie.

"Let me tell you something. My little empire isn't limited to Kansas City or the fifteen counties in the two states that make up our geographically complicated metropolitan area," McFadden said with pride. "I have, let's call them tentacles, and associates beyond the metro. Wichita, Omaha, Tulsa, Columbia, Oklahoma City, Springfield, Topeka, Hays, Des Moines. It's the Midwest, and it's all mine."

"Meaning?" Pascale asked. He was tiring of McFadden's

slow pace. "If you've figured something out and you're here to tell us, I'd appreciate you getting on with it."

McFadden smiled at Pascale, but it wasn't a welcoming look. "We don't know each other. I like to tell things at my own pace. I think we'll just stick with that approach, of course, if that's okay with you?" He shaped his right hand into a make-believe gun and raised the barrel to the ceiling. He didn't pull the imaginary trigger.

Pascale tried to ignore McFadden's barbed delivery and finger gun; he wanted to hear what McFadden had to say, so he nodded.

"Good. Because I'm intrigued by this whole unfolding story," McFadden said, turning back to 3J as he spoke. "I decided to look a little deeper. Here's what I learned: Franklin has a client—Martin Fillmore—in the oil and gas business who is not nearly as successful as Paxton. Old Marty wants to buy the same Stockton land Paxton wants to buy and drill the same wells Paxton intends to drill."

"I'm assuming there are others who are also interested?" 3J asked.

"It wouldn't surprise me. But only one has a brother-in-law at Franklin, and only one will pay above market for a loan to do this deal. Our boy Marty."

The room was silent. McFadden paused for effect. 3J and Pascale tried to absorb what they just heard.

3J broke the silence. "I'm torn, Mr. McFadden, between wanting to understand how you know all of this and feeling that it's better I don't know."

"Trust me. It's better you don't know. Just look at it as give and take. This for that. I scratch their backs. They scratch mine. I keep a record of who owes me a scratch. I call it my book."

3J didn't like the back-scratching analogy. The word was that he kept a book. Now he had confirmed it. A record of debts. A favor file. A little spiral-bound notebook where he kept track of who owed him favors. Name by name. Favor by favor. His list of chits to call in. It was precisely what Steele had warned her would happen if she pursued the matter with McFadden.

"And who is the brother-in-law at Franklin?" Pascale asked.

"Ah. You see, that's the interesting part of this story. The brother-in-law is a guy named Greg McCoy. Not an experienced oil and gas lender. He's a commercial real estate guy, but he dabbles in oil and gas from time to time. Does that name sound familiar to you, Ms. Jones?"

"He's the son of a bitch who brought Shumaker the video," 3J said in a very animated tone. "This guy Elkin was McCoy's expert. Supposedly used him on other matters."

"That's right. Now, in my line of work, sloppiness is dangerous. Dot all i's and cross all t's. Leave no breadcrumbs that someone like me can follow. But people aren't careful, and they drop them and leave a trail.

"That's not how I do things. I hate breadcrumbs in my line of work. But not Elkin. McCoy's alleged expert left some digital fingerprints in the file he created. According to my man Wilson, there may be a name or two buried deep in the encrypted tag. He's working on cracking the encryption right now. If I were a betting man, I'd put my money on the encrypted tag giving us some names, maybe some from the bank. That's what Wilson expects to find. If so, that idiot

Elkin made the video file for a banker and put the guy's name in the tag."

3J and Pascale pushed their chairs back and slouched for a few moments. Pascale pulled himself back to the table. "Why are you sharing this with us? You already got your fifty grand for Wilson's time."

"Her."

"Come again?"

"I don't remember inviting you. You kind of crashed our party. I'm sharing this with Ms. Jones. Not you and her. Just her. You're here to listen and observe."

"Okay, why me?" 3J asked.

"Ah. Another good question. Next time we have a confab at my office—The Bottoms Bar—I'll tell you. By the way, your view here is impressive. Way better than mine at the bar."

McFadden began to slowly push his chair back from the table while he continued, "But now, I've overstayed my welcome, and I need to get back to the bar. There's a client coming in to talk about… Well, you don't really want to hear about that." McFadden smiled.

His smile didn't send shivers down 3J's spine anymore. She was getting used to him.

McFadden stood, shook everyone's hands, and said, "Get the car, Stan, and bring it around to Walnut and 12th. I'll see you there in a moment." Then he turned to his other guard. "Will, you're still with me. Give her the package."

Will dropped an envelope onto the conference table and held the door open for 3J and McFadden. One half of McFadden's own Twin Towers and with manners to boot, 3J reflected. *At least his mother would be proud of that.*

McFadden turned to 3J. "Like I said, nice offices you've

got here. Impressive firm. I need counsel from time to time."
He smiled again. He turned to leave, and 3J walked them to
the elevator. That was the Greene Madison custom, as much
about extending a courtesy as it was about ensuring that no
one outside of the firm's lawyers and employees walked the
hallways.

When she came back to the War Room, Pascale was gone.
He left her a note: "In your office." He must have taken the
envelope with him.

She returned to her office, and there he was. The envelope was open on her desk. He buried his hands deep in his
pants pockets and stared out the windows, looking down at
the Power and Light District quad. The enormous area had
bars and restaurants on all four sides and a common area in
the middle, where revelers could gather and party. On the
north side of the quad, the developer had installed an iconic
two-story cowgirl, a playful nod to Kansas City's cow town
heritage. 3J's office faced the back of the cowgirl.

"3J, I thought I had seen and heard it all."

She looked over at her desk, deciding not to engage Pascale
in a discussion about what he had never seen before. She had
a pretty good idea it involved McFadden, and it wouldn't be
a good time to open that wound again. "Bill, what's in the
envelope?"

"A certified copy of a *lis pendens* recorded in Kiowa County,
Oklahoma. Take a look at it."

She skimmed the document, and looked up, eyes wide.
"There it is. The connection. Jeee-sus." She slapped the desk
with her left hand. "McFadden tells a good story, and he has
the ammo to back it up."

"Yes, he tells a good story. But now he's helping us, and

he's getting information using God knows what methods. And he's creating quite a chit we'll owe him."

"We? Maybe it's just me. You and he didn't exactly hit it off, anyway." 3J joined Pascale at the window, gazing out at nothing in particular.

"Bill, is it time to worry about the chit? Or is that a tomorrow kind of thing?"

"Has to be tomorrow. We have no time right now, and we have no choice. Now what?"

"I need to figure out if I have enough information or if I need to take this guy McCoy's deposition and quick."

"It's got to be the latter. You need to get this guy speaking under oath. Fillmore as well."

"They're both in Wichita, Bill. I can't make either of them come to court in Kansas City, Missouri. They're both beyond the subpoena power."

"That means you're off to Wichita to depose them. You can subpoena them to appear for a deposition there, and we have an office there. Use it as your base."

Pascale sat on one of the guest chairs. 3J sat behind her desk. They sat in silence.

3J spoke first. "Bill, why do you think McF—"

Pascale interrupted her. "3J, I have no idea what McFadden's angle is. None. And while he spoke, you know what went through my mind?"

"No, what?"

"What in God's name is our mutual friend Mr. Steele going to think about this? He's already had his fill of McFadden in life, and now this case. When he hears Robbie's name, he'll cover his ears and scream. This kind of meeting could send him over the edge."

"Should we tell him? Not me. Not yet."

"Me neither. 3J," Pascale concurred. "Get depo subpoenas out on McCoy and Fillmore."

"Will do. I also need to tell Ronnie that someone at the firm figured out the Stockton real estate question, so he can just go back to photographing a philandering husband for his client, the angry wife. He will be thrilled to return to sitting in his car with his camera while the husband does nothing."

3J grabbed her pad with notes for the Elkin deposition and made her way to the conference room where it would take place. When she arrived, Elkin, Davis, and the court reporter were in their seats and ready to begin.

Chapter 22

THE BIG THREE

THE ELKIN DEPOSITION was short and unproductive. Elkin had nothing to say that he hadn't already said in court in his four minutes on the stand. 3J didn't want to reveal the identity of her expert or even that she had hired one. She didn't want to reveal that Wilson had found a tag in the video that might identify the creator and the client he created it for.

She asked him some additional questions for the record.

"Mr. Elkin, who created the video?"

"I don't know."

"Is there no way to figure that out?"

"Not that I am aware of."

If Wilson figured out that Elkin created the video, she had shown on the record that he lied. Apart from that, she stuck to his background, and he stuck to his opinion. The whole matter ended in an hour. Elkin wasn't going to admit he had lied in court. He wasn't going to admit the video was MAI. 3J would have to prove all of it through Wilson, the McFadden employee.

෨

Later that night, 3J and Ronnie sat on the couch listening to Lester Young, Ben Webster, and Coleman Hawkins, all queued up on her Sonos. The Big Three. It seemed appropriate after 3J's visit to the Cherry Blossom Club's former location. Young, with his smooth, airy tone, played sitting down. Unusual, but it was his thing. Hawkins, from forty minutes north of Kansas City in St. Joseph, Missouri, was the king of the sax with his dense tone, whose career lasted over forty years. And Webster, with his warm, breathy tone, who was from Kansas City, and who wore a snap-brim hat with a tear-drop creased down the middle, and who ended up in the Netherlands, where he died in 1973, his style of jazz having fallen out of favor in the United States.

But The Big Three's style of jazz never fell out of favor with 3J's father. He passed on his love of the music to his daughter.

It was the kind of music that smoothed the edge off anything. Almost.

It wasn't smoothing any of the jagged edges in 3J's case.

3J had told Ronnie about most, but not all, of the Paxton Energy goings-on. It was public. No privilege involved. She omitted the Robbie McFadden get-together and his revelations. Also not privileged, but she wasn't ready for a rematch of their last fight. She deemed the McFadden twist not public and not ready for prime time with Ronnie.

As promising as McFadden's information was, it would be difficult to put it all together in an organized way for Judge Robertson to understand. And some of it—the important stuff—might not be admissible in the next hearing without McCoy and Fillmore on the record and under oath testifying.

Once she was in Wichita, if McCoy and Fillmore evaded service of the subpoena to testify in a deposition, she might be out of time and luck. To get them on the record, someone had to hand each of them a subpoena—a written directive to appear at a deposition. If they didn't appear, a marshal would bring them in to testify or even have them imprisoned.

Some witnesses would open the door and accept the envelope, read the enclosed subpoena to testify, appear at the appointed time and place, and give their testimony, agreeing to tell the truth, the whole truth, and nothing but the truth.

Questions posed. Answers given. Easy. No drama. Full compliance.

A few witnesses, however, didn't. They refused to open the door. They hid out. They ran. And sometimes, when there was a clock ticking and a deadline approaching, they evaded service and never testified.

Not a good outcome.

She wondered what would happen if McCoy and Fillmore tried to evade service. Who would she turn to for help? Steele? Perhaps. He was outstanding at tracking folks down. He had a knack. But Wichita wasn't his stomping ground, and she needed to find someone else who could help. Who could that be? Robbie McFadden and some of his goons in suits? Wichita seemed to be part of his empire. Would one of McFadden's goons be able to serve McCoy and Fillmore? Would they grab the witnesses by the arm in that vice grip she had come to know and "encourage" them both to appear for their depositions?

She was annoyed at how fast she thought of reaching out to Robbie McFadden again. One more entry in the book he kept under the Josephina Jillian Jones page with an ever-growing number of chits she would owe, awaiting the moment when

McFadden called them in. She didn't like the sound or feel of that. And she couldn't share her concern with Steele.

This was one time Ronnie Steele wouldn't be the one calming her down and talking her off the ledge, as he so often did. If she told him what was going on, maybe this time, he would push her off the metaphorical ledge. Or just leave… again… and maybe for good.

She wasn't ready to fess up with the stakes that high.

Chapter 23

THE LAST CHANCE

THE NEXT DAY, 3J found herself yet again in Robbie McFadden's "office" at the Bottoms Bar. The suited-up musclemen recognized her and never moved from their position at the bar.

McFadden saw her taking in the dimly lit, run-down bar, and smiled. "It's better to have a big idea while I sit in a small place like this. The idea matters. Not the surroundings. Keeps me focused."

It was an interesting comment coming from someone who lived in one of the largest mansions on Ward Parkway. Maybe he used the big house for his smaller, end-of-the-day ideas. Regardless, she was on his turf now, ready to explain what she needed.

Sitting across from McFadden at his table, she explained her Wichita problem. He seemed to enjoy that she needed his help.

"Let me get this straight. You're looking for help to corral two morons who are trying to run away from you? You want to serve them and make sure they come to your office to be deposed? Is that about it?"

"Yes, sir," 3J replied.

"Hmm," McFadden said, almost laughing. "Y'know, Kansas City has an interesting history of folks trying to evade those in charge. Ever hear of old Charles Binaggio?"

"I have not," 3J said. She was pressed for time and hoped he wasn't about to drag her into another Kansas City history lesson. But there was no way to avoid it.

"Charles was a guy who overpromised and underdelivered. And when the folks he worked for got tired of his unfulfilled promises, they came after him, and he made a run for it. Kind of a catch-me-if-you-can mentality.

"In those days, the mob influenced the appointments to the Kansas City police board. It wouldn't take much imagination to realize that if the mob controlled the police board, it controlled the police. Control of the police would make certain lines of work operate more smoothly. Charles promised he would get control of the board by getting three of the police board votes. No question, he was in the inner circle of the mob in those days."

McFadden paused to adjust his shirt cuffs clasped with expensive brushed silver cufflinks.

"It was 1948," he continued. "The way to control the board was a little roundabout. Charles was supposed to get Forrest Smith elected governor of Missouri, and he did. He promised the mob boss that Smith would stack the board. But Smith decided not to do it with Binaggio-friendly members, so the mob never got control.

"Remember, this was 1948. Truman, the gentleman from Jackson County, Missouri, who owned Truman & Jacobson Haberdashery before entering politics, had just won the presidential election, defeating Tom Dewey. Pendergast's reign as the Kansas City boss man had ended. The old man got out of jail, never regained his power, and died in 1945.

"Things were changing, and the mob bosses were tired of Binaggio's unfulfilled promises. They decide to bring him in. So what did Binaggio do?"

McFadden stopped for emphasis. This was his way of building tension to make a point. He was good at it.

"Binaggio made a run for it. The same as your Fillmore and McCoy might do. Somehow, he ended up at the Last Chance Tavern on Southwest Boulevard. You know, the one that was half in Kansas and half in Missouri. The one with the state line drawn down the middle inside the bar. When a cop from Kansas came in on a raid, everyone in the tavern moved across the line to the Missouri side. Kansas cops had no jurisdiction in Missouri, so they had to leave. The same thing happened in reverse when a Missouri cop came in.

"It was not altogether clear why Binaggio ended up there. The line down the middle wouldn't have mattered to the mob." McFadden cleared his throat. "Hmmph. The Last Chance Tavern. Turns out, that was Binaggio's last chance. The cops found him there, slumped in the chair and very dead. I can't say which side of the state line he was on, but in his condition, it didn't matter. Shot four times from close range. Everyone thought he must have recognized the assailant."

"Your point is?" 3J asked.

"The mob has always been good at tracking down folks and dealing with them. Here, in a coda fashion. I should point out, however, that it was never determined who offed Binaggio right there on the home turf of the United States president. Was it the mob? Or the FBI in an act of 'special merit?' Who knows? The point is simple. We've always been good at tracking down runners. 'No one gets away' might be one of our mottos."

The story was over. 3J got it: *No one gets away.* There was the Times Square looping ticker tape again, telling her to walk away.

But she didn't. "I don't want these guys killed. No coda. Just served and, if need be, brought in for the deposition."

"Of course. Not a problem. Not as good a story as mine if they live, but I get it."

"All right. I'm off to Wichita. I'll take a few days trying to serve these folks in a more conventional, lawyer-like way. If that doesn't work, I'll be back to you."

"Of course. Happy to help, Counselor."

But why? 3J wondered. *Why was he so happy to help?*

Chapter 24

C-R-I-M-I-N-A-L

"ARE YOU SOMEPLACE you can talk?" Greg McCoy asked his brother-in-law, Martin Fillmore.

He waited until Fillmore answered.

"Good. Listen, I have a real bad feeling about all of this," McCoy said. "Sure. I want you to get this loan and have a successful drilling endeavor. But now I'm joined at the hip with Wayne Shumaker, and all he gives me are bad feelings."

"It's the oil and gas business, Greg. It's all about risk. You live in the commercial real estate world. Same idea. But there's more of it in oil and gas."

"I'm not talking about the risk of drilling here. I'm talking about the risk of taking a bank group on a ride to the netherworld of lending. They don't realize what's going on. I'm talking about not liking the sound of 'C-R-I-M-I-N-A-L.' Like the word 'kickback.' Like 'felon' and 'jail.'"

"Jeez. Listen to you. Get ahold of yourself, man."

"Listen, Martin. I hear that this Jones woman has people out to serve you and me and make us testify. I don't want that at all. I think I—we—survive this by not raising our right hand and swearing to tell the truth," McCoy explained. "I don't want to testify on a stack of Bibles. I'm not going to. You can't commit perjury if you're not testifying.

"What makes you think we'll have to testify?" Fillmore asked.

"Shumaker told me about his deposition. It sounded pretty ugly, and in his testimony, he called me out. Christ! He mentioned me by name. Said it was Greg McCoy—me, goddammit—who hired this alleged tech expert. Your video guy, Martin. Your guy!"

Fillmore listened and began to understand the situation. "Greg, your name's out there, and you think she must be coming for me as well?"

"That's what I'm trying to get you to understand. It's us. Not just Shumaker."

"What did Shumaker say?" Fillmore asked.

"Shumaker outright lied in his deposition. Jones went down the path to show the bank had a conflict because it was going to fund someone besides Paxton to buy the Stockton land. Even though Wayne Shumaker was fully aware of your loan request to buy the Stockton land, he swore he didn't know about it. It's a bad sign if the only way out of this is to lie under oath."

Fillmore thought for a moment. "No, Greg. There's another way out. She needs our testimony before her next hearing. Here's what we do. We lie low. We go somewhere Jones won't find us until the hearing blows over. Paxton goes down, then you get my loan approved, I buy the Stockton land, and we're done."

McCoy said nothing. The thought of hiding out bothered him. But he didn't have a better plan. Fillmore continued,

"Listen, Greg. The most important things we have going for us right now are timing and the deadline. There are only days left before they all go back to court and the judge rules Paxton is a fraud. When that happens, it's the end of Paxton's Stockton land deal."

McCoy now realized he and Fillmore would have to go somewhere and hide, waiting for the clock to run out on Remmy Paxton. He wondered if he was the first respected commercial lender to have to make a run for it.

෴

The call ended and McCoy was agitated. He wondered how it had come to this: a plan to hide out from a process server as his mind raced over the events leading up to potentially having to testify.

He also had a growing sense of anxiety over his involvement with Shumaker in the scheme.

He had dabbled in and out of only a few oil and gas loans, mostly those related to commercial real estate. And he had made two very small oil and gas loans to Fillmore. But never an oil and gas loan of the size needed by Fillmore to buy the Stockton land. The mere size of the proposed loan worried McCoy. And his brother-in-law was just a small-time operator. Nothing like the size and sophistication of Paxton Energy.

McCoy knew he would need help to make this size loan to Fillmore. He turned to the bank's oil and gas group and enlisted Shumaker's help. Then, Fillmore discovered Remmy Paxton was already in line to buy the Stockton land, the same land where he wanted to drill.

McCoy had asked Shumaker for details of the Paxton loan,

and Shumaker delivered. McCoy conveyed those details to Fillmore. Armed with the details, Fillmore visited Bearfoot Stockton and made his offer, but Stockton turned down Fillmore on the spot even though it was for more money than Paxton had offered.

When Fillmore discovered Paxton was still in line to purchase and develop the Stockton land, McCoy talked to Shumaker, and at Fillmore's urging, Shumaker hatched a plan to advance Fillmore's interests by having the banks block Paxton's acquisition.

Blocking Paxton's acquisition was aggressive. To do so, Shumaker and McCoy needed to discredit Remmy Paxton. They hit upon the video idea and got Fillmore to find someone to create the video.

Their methodology was unethical, even illegal. But the plan could be lucrative for both bankers and included an interest in any oil Fillmore extracted from the Stockton land. It was all new to McCoy but not to Shumaker.

The plan might end Wayne Shumaker's career and McCoy's. But McCoy was in too deep to turn around so he went along. And now he was sinking into a legal quagmire and faced with only two choices: lie or run.

Or at least he thought there were only two ways his problem could end.

Chapter 25

WHERE WERE THESE TWO GUYS?

3J's DRIVE WAS two hundred miles from Kansas City to Wichita, through the Flint Hills and the Tallgrass Prairie, the largest in the United States. Rich in native grasses: bluestem, switchgrass, and Indian grass. Where ranchers send their cattle to feed. Many thought the cattle fattened there made the best-tasting beef in the world.

But by car, it was still two hundred miles of fields of nothing. Cattle looked up from grazing as the car sped by, as if it were the first vehicle they had seen in weeks. Life in the Midwest. Large urban areas outside of which was nothing. Ask someone driving from Kansas City to Wichita "Where are we now?" and the answer would be "Nowhere. We're in between."

The road stretched out in front of her and gave her lots of time to think. She hoped she would never need to turn to McFadden to serve McCoy and Fillmore. She shuddered at the notion that the twin towers who guarded McFadden would find McCoy and Fillmore, rough them up, and then, as an afterthought, hand them subpoenas and escort them to the deposition, where the witnesses would testify, trembling the whole time.

After several hours, she pulled into the Wichita metropolitan area. It was a vibrant city. Founded in the 1860s as a trading post on the Old Chisholm Trail, it was a cattle town, much like Kansas City, and grew into a key aviation manufacturing city, especially during World War II. From cattle to aviation. From beef to planes designed to drop bombs.

But 3J didn't need a steak or a plane—all she needed was a banker and an oil and gas guy. That's all. Nothing fancy.

Given the short timeline, 3J figured she had three days, maximum, to serve the two conspirators before turning back to McFadden. In Kansas City, the firm had used Steele and Anthony Rosino, a former Jackson County sheriff and now process server, to run down witnesses and serve them. Rosino recommended a process server with a similar background: Ali Little, a former deputy sheriff from Sedgwick County, where Wichita sat.

Most importantly, Little knew every nook, corner, alleyway, hideout, rock, and cave in Sedgwick County. She had contacted Little before she began her drive to Wichita, and he told her he would look for the witnesses even before she arrived. She emailed him the subpoenas.

Upon her arrival, 3J met with Little at the Greene Madison satellite office in downtown Wichita. He was anything but little. He was an imposing figure: six foot two, built like a tank, and he wore his muscles like armor. He had a voice like the lower register of Gerry Mulligan's baritone sax.

"*Ali?*" she asked.

"Yes, pronounced like the boxing champ. My dad adored him. I guess he wanted me to float like a butterfly and sting like a bee."

3J couldn't imagine him floating, but she sensed that his sting was painful.

Little had nothing for her so far. McCoy had taken some time off from Franklin Trust, and no one there knew where he was. There was no one at his townhouse. Fillmore worked out of his basement. No office in the city. No staff. Apparently, he was a one-man oil and gas show. The place was dark and locked up, and Little determined Fillmore wasn't home.

Little thought this would be a simple assignment—serving two prominent Wichita businessmen—but finding their whereabouts had proven difficult.

A federal court subpoena had to indicate the location for the deposition. To comply, 3J used the firm's Wichita office. It also had to set a date and time for the witness to appear for the deposition; it couldn't be open-ended. This presented another problem for her. The rules wouldn't allow her to command the witnesses to appear as soon as Little served them. That would be too open-ended. Instead, she had to write the subpoena with a date several days out to give Little time to find the duo and serve them.

This used up more valuable time. Too soon, she needed to be back in court for the continuation of the trustee hearing.

Where were these two guys?

Chapter 26

OFF TO LIBERAL

LITTLE HAD COME up empty in his efforts to find Fillmore and McCoy in Wichita. He had turned over every rock he knew of, and nothing but varmints scooted out. Fillmore and McCoy weren't there; he was sure of it. He had interviewed friends of both men, and the ones who cooperated said they didn't know where either one was, nor did they know where the men might go if they wanted to get lost.

"If they're at all findable, I'll find them," he told her. But the "findable" part was the problem. If they weren't, she would soon be out of luck, and Paxton would be too.

That night in her Wichita hotel room, her phone rang. The call showed a blocked ID.

"Hello?"

"You decided to take care of this on your own, eh?"

It was McFadden.

"At the moment, yes."

"Tell Little to look here. I'll text you a map."

"Mr. McFadden?" She took her phone off her ear and

looked at the text he had sent. She didn't recognize the map location. "Where is this?"

"It's a couple of hunting cabins near the Oklahoma-Kansas border in Southwest Kansas."

"How did you find this out?"

"Look, tell your man to look there."

"You're saying these two folks are now in Oklahoma?"

"Not quite Oklahoma. They're outside Liberal, Kansas."

Liberal was in the extreme southwest of Kansas. The last town you came to heading south before leaving Kansas and entering Oklahoma. She'd never been there.

"You better tell him to bring a fast vehicle. If they make a run for it, he'll have to be faster than they are."

"Thank you… again," she said, and the line went dead.

She shook her head as she imagined McFadden putting down his phone, opening his vintage Montblanc fountain pen, dipping it in ink, and making another handwritten entry in his book in the ever-growing "3J section."

3J wasn't familiar with Southwest Kansas. Google Maps told her it was 211 miles from Liberal to Wichita. If that was where Fillmore and McCoy were hiding, she would have to modify the subpoenas to take the depositions at a court reporter's office in Liberal, not at the Greene Madison office in Wichita.

She called Little. "Ali? This is 3J. I just got some information from a source. Apparently, McCoy and Fillmore are in hunting cabins near Liberal, Kansas."

"Who told you?"

"I'd rather not say."

"Reliable? It better be. That's a hike from Wichita. I wouldn't want it to be a journey to nowhere."

"Reliable, yes."

"Let's make sure I'm clear. You're sending me to Liberal?"

"Yes, sir. I'm paying you to go to Liberal and find these two guys. Please. I have a map that I'll text to you. It shows two cabins. I need to find a court reporter in Liberal who'll transcribe the depositions and let me use their conference room, and I need to change the subpoenas to reflect the new location."

"When will they be ready?"

"Come by our office at 8:30 in the morning."

"Okay. Will do."

"And Ali?"

"Yes?"

"How fast is your car?"

"Very. I'm pretty proud of it. It's a Mustang I've modified over the years. Black, gleaming, supercharged, tuned, and loud. It growls. Front splitter, rear spoiler. Performance springs. Heavy-duty clutch. Four on the floor."

"Okay. Okay. I get it. Good. You may need some speed."

"Understood."

"And Ali?"

"There's more?"

"If you get into a chase with these guys, catch them close to Liberal. If they get more than a hundred miles away, I may have to get yet another new subpoena. Understood?"

"10-4."

Chapter 27

THE MUSTANG

LITTLE PICKED UP the new subpoenas at 8:30 and headed out for the three-and-a-half-hour drive to Liberal. A straight shot southwest on US 54. It was just like 3J's trip to Wichita, a whole lot of being nowhere and in between.

He had served process a few times before in Southwest Kansas. This part of the country had many long, two-lane, paved roads intersecting with dirt and gravel roads that took him deeper into nowhere land. All he saw were cattle, tumbleweed, oil wells, some wind turbines, and farmland. The occasional coyote. Precious few trees. No humans.

Eventually, he arrived at an area he hoped was near the hunting cabins where Fillmore and McCoy were supposed to be, according to 3J's map. It was farm country—cropland and pastures stretching to the horizon. There were billowing clouds that looked like they caressed the distant fields where the wheat had been harvested ten weeks before.

Up ahead was an intersection. Little pulled over, looked at the map, and believed he was close to his destination. He got out of his car and scanned the horizon with his high-powered binoculars. Off in the distance to the north, he saw two small cabins on a dirt road that eventually connected with another paved road that ran east and west.

One thing was certain. He would have no element of surprise. If the witnesses were paying attention, there would be no way for him to sneak up. They would see him coming. His best bet: drive fast and hard, kick up lots of dust, and chase them down if they fled.

He got back into his car and started toward the cabins. He hated taking his Mustang on off-road trips. The faster he went, the more dirt and gravel kicked up against the car's mirror-black finish.

As he approached, he saw one pickup truck in front and one behind the cabins. "Shit. Two trucks," Little muttered.

Both were standard-issue Kansas pickup trucks. One was a Ram Heavy Duty. Cherry red. The other, a Chevy Silverado. Bright blue. Both were fine trucks. But neither had the horsepower under the hood to outrace his Mustang.

But he hadn't counted on chasing down two vehicles.

The witnesses must have seen the Mustang's dust storm. Before Little got to the cabins, the door of one cabin flew open, and the two men raced to their trucks, then headed north and quickly turned east. Little was closing in quickly. But in half a mile, all three came to a north-south intersection. McCoy, in the red Ram, headed north. Fillmore, in the blue Chevy, went south.

Time to pick one, Little thought. He decided to chase the pickup heading south for the Oklahoma border. "Try to keep him close," 3J had requested. He'd have to figure out what to do about the Ram later.

As he raced along, Little ignored the tumbleweeds lodged

against the fences. He was laser focused on the blue Chevy and narrowing the gap.

The blue Chevy was no match for Little. He caught up to Fillmore, pulled out into the oncoming lane, and drifted over to Fillmore's driver's side door, forcing him off the road into a ditch, smacking into a sign: "Oklahoma, The Sooner State—One Mile."

At first, Little was worried, afraid that Fillmore's truck would flip over. Luckily, he somehow kept control of the truck, and it didn't flip. But his airbag deployed. When it struck Fillmore in the head and chest, it knocked the wind out of him. He thought he broke a rib or two. While he gasped for air, he unlocked the door and tried to get out from behind the airbag. But between the bag and his injuries, he had no way to escape. There was blood trickling out of one eyebrow and his nose. His left eye was swollen, and it would shortly be closed.

Little bounded over to the truck and reached it in seconds. He looked menacing, as if to say, *Don't fuck with me, dude. It won't be good for your health.*

He opened the door from the outside, reached in, grabbed Fillmore by the shirt collar, and with one arm, lifted him out. He held Fillmore above the ground for the count of three and then released him. Fillmore's kneecaps and elbows broke his fall. He grunted loudly in pain. He stayed there on all fours, panting.

"Get up, sucker," Little boomed at him.

But Fillmore was in no condition to get up.

"Here you go." Little threw the subpoena on the ground next to Fillmore. "You've been served, asshole. Be in town tomorrow morning at the address in these papers. You'll raise your right hand and then you'll answer Ms. Jones's questions.

You understand? You do that, or I swear, I'll come back for you. I won't be as nice next time."

He paused and then concluded, "Pleasure doing business with you, my friend."

Fillmore lifted his head and watched Little pull away, kicking up dust and gravel that landed all over him. His body shielded the subpoena from getting covered in dirt.

Little pulled a U-turn and headed back north. After ten minutes, he saw an old-style filling station up ahead. The kind that might have been around in Mayberry RFD. Two pumps, and a squeegee in a dirty pail of water.

To Little's surprise, a chubby, balding man next to a red pickup was pumping gas. It was McCoy, and he had a very casual air for someone who was just in a car chase.

Little got lucky. He downshifted, slowing the Mustang. McCoy had only caught a brief glimpse of the car at the cabins before jumping into his pickup truck, and it made sense that at first he didn't recognize the car. But as Little exited the Mustang, McCoy's brain lit up.

He yanked the nozzle from his tank, slammed it into the pump, and ran back into his pickup, then roared his engine and floored it.

Under his breath, Little said, "Shee-it. Not again. Stupid sucker." He jumped back into his car, gunned the engine, and took off after the Ram.

McCoy's truck kicked up dust and gravel as he sped onto the state highway. He leaned forward in the cab, resting both forearms on the steering wheel. He had watched his father drive that way growing up on their family farm. It was his way of concentrating while speeding.

The air conditioning worked perfectly, but McCoy was

sweating profusely. He didn't really have a plan; he just needed to get away. He was a real estate banker. No one had ever chased him before, let alone a souped-up Mustang going at high speed.

As he drove, Little talked quietly to the pickup driver in front of him. "Slow down, man. Slow down and pull that heap over. I don't want you to get hurt, but I'm not going away. I just have some papers for you. That's all."

There was no oncoming traffic, and Little downshifted again, floored it, and once again, pulled into the oncoming traffic lane, driving the Mustang right next to McCoy. Little mashed his horn and signaled with his hand for McCoy to pull over. McCoy took his eyes off the road and saw Little yelling. The windows were up, and he couldn't hear Little. But he knew what the man wanted him to do.

McCoy just had no intention of complying.

As McCoy resisted Little's order, a thought occurred to Little. *Here, in the middle of nowhere rural Kansas, on a two-lane highway, is a large, powerful Black man chasing an overweight, aging White male banker. Right here in modern-day America.*

Little was still in the oncoming traffic lane when he saw a tractor up ahead. Frustrated, he banged the steering wheel, slowed the Mustang, and pulled back behind McCoy.

McCoy saw the tractor and saw Little maneuver back into the proper lane, and he took his eyes off the road again as he and Little sped past the tractor. As McCoy glanced away from the road, his truck drifted a few feet to the right, and the front right tire lurched off the paved road onto the gravel of the shoulder six inches lower. It happened too fast, and there was nothing McCoy could do. His steering wheel spun, and he lost control of his truck. He screamed, but no one heard him as the truck veered into the ditch, flipping over a full 360 degrees twice, then came to rest on its side.

A second later, Little screeched the Mustang to a stop, skidding on burning rubber. He popped out of the car almost before it shut off and started running toward the Ram. But before he could get to the pickup, to his horror, the truck burst into flames. He shielded his eyes with his left forearm as he began slide-stepping slowly toward the truck. He could feel the air getting warmer from the growing fire. As he got closer, he saw gas leaking onto the ground; the gas tank must have ruptured.

"Jesus!"

He worried the pickup might be about to explode and decided he couldn't get near enough to get McCoy out. As he backed away, his mind raced, scrambling to figure out how to save the man.

Then, in an instant, the truck went from flames to an explosion. The reverberation sent Little airborne. He landed on his back, then, after a moment, slowly got to his feet, his ears ringing and a little unstable as he stood up. McCoy wasn't dizzy and had no ringing in his ears; he was dead, roasting like a cut of Kansas beef in a hot oven.

Little was pretty sure of three things: first, McCoy's time on planet Earth had just expired and he wouldn't be testifying in 3J's case, or any other one, for that matter. Second, you can't serve a dead man. That was a hard and fast rule in the biz. And third, most importantly, even though it was modern-day America, Little was still a Black man in the middle of nowhere, and he really didn't want to have to explain to a local White sheriff and any Wild West posse members what had just happened.

He knew there were no high-tech traffic cameras on the road which meant there wouldn't be footage of a Black man leaving the scene. No record he was ever there. He went back to his beloved Mustang and drove off.

He called 3J as he made his way to US 54, heading northeast for Wichita. He told 3J that he served Fillmore and put the fear of God into him as well. He took a deep breath as he reported McCoy's death. He apologized and told her there was nothing he could have done to prevent the accident.

"He was a damn fool," Little said.

Not the outcome she expected and 3J seethed. But quickly she began to panic. Her case had little margin for error. The loss at the hands of her process server of a potentially important witness who might shed light on the video was almost too much for her to process.

She said nothing and Little, uncomfortable with the silence, filled the void and told her he was heading back to Wichita.

"No," she replied sternly. "I need you to stay the night in Liberal. Fillmore may or may not show up for the deposition tomorrow. If he does, you can head out after a bit. But if he doesn't, I may need your help in getting Fillmore to the court reporter's office to testify." After pausing a beat, she added, "Hopefully alive."

"Sure thing, 3J. I'll just meet with you at the court reporter's office in the morning," Little replied softly.

Little checked into a Liberal motel on the edge of town. It was clean and quiet. That's all he cared about. He sprawled out on the bed and saw a booklet on the nightstand about Liberal. Despite the name, the town was as politically red as they came. In the booklet, he learned that a local settler in the 1880s gave away free water to anyone passing through. He told the travelers to "help themselves," and the story goes they would reply, "That's mighty liberal of you." The comment stuck.

The town was known for Kansas's "big three": wheat, oil and gas, and cattle. Little wasn't too interested in the first ones, but cattle would work fine for him. He was hungry. Car chases can do that to a process server. He asked the motel clerk who served the best steak in town. Without hesitating, the man answered, "Cattleman's II Café, my friend. Get the ribeye."

It had been quite the day for Little. Not his best. One out of two served. One out of two survived. And he hoped that one out of two would testify. It wasn't perfect and wasn't what 3J had hoped for, but all they needed was one witness to cement the case for her.

To cap the day off, he looked forward to a big Kansas grass-fed ribeye, medium rare, with a loaded baked potato and a glass or two of red wine. He'd see 3J in the morning at the court reporter's office and hoped Fillmore had the good sense to just show up and answer her questions. That wasn't too much to ask, was it?

After her call with Little, 3J knew she'd have to get up at the crack of dawn and be on the road to Liberal in time to take a deposition. Only one. Fillmore.

She tried to fall asleep but couldn't. Losing McCoy was a hot mess even though no one knew what he would say under oath. *Would he have been another lying Franklin banker?* She'd never know. One thing was now certain. He wouldn't need to contemplate the consequences of lying and getting caught. He wouldn't need to hide out. All he had left to do was deal with St. Peter at the pearly gates and answer for whatever was on the heavenly clipboard. In McCoy's case, his role in the whole Fillmore affair might make it a long shot for him to ever march through those gates.

St. Peter had the clipboard. McFadden had the book. It was going to be a rough night of sleep for 3J.

She'd still have to figure out what to do about losing McCoy's testimony, whatever it might have been. But not now. She tried to force her brain to shut down hoping she could fall asleep. She could deal with the case and its problems on the drive in the morning. She'd call Pascale from the road. Maybe he could help; maybe not. He'd been known to say, "Not every problem has a solution."

As she tossed and turned in bed, she worried whether she could win the case with an expert who worked for McFadden. Davis might have a field day with that on cross-examination. She imagined Davis's questions and how that might go.

"Mr. Wilson, I understand you're employed by Robbie McFadden?"

"Yes."

"The biggest crime boss in modern-day Kansas City, correct?"

"Yes."

"But you're not in Mr. McFadden's Death and Mayhem divisions? Just his Fake Video Creation division?"

"Yes."

"That's what you do, after all. Create fake videos for pay?"

"Yes."

On and on and on. Imagining the cross-examination did nothing to help 3J drift off to sleep, but she couldn't turn it off.

And of course, the other "expert" was Linda Knoll. Remmy Paxton's right-hand person for decades. Davis would have another field day. More hypothetical testimony ran through her mind.

"You've worked for Mr. Paxton for decades?"

"Yes."

"He pays you a salary?"

"Yes."

"He decides whether you get to come to work tomorrow or need to find a new job because he fired you?"

"I suppose."

"In fact, you have a duty of loyalty to Mr. Paxton?"

"I suppose I do."

This was just more things for 3J to worry about. Throughout her career, she'd heard plenty of cross-examination in the courtroom. She really didn't need it running through her head like a B-movie when she was trying to sleep.

She went to law school to become an attorney. But in moments like this, she wasn't just an attorney. She was a professional worrywart. One of the best. Seeing bad things at every turn.

Chapter 28

KEMO SABE

3J STAGGERED OUT of her Wichita hotel at 5 a.m., already exhausted. She imagined that someday she'd have a private jet and a pilot on retainer who would fly her wherever she needed to go. Her own stocked bar and munchies in the plane's rear cabinet. Yeah, right. For now and the foreseeable future, she would have to settle for piloting her Prius down the interstate.

She had a cup of tea from the hotel, and even though she wasn't a coffee drinker, she considered grabbing a cup of coffee for the road.

Music would help the miles melt away. She decided on one of her favorite jazz albums, Phil Upchurch's *Tell the Truth*.

The album's message resonated. Fillmore needed to tell the truth, and she too… at some point. She hadn't told Steele or Pascale everything that was going on as, inch by inch, Robbie McFadden drew her into his vortex. As the title song played, it was as if it was telling her to disclose everything. Ronnie Steele might fly off the handle again. The song must have been saying to tell Pascale. At least he might be able to handle it.

Remmy Paxton was an early riser. He sat in his office in downtown Wichita. He felt as if something had invaded the company. As if Paxton Energy had a virus moving through the hallways and offices unimpeded, infecting the employees, the morale, and the company's very being, and even him. But there was no vaccine for it.

The virus had a name: Asher Williamson. He came with a court order from the Honorable Daniel Robertson appointing him the examiner of Paxton Energy. What would he examine? Apparently, there were no guardrails. Anything he wanted. Anything.

Williamson had access to the servers that held the company's secrets, and he could interview anyone.

But he didn't use the company's Wi-Fi. He used his personal hotspot. A cautious man.

He wasn't much to look at: short, maybe five foot six, and skinny, maybe one hundred thirty-five pounds, with no wedding band, unpressed, oversized white shirts that went untucked, black ties with loose, knots, dark gray pants that were too long for his inseam, and soiled tennis sneakers. He sported a Mickey Mouse wristwatch, and when he spoke, he sounded like the famous mouse. His five o'clock shadow showed up by 7:30 in the morning when he arrived at the Paxton Energy offices.

Remmy Paxton had instructed the employees to give Williamson their full cooperation. There was nothing to hide, he told them.

And… there wasn't. At least not anything Williamson could find.

In Paxton's initial meeting, Williamson conveyed that he was the company's number one priority. Whenever he showed up, they should drop everything they were doing and address his needs. They should answer every question he asked. If they didn't know the answer, they should find it. If they didn't have the information, they should get it.

Paxton nodded. *What an asshole!*

He asked them questions about Remmy Paxton, and the next day, he asked about Linda Knoll. About their lives at Paxton Energy. About their lives outside Paxton Energy.

Paxton thought Williamson was too much. He was supposed to examine the company, not the private lives of its CEO and the head of valuation.

The examiner's abrasive personality seemed designed to establish an underground resistance as he wandered through the company's hallways and books and records. Nobody was inclined to comply with his demands, nor did they want to drop what they were doing.

It left Paxton unwilling to give Williamson everything. He felt it was appropriate to stop short of complete transparency. He wouldn't hide or lie or cover anything up, but he wouldn't go out of his way to cooperate either. He'd answer only the question asked. No more. He wouldn't make it easy.

Paxton had a company to run. He had wells to drill. He had oil to find and extract. Americans were energy hogs, and he had a duty to do his part to keep them well fed.

Williamson's presence activated a darker side of Paxton's personality. Most of the time, Paxton could keep his paranoia on a short leash, but he was struggling now as Williamson roamed his hallways.

He even wondered if Williamson would tap the company

phone lines and listen in on his calls. The anxiety over the possibility of phone tapping ran rampant in his mind. As improbable as that was, paranoia is a strange thing. In fact, on this day, he worried more about potential phone taps than reviewing a new drilling equipment lease.

The only way to manage everything about the examiner's invasion was to keep thinking of Williamson as nothing more than an annoyance.

But just in case, to ease his mind about his fears, he vowed to only use his cell phone rather than his desk phone. That would put an end to any worries about a phone tap.

Promptly at 7:15 a.m., his cell phone in hand, Paxton stepped out of his office, went to the elevator, rode it down to the underground garage, got into his car, locked the doors, and called 3J. She was speeding to Liberal for the deposition and wanted to put all her waning energy into the Fillmore deposition. But Remmy was the client, and she took the call.

"3J, Examiner Williamson is in here reviewing books and records, analyzing assets, interviewing employees, and impeding the day-to-day operations of Paxton Energy. It's worse than a proctology exam," Paxton complained. "He's wasting valuable time asking about our personal lives, Knoll's and mine. Isn't there anything we can do to end this madness?"

3J had heard this kind of complaint in other cases. Examiners were not there to help the company run more smoothly. They were there to find fraud and mismanagement. They were there to find the smoking gun and then report to the court and the United States Trustee that the debtor was a fraud. The process was a significant disruption to day-to-day operations.

"Is he going to find anything, Remmy?"

"Of course not."

"I assume that's because there's nothing to find?" She was withholding the alternative that someone had hidden secrets well enough that the examiner would find nothing.

Remmy paused for a moment and then said, "Correct. Of course not."

3J noted his hesitation. Like someone gathering themselves to tell a lie. "Good. Then try to ignore the intrusiveness of the process and carry on as best you can. That's all we can do."

Remmy sighed. "I understand. It's damn frustrating. The guy makes me paranoid."

She refrained from asking, *Paranoid about what?*

"3J, have you met this guy?"

"I have not. What is he looking at?"

"As far as I can tell, just books and records. Linda Knoll's domain. This guy's background is numbers, not geology and engineering. For that, he'd need an expert. Up to now, it doesn't look like he's focused on our analysis of what's going on underground."

3J worried that the examiner might bring in experts later.

"You told me Paxton Energy would have to pay for the examiner's time," Remmy said. "Now that I've met him, it's hard for me to swallow. He's a joke, a dangerous one. I'm powerless at the moment. It's difficult to swallow that I'll have to write this man a check."

She had fulfilled her duty in letting Remmy rant. There was nothing she could do about the examiner in the short term. The way to eliminate the role was to win the trustee hearing. She tried to move the conversation to a different topic.

"We're getting ready for the next round of the trustee hearing to restore power to you. I have some things to share with you." McCoy was dead, she told him, in a husky voice reflecting how shocked she was. Then she added quickly she was off to depose Fillmore in Liberal.

"Dead? Liberal? Jesus! Pretty far from Kansas City. How did he die?"

"Not of natural causes, I'm afraid. He refused the subpoena to testify, and he made a run for it, which ended in a ditch and a fiery crash. I'm not very clear on the details, but our process server tried to force him to slow down and pull off on the shoulder. Instead, McCoy sped up, lost control, and went into the ditch at full speed. He rolled his pickup truck, and… well… You get the picture."

"I never met him. It sounds gruesome."

"It was. Things have been unfolding, I'm down one witness, and we're running out of time. I need some information from you."

"Sure, anything."

"Do you know Martin Fillmore?" she asked.

"Unfortunately, yes."

"Tell me about him."

"He's a small-time driller. He once worked for one of the bigs in the oil industry. I heard it was Exxon. I'm sure he learned a lot about oil and gas production there. He left the company, and I heard he works out of his basement now. No staff. He contracts with outsiders for all his support needs. Books, records, geologists, and engineers. You know, the works. He's got some setup. But he's not in Paxton Energy's league at all. I'll give him this. He knows Southwest Kansas and Northwest Oklahoma well. Remember that witching stick I mentioned to you? He doesn't use one, but he has a nose for where the oil and gas deposits are."

"I'm starting to believe he's the one who hired the video guy who testified in the first hearing," 3J mused. "But the engagement wasn't to review the video. I think it was to create it."

"You're kidding!"

"I'm afraid not."

"How did you figure that out?"

"Darius Wilson, our expert, found an encrypted tag in the video," she explained. "He's trying to break the encryption, but he says there are names in the tag. I'm waiting to hear what they are."

"You served Fillmore?"

"We did. Similar car chase near the Oklahoma border, but no deaths. And our guy served Fillmore to appear this morning at a court reporter's office in Liberal to testify. I'm in the car now heading there."

"Where did you find him?"

"Hunkered down in a hunting cabin outside Liberal."

"Hmm. How did you learn about the cabin?"

"I'd rather not say right now," 3J responded. Paxton had enough on his plate. She didn't need to add to his woes by telling him that a mobster on their team had been feeding her information. "What else about Fillmore?"

"He doesn't much like Native Americans—Kiowa, like me, in particular."

"Why do you say that?"

"We were at an oil and gas conference," Paxton said. "He saw me with some of my employees. He came over and made a comment to my group and mentioned that times have changed considerably, something like, 'Back in the day, Remmy, you would've been Tonto working for your crew rather than the other way around.'"

"Tonto?"

"Yeah. From the old *Lone Ranger* television show. Tonto was the Lone Ranger's Native American sidekick. They rode together, righting wrongs, and in the show, he called the Lone Ranger 'Kemo Sabe'—trusted friend."

3J stretched her neck as she drove. It was more Lone Ranger than she needed right now. "Geez. Why me?" she said out loud.

"Not sure if that was a question for me, 3J. But I'm sure you've already figured out the world is full of all kinds. Fillmore is just one of them."

"For sure. But one other thing. I have a certified copy of a document that was recorded in the land records of Kiowa County, Oklahoma, where the Stockton land is located. As far as I can tell, Fillmore wrote it. It claims he has an interest in the Stockton land you're trying to buy. He claims he has the right to buy it. Were you aware of that?"

"No. We hadn't gotten as far as checking the title. Was it signed by Stockton?" Paxton asked.

"It was not," 3J replied. "He just says Fillmore has a deal with Stockton to buy the land."

"I doubt it," Paxton offered. "Bearfoot Stockton and his family have been in the oil and gas line of work for decades. Bearfoot knows what he's doing. A handshake might be a friendly gesture. But a legal contract? No. It's not worth diddly once the lawyers show up. Stockton knows that. Handshaking is not his style. Signed written contracts are his only way of doing business."

"Could you ask Stockton if he's aware of it and, if he is, what he thinks of it? Did he agree to it? Was there a handshake? Was he going to sell to Fillmore? Has he done other deals with Fillmore? That sort of thing."

"Sure."

"Any chance I could get you to do that now while I'm driving?" 3J asked.

"Of course. I'll call you back after I talk to Stockton."

∽

Forty-five minutes later, Paxton called her back.

"Here's what Stockton had to say. He's never sold any land or oil and gas interests to Fillmore, and he never will. Not the Kiowa County land I'm trying to buy. Not any other land. Not any other drilling rights.

"He says the guy's a snake. All hustle, no honor. Stockton is all about honor. Not only wasn't there a handshake, but he also told me he'd never touch Fillmore's hands. He was worried he'd get some disease."

3J chuckled. "Okay. I get it. What about the filing?"

"He says Fillmore met with him at his house and floated a price for the same land. On paper, it was more than we had offered, but it had too many contingencies including bank financing, which Fillmore didn't have. And Bearfoot was concerned that Fillmore didn't have a big enough operation to handle the drilling. He said, 'Sometimes the best price isn't the best deal.'

"He told Fillmore a flat-out 'no.' Fillmore said it was more money, and Stockton told him 'no means no.' At the end of the meeting, Fillmore accused Stockton of only wanting to sell to a Kiowa even if the price was less. Apparently, Stockton laughed and the meeting ended. Stockton said he muttered Fillmore was 'a stupid White man,' and he's pretty sure Fillmore heard him.

"As for the filed document, he found out about it only a

few days ago. You can file just about anything. Hell, I could file a deed to some dilapidated land and purport to transfer it to you even if you didn't want it. Anyway, Stockton's got his lawyers preparing papers to file in state court to clear the record and expunge the document. He's considering whether to sue Fillmore for slander of title. He swears this won't take long, and then he'll be able to give Paxton Energy clear title." His voice trailed off. "That is. If we can ever borrow the money to do the deal with Stockton."

"I'm working on it," she said. "Sounds like I'm going to have my hands full with Fillmore if he shows. Look, Remmy, just hang in there. The examiner is a headache, no question. But things could have been worse. Judge Robertson could've hit us with a trustee. Then you'd be out of the company. Barred from coming into your office or even conducting business. The examiner's bad, but it could've been much worse. At least you're still running the company and it's still operating."

She was about to end the call when another question came to mind. "Would Bearfoot Stockton come to court for the next trustee hearing and testify for us?"

"Let me ask. I bet he would. He'd be an impressive witness. He flew fighter jets for the Air Force, supposedly in Southeast Asia missions in the 1970s. He'd tell you he flew on the front lines. That was his standing assignment. Kind of an Air Force tradition of how the brass treats us Native Americans. He's a stand-up guy, and he'll always tell the truth."

"Thanks. I think he would be a powerful witness for us."

"You know, 3J, I once asked him if he was sorry they didn't name Kiowa County *Stockton* County. He and his family are extremely prominent there. Without hesitating, he said, 'Absolutely not. The county's name honors our people. I am one of them, so I am honored. People over person, Remmy, every time.'"

❧

3J was about twenty-five minutes from Liberal. The drive gave her time for some soul-searching. She decided she needed to tell Pascale everything about her interactions with McFadden and called him to explain the status of the deposition. "There's something else I have to tell you, Bill." She told him all about her dealings with McFadden.

"My Lord, 3J. I had no idea he was your Deep Throat source. I want to ask how he knows all this stuff, but I also don't think I could handle the answer. Why the hell is he helping you?"

"Bill, I have no idea. I've signed no agreement with him."

"That might be your view, but he could see things through an entirely different lens. A mobster's lens. Like a fisheye, distorted. No signed agreements and nothing is free, everything has a price, and until there's payback, there's also interest. Jesus, 3J. In his world, you'll owe him favors, even more than he's done for you."

"I understand. But his help has been invaluable. And payback's coming. I get that. When he comes for his favors, I guess I'll just have to figure out what to do."

"Wrong. *We'll* have to figure out what to do."

"Thanks, noted and appreciated. I'll make sure to lose the 'I'm in this alone' mentality. For now, when he feeds me information, it doesn't seem like the devil's coming for my soul. It feels like he's a Good Samaritan just doing his civic duty. But you don't need to say it... McFadden's no saint."

"Have you told Ronnie?"

"What do you think?"

Pascale drew a long breath. "What about Fillmore? Do you have a plan?"

"Sort of. First, he has to walk into the conference room for the deposition. And then stay. I have no idea if he's bringing an attorney to represent him. I'm not even sure if he's coming. If he shows up, I have the video questions, the document he filed in Kiowa County, Stockton, his view of Paxton Energy, and his relationship with Greg McCoy, both personal and professional. I have some new information from Remmy about what went down between Stockton and Fillmore. But I'll hold that back for the trial. Remmy says he can convince Bearfoot Stockton to come and testify."

"Full plate. Finish up there and get back home as soon as you can. We don't have much time left to put all this together for Round Two. If Stockton would come to the next hearing, that would be huge."

"Yep. Thanks, Bill."

The call ended just as 3J arrived in Liberal, found the court reporter's office, and went inside to set up for the deposition.

Waiting outside the conference room was Little. She asked him to sit with her in the conference room. She didn't want Fillmore to see him outside the room, get cold feet, and run. And she decided that if Little stayed for at least part of the deposition, Fillmore might feel compelled to be on his best behavior—or at least whatever his definition of that was.

All they could do now was to wait and remember rule number one of depositions: *you need a witness who will testify.*

3J had no idea if she'd get past rule number one.

Chapter 29

LIMPING ALONG

RIGHT AT 9 a.m., Martin Fillmore entered the court reporter's office, limped into the conference room, taking his time as he entered, and sat. He was in pain and moved gingerly. But he offered no drama or resistance. No fireworks or lawyer at his side. He came, he sat across from 3J and Little, he swore to tell the whole truth, and the deposition began.

His left eye sported a shiner and wasn't fully open from the airbag's impact. His face showed bruising as if he had gone three rounds in the ring with a professional boxer.

As bad as he looked, he was there and ready to testify. He noticed Little. Fillmore was already hurting; he didn't need Little to add to his misery.

After the preliminaries, 3J asked, "What was your relation to Greg McCoy?"

"Was? What does that mean?"

"Mr. McCoy is deceased. You didn't know that?"

"Jesus. How would I? You're kidding. What happened?"

"I don't really want to get into that now. Ask me during

a break and I can share what I've been told. Do you need a moment to gather yourself?"

"No, it'll take more than a moment to deal with this news." He rubbed his corner of his eyes and nose bridge with his left thumb and pointer." There were tears he fought back. After a few moments he said, "Let's proceed. My relationship: I married his sister. He is... He was my brother-in-law." He paused. "A good man," he said in a husky voice.

"Where did he work?"

"Franklin Trust. A bank in Wichita. He was a loan officer."

"Have you ever borrowed money from Franklin?"

"Yes."

"Was Greg McCoy your loan officer?"

"Yes."

"Did you ever default on any of those loans?"

"What? No. Never."

"Were your loans from Franklin real estate loans?"

"A couple of real estate loans. A few small oil and gas loans. I've also borrowed money from a different bank when I needed money to buy rights to drill for oil and gas. That's what I do."

"Was McCoy in Franklin's oil and gas department?"

"I don't think so. He was a real estate lender, as far as I knew."

"Are you familiar with land in Kiowa County, Oklahoma, owned by Bearfoot Stockton?"

"Bearfoot... Yeah. Him and his family own a lot of land in that part of Oklahoma."

"Well, are you familiar or not?"

"You'd have to be more specific."

3J handed him the *lis pendens* document and said, "I hand you Exhibit 1. Identify it for the record, please."

"It's a document I recorded in Kiowa County, Oklahoma."

"It covers certain land, correct?"

"It appears to, yes."

"Who owns the land covered by Exhibit 1?"

"Bearfoot Stockton."

"Did you ever go to Bearfoot's house to talk about the land described in Exhibit 1?"

"I may have?"

"It's a yes or no question. Yes you did, or no you didn't."

"Or maybe I don't remember."

"You're saying you don't remember going to Bearfoot's house to discuss the land described in Exhibit 1?"

"No. I went there, and we talked."

Fillmore seemed committed to making her work for answers. He was uncooperative at times. 3J made a strategic decision to let him. If he acted this way in court, Judge Robertson would see through it. If he didn't come to court for the next hearing, she would use the transcript of the deposition in lieu of his appearance. Judge Robertson would read it and see Fillmore wasn't the most cooperative or the most trustworthy witness around.

"Describe the conversation."

"Me and him… We agreed he'd sell me the land for the price I offered."

"It's your testimony that you and Mr. Stockton agreed?"

"That's what I said. Yes."

"Did Bearfoot Stockton ever sign an agreement to sell you the land in Exhibit 1?"

"We were going to. We hadn't yet. We just shook hands. He's Bearfoot Stockton. His handshake is good enough for me, and mine is good enough for him."

"Is that the usual way you conduct oil and gas business? With just a handshake?"

Fillmore tried to smile, but smiling made his bruised face hurt. "That would be a big mistake given some of the folks I have to deal with in my line of work. There are some real lowlifes who I cross paths with. Not Bearfoot. But others. The others, I get 'em to sign and then record the sale agreement. My lenders require that anyway. They won't lend me money on a handshake. They want lawyers involved. It's gotta be legal. I'm sure you understand that, right?"

"Then why didn't you get Bearfoot to sign?"

"I was gonna until all of this stuff blew up."

"What stuff?"

"All the Remmy Paxton stuff and the bankruptcy and the fraud."

"Do you know Remmy Paxton?"

"I do. We've crossed paths before."

"What does Remmy Paxton have to do with Stockton's land and alleged handshake with you?"

"Well, nuthin' and everything."

"How so?"

"Remmy claimed he had a deal to buy Stockton's land in Kiowa County. But it was for less money than I offered. And if they signed an agreement, they didn't record it in the county office like my document. Remmy also needed a loan, and as I hear tell, he didn't get that loan approved by Franklin. It's a shame when plans don't work out worth a damn." He tried to smile again but just grimaced.

3J wished she videoed the deposition. There just wasn't time to arrange that.

"How did you learn that the banks didn't approve Paxton's loan request?"

"Common knowledge."

"You didn't learn it from Greg McCoy?"

Fillmore paused, closed his eyes, and tilted his head up. "He may've said something to me about it."

"Why did Greg McCoy talk to you about a different loan at his bank—the Paxton Energy loan?"

"Same land. Same line of work. Competitors, I guess you'd say. Greg was just giving me a heads-up because I let him know Bearfoot had promised to sell me the land."

"A little while ago you said, 'All that Remmy Paxton stuff and the bankruptcy and the fraud.' Do you remember saying that, or should I have the court reporter read that testimony back to you?"

"No need. I remember."

"Didn't 'all that Remmy Paxton stuff' make it easier for you to buy the Paxton land described in Exhibit 1?"

"I'm sure it did. Yes, ma'am. I'm sure it did." He crossed his arms across his chest and looked suddenly aggressive.

Little leaned forward. Fillmore uncrossed his arms and put his hands back on the table.

The deposition ground on as Fillmore shared minimal information with 3J and told her nothing new. But she needed him on the record, taking whatever position he took. She had decided not to press Fillmore on his rendition of the meeting he had with Bearfoot Stockton. Remmy was sure he could get Bearfoot to come to the next trustee hearing and testify, and he was confident Bearfoot would make Fillmore look like the liar he was.

She looked down at her outline. It was time to turn to center stage: the video.

"Are you familiar with a gentleman named Paul Elkin?"

"You mean the little guy who testified against Remmy last week? I just know him, or of him, in passing."

"Do you know him or not?"

"I've met him. Can't remember when or why."

"Have you worked with Elkin in the past?"

Fillmore paused, twitched, and blinked. "Not that I can recall."

3J saw the body language. He was lying.

"It's your testimony that you've never hired him to do work for you?"

"For me, no."

"Did Greg McCoy use Elkin for any projects?"

"Hard to say, and we can't ask Greg anymore now, can we?" He glared at 3J.

"Are you familiar with the video used by the banks in court last week against Remmy Paxton?"

"Sure. Greg showed it to me. Damn shame. Pulling the wool over the banks' eyes like that. But that's Remmy for you."

"Who filmed the video?"

"I don't know."

"How did the banks get the video?"

"All Greg told me is that he gave it to another banker at Franklin. A guy named Wayne Shumaker, who was in charge of the Paxton loan."

"You didn't give it to Greg?"

"Negative. I did not."

"Did Elkin give it to Greg?"

"Maybe. Don't know."

"Have you met Wayne Shumaker?"

"Negative. Never met the guy."

Again, 3J decided not to question Fillmore further on the video. She wanted him on record, and Elkin was under court order to return and testify. As important as Fillmore was in the story, the real story was going to be Paul Elkin versus Darius Wilson.

"Do you ever do business with Remmy Paxton?"

"Remmy? None. Remmy wouldn't do business with me. He would do anything to put me *out* of business." He lingered on the word *out*. "This whole Bearfoot thing is just another example. I'm Remmy's competition. He's programmed to crush the competition. Whatever it takes. Neutralize all threats. Whatever he's told you, it's all lies."

"And Bearfoot? Are you suggesting that Remmy reached a deal with Bearfoot Stockton to hurt you?"

"I ain't saying any more on the topic. What else you got for questions?"

It was time to wind up the deposition. Fillmore stood, grimacing, and left. Maybe he'd want to stop at an urgent care center, but he wasn't going to be asking for any health advice. She thanked Little for staying for the deposition and told him it helped.

"I kind of enjoyed it, 3J. Not a problem. Happy to assist."

3J packed up her papers and gear and headed out for the long drive to Kansas City. Over four hundred miles and seven hours if she didn't stop. Kansas wasn't the biggest state in the lower forty-eight, but it was big enough. Driving through nowhere to get home to Kansas City, it seemed the roads stretched across an expanse that could swallow Texas four times over.

How did I ever end up in Liberal on this case?

She put on a long Buck Clayton playlist she had made. In

a 1936 visit to Kansas City, the Parsons, Kansas native joined the Count Basie Orchestra, replacing Basie's trumpeter, Hot Lips Page, and remained in KC for years, swinging the jazz tunes almost every night. He played with all the giants of jazz with his characteristic melodic dexterity. More Kansas City swing for her to get through the long drive back to civilization.

She wondered about Steele and how tenuous the relationship had become overnight. She felt like she was walking on eggshells as she handled the Paxton Energy case and kept her burgeoning business relationship with McFadden from Steele. She couldn't face telling him how deep into the McFadden world she had fallen, and she was sure Steele would leave again if she told him everything. She wanted him to stay. She needed him to stay.

As she thought about Steele, she realized it wasn't melting the miles away at all. Then her thoughts turned to Fillmore and his lies, and she realized they wouldn't melt the miles away either.

It was just going to be a damn long trip, and when she got home, there were problems everywhere to deal with, most of which she would have to set aside while she tried to save Paxton Energy.

Chapter 30

BUT NOT THAT GOOD

Wayne Shumaker sat in his historic home in the Delano neighborhood in Wichita on the west bank of the Arkansas River as the daylight waned. As the neighborhood had originally formed in the 1870s, saloons, gambling establishments, and brothels sprang up to cater to cowboys who stopped in after a long day driving the cattle.

After Wichita annexed the area, the booze, ladies of the evening, and the gamblers' faro tables gave way to a mixture of residential and commercial structures. Craftsman bungalows appeared along with larger American Foursquares, some with high wrought iron fences surrounding the property and pillared, two-story front porches.

Shumaker had one of the Foursquares that had been built in the early twentieth century. An elegant white house with a lantern hanging from the porch roof illuminating the stylish wood-stained front door.

He lived there alone. Or at least he lived there alone now. His administrative assistant of many years, Leah Belle Thomason, had also been his live-in companion. They met in a bar a few blocks from the house. You might say she picked him up. She was hard to miss, even when the lights were low. Even in the dim glow of the barroom lanterns, her gentle curves and angular face were apparent. Strawberry-blonde hair, blue eyes, an alluring smile, and a silky voice. Far better looking than Shumaker figured he'd ever meet. That first night, they went back to his house, and the romance began.

Soon after, he hired her as his trusted assistant, and then he began to knock her around. His father had abused his mother and him, and Shumaker grew up learning that women were there to be loved and pushed around. Shumaker never hit her in the face to ensure that the clothes she wore to the bank always covered up her bruises.

She stayed when it would have been easier to walk away from Shumaker and never look back, but she was a member of the Stockholm Syndrome club. She had a psychological attachment even through the abuse. He hit her and then apologized and promised to change and then lavished gifts on her. Wanting to believe him, she stayed.

No one at the bank knew Shumaker abused her. If they had, they might have pitied her. But they didn't know, and many at the bank talked about her behind her back and resented her. She always wished Shumaker would put the backbiters in their place. But he didn't. Maybe he couldn't. Or he wouldn't. It would've been the right thing to do, but he didn't have a reputation for doing the right thing. He was all about the Wayne thing.

At first, they had a relationship even through the abuse. But the relationship cooled, and it turned from love to an arrangement. He slept around, often. She slept around from time to time, and they slept together when they weren't with others. But she needed to be available for him for a roll in the sack and when he needed to slap her around.

At work, he kept a personal ledger of all the loans he booked, his bonuses, and the completed transactions where he colored outside the banking lines—times when he would get paid a bonus by the bank and an under-the-table payment from a borrower to push a loan through.

As his assistant, she knew many of Shumaker's habits, including the corners he would cut to pad his income. And she had access to the ledger.

But they had a falling out. While they had an arrangement, she had told him early on that she never wanted to see him sleeping in their bed with another woman. He promised he wouldn't, and he honored the promise until one night. After all, it was his bed and his house, and he didn't think she'd come home that night.

But he was mistaken, and then it was over between them. No more girlfriend, and she also quit the bank, and her administrative assistant position.

"It's not bad enough, Wayne, that I catch you with another woman in the very bed we share. It's not bad enough that you broke the only promise I ever asked you to make. Not only am I your personal punching bag, but the things you do at the bank that make it into your ledger also make me nervous. I don't want any part of it anymore."

He tried to talk her into staying, but for Thomason, there was no going back. It was time for her to move on. She needed to get control of her life, and up to then, it had not been an easy one. At the door, she said over her shoulder, "Don't call me, and don't come looking for me either."

The next day, she left her things behind, left Wichita, and moved back in with her mother in Kansas City.

It was now dark outside, and Shumaker brooded. On his couch, he thought about his job, his sharp practices at the bank, the way he treated Thomason, and how his life was racing toward its horizon. He was stuck in his own riptide with no way to swim out. He would miss going out with Thomason on his arm while everyone in the room turned to catch a brief look at her, not the couple. He would miss pushing her around.

And now, he was starting to have trouble at the bank. He had expensive tastes. Bankers make good money... but not that good.

He didn't want to be alone, but he would have to accept it and the benefit to his bank account that went along with it. The house was a money pit—the taxes, the upkeep, his mortgage payments, the landscaping, and the elaborate interior decorating that he commissioned to fill the home with authentic period pieces. His attempts at restoration also led to costly squabbles with local authorities, who regulated what he could and couldn't do.

How could he ever make ends meet? Truth be told, he couldn't. He had spent almost all of his modest inheritance buying and then fixing up the house. His dream was that someday he would be the owner and president of a bank, and he would entertain the masses at home with Thomason by his side. That was ten years ago. He still wasn't president, and, given his work ethic, he wouldn't be anytime soon. And now she was no longer around either.

He thought about how much money he needed and how

he could take in more than just his bonus when he placed a loan.

Paxton Energy was his first triple-dip. He got his bonus for placing a $28 million loan, and it was substantial. The rest of the plan would follow. Shumaker would discredit Paxton and shut down his borrowing. Then, Shumaker and McCoy would make the loan to McCoy's relative to buy the same land Paxton hoped to. Shumaker would get two bonuses for the same oil and gas project. As a condition of making it all happen, under the table, McCoy's relative, Martin Fillmore, would also grant Shumaker an interest in the oil produced.

He recorded all of it in his ledger. The one he didn't bring with him to the deposition. The document he testified didn't exist.

Sure, his plan would signal the demise of Paxton Energy, but borrowers came and went. It was risky, but he needed the money.

Sure, he lied under oath, but sometimes you just need to do what you need to do. And he might get caught, but he'd done the dip before, and it always went off without a hitch.

He didn't expect Greg McCoy to die. *Damn fool.* He shouldn't have run. He shouldn't have panicked. He should have just testified and denied everything. No one would have figured it out. Instead, McCoy ended up in the ditch in a fiery inferno. But sometimes, loan officers came and went.

Now there was only one loan officer involved with Martin Fillmore—Wayne Shumaker—and no one left to split the Fillmore bonus with.

Shumaker smiled. *More for me.*

Chapter 31

THE CREATOR

THE TECHNOLOGY TEAM working for Paxton Energy reconvened on Greene Madison's twenty-ninth floor. When the firm first moved into the building, the floor housed its award-winning library. As technology advanced, books on shelves gave way to online research at each attorney's desk. The firm converted the library into a dozen conference rooms with state-of-the-art technology. Shelves and library stacks gave way to touchpads, technology, movable walls, and configurable spaces.

As 3J and Pascale entered, Darius Wilson and Millie Brownstein were already there, lowering the room-darkening shades and readying the technology necessary for Wilson's presentation. Remmy and Bree Paxton had driven up early that morning from Wichita to attend and took their seats. Several paralegals for 3J and Pascale sat at the back of the room.

Brownstein's team had set up tables facing the front of the room, and she pushed a button on a control tablet. The projection screen slowly descended into position.

Wilson had prepared a PowerPoint presentation to explain

his work and support his opinion. Up at the podium, he connected his laptop to an HDMI cable.

3J thanked everyone for coming on short notice. "Okay, Darius. It's your show."

Neither 3J nor Pascale had screened the presentation beforehand. Everyone in the room was about to see Wilson's work for the first time.

Wilson opened with a brief explanation of deepfakes and a bit of history. His information mirrored what Rome had told 3J. It felt like 3J had talked to Rome months before. But it was days ago, not months.

Wilson then played the video at normal speed. When it finished, he showed a still image of a scene taken from the video and said, "I'm going to play the video two more times. Slow and super slow. When I do, try not to watch or listen to Remmy. I want you to focus on two other things. First, keep your eye on this person in the foreground to the right of Remmy, and second, please study the light coming through the curtains in the background."

Wilson used a red laser to circle both areas.

"What are we looking for?" Remmy asked.

"I would rather not give away any possible tells. I want you to observe with no preconceived ideas except for where I'm asking you to focus your attention. Pay attention. We can talk after the second video ends."

"Very well." Remmy looked at the slide.

"Okay, folks. Here we go."

Wilson played the video twice at the two slow speeds. As he did, everyone in the room leaned forward and concentrated on what they saw. When they finished, Wilson went back to the still slide of the scene.

"What did you see?"

"The light in the back of the room looks off somehow," Pascale noticed. "It seems to shimmer and jiggle. Shiver might be a better word to describe it. Wait, I know what I'm getting at. In the summer, off in the distance where a tarred road meets the horizon, you can see a wavy image. The light refracts it. Here, it looks that way to me. The light in the video wasn't streaming into the room."

"That wavy phenomenon over the tarred road you're referring to," Wilson answered, "is called 'heat shimmer' or the 'mirage effect.' It happens when the heat from the road rises into cooler air. The light rays from the horizon bend as they pass through different air temperatures. Of course, in an air-conditioned or heated room like the one in the video, we can assume there wouldn't be such air temperature changes, and there shouldn't be the shimmer or shiver you described."

"Fascinating," Pascale remarked.

"Anything else?" Wilson asked.

"The image of the man you asked us to focus on seemed to have uneven edges around his face. As if there were a pixel or two out of alignment," Bree noticed.

"Perfect, folks. Neither of those two artifacts should be present in an iPhone movie of an indoor scene like this shot at 1080p. And now, I need to get a little technical with you, but it's relevant. Just bear with me. You may have heard of 1080p? Maybe when buying a television? Sometimes people just call it high definition or HD. 1080p is a video resolution standard that means the picture has 1,920 pixels across and 1,080 pixels down, with the 'p' standing for progressive scan. We measure the resolution by multiplying 1920 by 1080 pixels for a little over two million pixels. In every cycle, a progressive scan draws each frame in full, top to bottom. This is in contrast with what we call 'interlaced,' where there are odd and even lines of pixels that alternate. In a nutshell, a progressive scan is smoother. The image is clearer."

Wilson waited for his audience to process his explanation and then continued, "In a true progressive video, I shouldn't see jagged edges on this person's face," at which point he pointed the laser and circled the face in question, "and there shouldn't be any jiggle and shimmer in the light." Here, he pointed the laser up and down to trace the curtains.

Wilson advanced to the next slide. It was a still frame he had extracted from the video, blown up to show the face of the subject man.

"Here's the man blown up."

In the zoomed image, everyone saw the prominent jagged edges around the outline of his face.

"Now, one more scan of the area around the curtain. What do you see in the still capture on the screen?"

"I see two tables, one on either side of the curtains, each with a table lamp on it," Bree said.

"Good. What's missing?"

No one said anything.

"Where are the shadows?" Wilson asked. "There should be a shadow cast by one or both of the table lamps as the sunlight hits them. There are no shadows."

Everyone nodded.

"Okay, two more passes through the video. First at normal speed and then slowed down. This time, look only at Remmy."

When the passes finished, Wilson asked, "What did you see this time?"

"He never blinked," Bree said.

"Correct," Wilson agreed. "It's hard for AI to replicate eye movements. Sometimes, if someone creates a deepfake video on a tight schedule, the eyes are a giveaway. They either don't blink or the blinking is too pronounced and unnatural. Almost robotic. Anything else?"

Pascale jumped in. "He looks a little emotionless. He's touting his ability to fool the banks over an extended period, and yet he doesn't smile, he doesn't frown, and he doesn't act triumphant. He looks... well, empty."

"Correct. Also challenging to have facial expressions sync up with the words. Expressions of anger, surprise, happiness, and, as you said, a sense of triumph. The result is sometimes an emotionless face. Our brains match our expressions to our emotions at the time, and our emotions often come from the words we're speaking. AI has a harder time with that. Let me run it one more time at normal speed. Now that you know what to look for, watch Remmy's eyes and his facial expressions in real time."

The group saw eyes that now looked peculiar. No blinking. And a face showing no emotion. In the video, he wasn't human. He was Remmy, the android.

"Let's turn to the voice and the background noise in the video. I'll start by telling you that cloning a voice is becoming easier. You can download a sample of someone's voice—in Remmy's case, a clip from one of the speeches he has given—and use the AI synthesizing tools to create audio content. Creating something Remmy never said from something he did. Commonly called a voice skin or a clone.

"I compared Remmy's voice in the video to his voice in the company-created videos he provided. It's different in the video. And when I filter out the background noise, you get this."

Wilson advanced to the next slide, and the group listened to only Remmy's voice in the video. "What do you hear?"

"His voice warbles a little. Like he was trying to speak while he was running on a treadmill or something," 3J said.

"Correct again. That's the audio AI missing the mark by a little."

"Last slide before I wrap it up. A comparison. Remmy provided me with other videos. Corporate marketing videos showing him promoting the company. Real ones taken by real videographers. I've compared the real ones with the banks' video. In the real ones, he blinks. No jagged edges. His voice is firm and doesn't quaver, just like I've observed his voice hasn't quavered here today. When you compare the two side by side, it's even clearer that there are distinct differences."

Wilson advanced to a slide that said "Conclusion" in bold letters.

"And now for the moment you've waited for. Here's where we are in the analysis. It's clear to me that the banks' video is a deepfake. The tech used to create it was not state-of-the-art. Given the artifacts, someone either wasn't skilled, wasn't careful, or more likely, had to rush to create it."

He advanced to the last slide: "The Tag."

"There are tags in the video. Not uncommon. The creator seems to have encrypted one tag. It took a while, but I was able to crack the encryption." He advanced the slide to one that had the words "Elkin: Fillmore: McCoy." Pointing to the slide, he said, "This is what the tag says: Elkin:Fillmore:McCoy."

Wilson pointed at Millie Brownstein, and with a tap on her tablet, the lights came on. "Does this mean anything to you folks?"

"All names in our tangled web," 3J said. "Is there any standard way someone tags a video after they've created it?"

"No standard way. But this way isn't uncommon," Wilson said. "The creator lists himself first: Elkin. I'm betting that's Paul Elkin. Then the next two names are likely the parties for whom Elkin created the video. Judging by your expressions, you know these folks."

Pointing to the slide of the tag, Wilson concluded, "My final opinion is this: Elkin's task wasn't to review the bona fides of the video. He was hired to create it."

No one in the room said a word as they processed Wilson's revelation. *That could change everything*, 3J realized.

Chapter 32

Q39

AFTER THE PRESENTATION, 3J and Pascale decided to grab an early lunch, this time at Q39, one of Kansas City's top barbecue joints. They had a great deal to discuss. They headed for Pascale's twelve-year-old manual transmission Toyota Camry with almost 200,000 miles and drove to 39th Street near Southwest Trafficway and Q39.

"Are you ever going to enter this century, Bill, and buy a modern automobile?"

"Why? What's wrong with this car? I love it."

"There's a lot to love if you're displaying it at a vintage car show," 3J quipped.

"I don't like change. You know that. There's no need to flood my brain with computer readouts and large high-definition display panels. I'm good with my retro wheels, thanks."

They parked and headed for the restaurant. They had arrived early enough to avoid the large lunchtime crowds. By noon, the line to get in would stretch far from the front entrance.

Rob McGee, a Culinary Institute of America graduate,

perfected his barbecue skills on the famous Munchin' Hogs barbecue team. He then opened Q39 in 2014. It was an instant hit on the very competitive Kansas City barbecue scene, attracting people from all over the country to dine on the chef-driven, from-scratch barbecue.

3J ordered the Pitmaster Brisket sandwich with provolone and onion straws on a toasted bun, slathered with the Q39 classic BBQ sauce. Pascale went for the Southern Pride sandwich: pulled pork and southern slaw on a toasted bun, covered with a zesty BBQ sauce. They shared beans and fries.

As the food arrived, 3J started the discussion. "Wilson was great, but we've got issues, Bill. Shumaker's name's not in the tag. McCoy's dead and won't be in court. I'm not sure what Fillmore might say apart from what he's already said under oath. I'm not sure if Fillmore is even coming to the hearing. He's over a hundred miles from the courthouse, meaning we can't make him come."

Food always won out before analysis when there was barbecue on the plate, so she stopped to take a bite and then continued.

"We're close. But we're not home free yet. Where do we go from here?"

"I'm not sure, 3J. We need to figure out a way to crack through Shumaker's story. In his world, it's all fine, the video is real, and the banks had every right to block Paxton from drawing on the line. Given what they saw on the video, they were right on that score. They saw Paxton admit to committing a huge no-no and responded by saying, 'No more.'"

"Shumaker denied knowing anything about Fillmore seeking a loan to buy the same land Paxton was after."

"Here's something. What would Bearfoot Stockton have

to say? Maybe he'd come to court and explain what really happened when he met with Fillmore."

"I asked Remmy to reach back out to Stockton and have him come to the hearing. Before Wilson started, Remmy let me know Stockton said he'd come and testify."

"That's great news. I'm guessing he'll say 'hell no' to the Fillmore story. That'll discredit Fillmore once and for all. Stockton's testimony will show Fillmore lied. Then, we'll have Wilson give his presentation to Judge Robertson, discrediting Elkin. Knoll will offer her opinion that there was no fraud. Then, all we'd have left is to figure out a way to blow up Shumaker's story."

"I agree, Bill." 3J still looked concerned. "All of that's the play, but we still have issues. Wilson works for the mob. No, check that. Wilson is now part of the mob. I've had nightmares imagining Davis's cross of Wilson on that point. Knoll is beholden to the alleged fraudster, Remmy Paxton. I've had more nightmares. Bearfoot and Fillmore belong to the same society of mutual dislike of each other. While I'm sure Bearfoot Stockton will carry the day and trump Martin Fillmore, the truth is the judge will have to decide who he believes—Stockton or Fillmore. Hopefully, Stockton won't let his distaste for Fillmore color his testimony.

"The judge will have a good deal of conflicting evidence, and he'll have to weigh the witnesses' credibility. There's too much conflicting evidence for us to be certain how he will come out. And right now, we still have nothing to counter what Shumaker will say. We can't submit the deposition transcript with a sticky note on it saying 'Liar.'"

3J shook her head. Pascale smiled.

"What?" she asked him.

"Hey, Papa never said it would be easy."

"Ain't that the truth."

3J was quiet on the drive back from Q39. She knew what she had to do about her Shumaker problem, but she didn't want to share it with Pascale. The continued application of Rear Admiral Grace Hopper's advice about asking for forgiveness, not permission, when it came to Robbie McFadden.

She was certain of one thing. Without the rear admiral, she might have already moved this entire case into her loss column.

But she wasn't ready to concede defeat.

Chapter 33

THE SPECIAL SAUCE

AFTER THE WILSON presentation, the Paxtons returned to Wichita in their Tesla Model Y. Remmy drove an electric car even though he was in the business of extracting oil and gas to feed the world's endless appetite for fossil fuels.

He noted the irony often to Bree. He joked that his career trapped him into pulling hydrocarbons from the earth. It was how he put food on the table. Bree would answer that food is a necessity. But even though Paxton Energy was in the hydrocarbon business, the Paxtons' house was all electric, heat-pumped, with solar panels on the roof and battery storage in his garage, and his car was an EV fueled by his Tesla garage charger.

Ironic indeed. But humans were enigmas wrapped in paradoxes.

That night, when they finished dinner, he and Bree lingered before clearing the table. Paxton twirled his fork aimlessly.

"Wilson was impressive," Bree offered.

"Yes. Very focused on the details." Remmy didn't look at Bree as he spoke and instead played with his fork.

"I like that. It's always the little things that are the most important and the hardest to identify," Bree responded.

Remmy put his fork down and looked across the table into her eyes, which seemed to shimmer like winter light. "At first, I thought a second hearing coming soon after the first would doom us. How would we ever find someone with cred to reveal the video was fake? I have to give the nod to 3J. She done good."

"Yes, she did," Bree agreed.

"What next?" Remmy asked.

"Now that we have the video under control, I think the short time before the next hearing is to our advantage," Bree responded.

"How do you figure?"

She unpacked her thoughts. "The examiner doesn't have time to hire experts and kick the tires on all your work. He's focused on your numbers in the books because he's a numbers guy. Aside from the video, the trial seems focused on the same thing: whether Linda's work on the numbers and your work to tweak them created significant discrepancies. We know they didn't, right? Your tweaked numbers were almost the same as Linda's initial work product. The numbers are fine. You and Linda always do an impressive job."

Bree paused for a drink of wine.

"But while everyone is studying the numbers," she continued, "no one has had time to hire an expert to dig into your reserves analysis. No one has come at you with teams of geologists and engineers, and nobody is challenging what you claim is underground. Even the examiner all by himself won't figure that out."

Remmy smiled. "This is true. Pascale asked a few questions

at one of the first meetings about the reserves. We even talked about witching sticks. But in no real depth. It's a complicated business. More than just a bookkeeper's numbers in an Excel spreadsheet. Countless little things. Numerous nooks and crannies where all those hydrocarbons are hiding. It can be tricky to determine the extent of the hydrocarbons under the earth. Lots of underground formations and wiggle room and the opportunity to massage the reserves after the geologists do their thing."

Bree nodded and smiled back. "Assuming we win this hearing, Remmy—and I like our chances—the examiner goes away empty-handed, he reports to the judge he found nothing, you go back to running the company, and the banks rethink their view on the loan request.

"Going forward, the banks will keep approving the work." Bree smiled. Between her eyes and her smile, she was enchanting.

"Just business as usual," she continued. "You'll tell them where the hydrocarbons are hiding and how much you think is there. Like you've always done. After the geologists count those molecules, you have the chance to generate new special reserve numbers after you apply the customary special sauce. Adjust upward what you expect to produce and report it to the banks. Net result: bigger reserves, bigger loan."

"Just like usual, the banks won't hire a geologist," Remmy added. "They trust us, and they save money. Too bad for them."

"You're always right. It's the little things that matter the most, right? Bree asked. "And the smallest lies that can unravel the truth, but not everyone consistently looks for those little lies, now do they?"

Chapter 34

DO YOU KNOW HOW BANKERS GET PAID?

BACK AT HER desk, 3J focused on Shumaker. She had to break through his story. As much as she hated the idea, and with no obvious alternatives, she had to pay Robbie McFadden yet another visit. Twenty-five minutes later, she was in the Bottoms Bar at the usual table, having what was becoming a usual conversation with a well-known, but unusual, gangster. Her appointments with him were likely squeezed in between his typical daily business meetings: murder for hire, drugs, women of the evening. She couldn't tell if he was humoring her or if he looked forward to talking about something that was a departure from his usual business.

She gave him a quick rundown of where the case stood and then came to the Wayne Shumaker problem.

He listened, drowning out the other demands on his time. When she finished, McFadden said, "Loans have always been good business. Back in the day, Jim Pendergast, bossman Tom's brother, ran the American House down on St. Louis Avenue just below the West Bluff at 12th Street. Close to here. He cashed workers' paychecks and made loans to them. It was good politics to develop a large group of blue-collar workers indebted to him. They voted as he directed them to vote. They filled the political offices with men who did the Pendergasts' bidding."

Another story, 3J groaned silently. She hoped her face showed nothing but interest.

"Back in those days," McFadden continued, "I'm guessing lenders like Jim didn't get an incentive bonus for making a loan. These days, they do. They get paid a base salary plus a bonus. A good producer at a decent-sized bank might rake in three hundred grand, of which over one hundred was a bonus based on the loans he originated. Not Elon Musk money, of course, but not chump change either.

"Ms. Jones, I hear your Shumaker problem, but you're not focused on anything except reporting the problem. My suggestion: focus on the bonus."

He raised his eyes as if to ask if she understood, and she nodded.

"In your little developing saga, who works for the biggest bank? Shumaker," McFadden answered his own question. "Who originated a loan to Paxton? Shumaker. Who seems to have had something to do with Fillmore, although it's murky? Shumaker. Who might get a bonus if Fillmore gets a loan? Might have been McCoy, but he's joined the dearly departed list. Who else? Maybe Shumaker? Could be."

"How do I prove all that?"

McFadden chuckled. "Ever hear the story of Arlyne Brickman?

Another story. 3J took a deep breath and shook her head answering McFadden's question.

"Arlyne was the shapely, sometime-redhead who set out to sleep with every mobster in New York. She wanted them to owe her favors. I read she had more than eight abortions and thought little of her mobster lovers' prowess in bed as sexual partners."

My Lord. Where is he heading this time? 3J wondered with that look on her face again, but this time McFadden ignored it and continued.

"After a while, some gangsters beat her and raped her. None of her Mafia friends and lovers came to her aid. None sought payback from the abusers. Her mobster lovers didn't reciprocate her services when she needed help. And then a loan shark threatened Arlyne's daughter. That was all she could stand."

McFadden stopped and directed one of his bodyguards to bring him a cup of coffee. He asked 3J if she wanted one and she declined. He took the coffee mug in both hands and continued.

"Arlyne got her revenge. She turned on the mob. Supposedly, she wore a wire in her bra. That must've been quite a wire." McFadden chuckled at the image of an FBI agent installing the wire on a busty mob mole. "The gov gave her a plea deal and paid her debts off. She worked for the FBI as an informant for a decade. She helped put Anthony Scarpati of the Columbo crime family in prison. She helped convict several other family members of racketeering.

"Arlyne and folks like her are why I don't have a secretary. I don't need anyone who might turn on me. I surround myself with all kinds of folks, but I have to remain a man unto myself, I guess." He paused, his face showing surprise at sharing that with 3J.

"Funny gal though." He smirked. "She rejected the witness protection program. Said it was the quickest way for her to get killed. You can find some of her interviews on YouTube. I think she gave one to Larry King on CNN. Quite an interview. A real hoot to watch."

McFadden paused and studied 3J's face. "Counselor, once again you have that look on your face. The look of 'why is he telling me this?'"

"Sorry, it's not about you. It's the look of a lawyer worried about losing a case for a client who doesn't deserve that outcome."

"I once heard a lawyer friend tell me that lawyers lose cases."

"Yes, news flash. We do occasionally."

"Well, let's see if we can hold off the loss for another case. Right? The question is, what to do now? Simple. Find a woman who'll help take down your man, Shumaker. Your own Arlyne Brickman, if you will. In my experience, Counselor, it's always the scorned woman."

"Is there one?"

"Would I be telling you this story if I didn't think there was one? But I can't keep all the fun for myself. I'm not going to get you much more on this right now. Get Ronnie Steele to help you figure out this part of the puzzle. And hey, you've got this. Give Steele my regards. He'll find that woman for you. Me? I gotta get back to some paying clients."

⌁

"Ronnie. I need your help badly." 3J told him the story of Shumaker and the need to find a woman scorned, if there was one. "I need to find out if Shumaker had a girlfriend and an ex-employee who might find a little retribution by testifying against him."

"Is there a woman?"

"Isn't there always?" 3J asked rhetorically, mirroring McFadden.

"Not sure. But if there is one, I'll find her for you."

3J breathed a sigh of relief. Ronnie didn't ask her to fill in all the blanks and asked nothing about McFadden. She didn't utter the mobster's name and decided to keep the Arlyne Brickman story to herself. McFadden's story was definitely relevant here. 3J needed to find the crooked banker's mole to put her case in the win column once and for all.

One day, she'd have to tell Steele everything... and face the blowback again. Someday.

Chapter 35

LEAH BELLE THOMASON

THE NEXT DAY, Ronnie called 3J to report he had a lead. There was a girlfriend. Now an ex. There was also an administrative assistant.

"Ronnie, how on earth did you figure this out?"

"One part pretense, two parts luck. I just called the bank and asked to speak to the president's administrative assistant. I got transferred, and a very helpful woman spoke with me. I told her I was with an employment agency trying to make connections. You know, put my name away for a later time, should she ever need to seek other employment.

"We got to talking, and I offered that if there were any admins who had recently left the bank who might be looking for employment, I might be able to help. She volunteered that Leah Thomason had recently resigned. She called her Leah. Told me Leah had worked for—wait for it—Wayne Shumaker for many years but had just left the bank. Turns out, the president's admin was friends with Leah. A lot of folks at the bank didn't like her. She was pretty, even sultry, according to my source. Maybe they were jealous? I'm not sure.

"I asked why Leah left. Answer: It would be better to ask her. Then I asked for an address. Answer: Leah moved up here to be with her mother. Somewhere in Brookside. And then I asked if there was anything else she would be comfortable sharing. Answer: She lowered her voice to almost a whisper and told me—wait for it—Leah and Wayne used to be an item, but they broke up. It's not just an ex-employee or an ex-lover. A BOGO. A package deal."

"Wow. Lots of info from a chatty admin."

"My clear impression is that the admin isn't a fan of Shumaker but *is* a fan of Leah Belle Thomason. Did her name pop up at all in your case?"

"Not at all."

"Okay, kiddo. Give me a few hours, and I'll dig out an address and Leah's mobile number."

"Great work! Thanks, babe. Thanks a bunch. Get me as much contact info as you can, and I'll take it from there."

Steele figured out that Thomason's mother lived on 60th Terrace, a few houses in from Brookside Boulevard. Kansas City's Brookside area was part of a turn-of-the-century residential development by J.C. Nichols as the city spread south. Today, it is a collection of smaller subdivisions, like Crestwood, Countryside, and Morningside. The homes are older: Tudors, Colonial Revivals, and other popular early-1900s styles. Many of these subdivisions are now quite affluent.

Steele gave 3J the pertinent information. Real estate records showed Jane Thomason owned the house. No co-owners. 3J assumed Jane was the mother. She drove to the house, heading south on Main Street and picking up Brookside Boulevard just as it intersected the Plaza. It was only about fifteen minutes south of downtown, depending on traffic. 60th Terrace was quiet and heavily tree-lined. Jane's house had a stone retaining wall in front, an off-white stucco façade, and accenting brickwork that looked original to the 1920s.

3J decided a visit was better than a phone call. She rang the doorbell, and in moments, an elderly gray-haired woman answered. Jane. 3J introduced herself and asked if she could speak to Leah Belle Thomason.

Jane's features were soft, and her voice was as well. "May I ask what this is regarding?"

"Of course. Here is my card. I am a lawyer at the Greene Madison law firm downtown. We represent a company on the Plaza, Paxton Energy, that filed a bankruptcy case here in Kansas City. There is an ongoing trial. One witness for the other side is Wayne Shumaker. I understand that Ms. Thomason was Mr. Shumaker's administrative assistant at Franklin Trust in Wichita for many years. I am hoping Ms. Thomason would talk to me and give me some background information to help me in my trial."

Jane Thomason studied the card and then looked up at 3J. "Leah is no fan of Wayne Shumaker." She frowned. "But I can't judge her interest level in getting involved. She's back home here in Kansas City, staying with me to put Wayne and the bank behind her. I'm hopeful she'll figure out her path forward now. It's best that you speak with her rather than have me surmise her response." She spoke in an even-keeled voice.

"That's fine. Is she home?"

"She's out, I'm afraid. I expect her back in about fifteen

minutes. If you'd like, you're welcome to come in and wait on the couch."

"I would like to, thank you. But it might be better if I waited in my car rather than assuming she's willing to speak with me. I need her help, and I hope she'll at least hear me out."

"I'm sure she'll at least listen to you. She parks in front. She has blonde hair. She'll come up the walkway." Jane Thomason smiled as she described her daughter. "Give her a second, and then feel free to ring and ask to speak to her."

"Thank you so much for speaking with me." 3J returned to her car and waited. She had parked under a tree in the shade. It was one of those "almost fall" afternoons in Kansas City that could make you forget the intense summer heat and humidity that was a hallmark of the Midwestern city on the river. More than a century earlier, someone dubbed it the Paris of the Plains for the winding boulevards and fountains dotting the city. The naming committee might have ignored them and instead named it the Midwestern Jakarta if they had convened in Kansas City at the end of July when, for weeks on end, the television meteorologists reported inhumane temperature and humidity—over 90 degrees and over 90 percent.

Fifteen minutes came and went. Then thirty. Then forty-five. 3J worried she was on a hopeless stakeout, like Ronnie when he was hoping to photograph a wayward husband's indiscretions, but the husband never showed up.

At last, a silver Honda Civic pulled up. A tall blonde with a perfect figure got out of the car. She didn't quite walk toward the front door. It was more like a sashay, with a bit of showiness and attitude. An Ann-Margret stroll designed to attract attention. It looked good on her.

She let herself in the front door. 3J waited five minutes and then went back to the door and, for the second time, rang the bell.

Leah Thomason answered. 3J started to explain the situation again, and Thomason interrupted. "I don't mean to be rude. It's not in my nature. But my mother already told you I'm here, back in Kansas City, because I want to leave Wayne and that bank behind me. The image in my rearview mirror is shrinking fast."

"I understand. I'm not here to harass you. If I could just come in and explain what's going on, then I'll leave and you can decide whether you will talk without me here pressuring you."

"You really don't expect me to talk to you?"

"I would love it if you would, but you don't have to, and I'm prepared to leave without you saying a word. I can follow up in a day, then see if you'll have me back for a conversation."

"Alright. Come in. We can sit in the front room on the couch, and I can hear what you came to say."

"Thank you."

Thomason stepped aside and cleared a path for 3J to enter. They turned left into a beautiful and inviting sunroom at the front of the house.

After they sat down, 3J explained the case, what had happened to Paxton at the bank group meeting, the video, why 3J believed it was fake, and her concern that this was all happening because of Wayne Shumaker's personal desire to profit from the Paxton Energy misfortune.

"What's your understanding of how Wayne will profit?" Thomason asked.

Maybe this was the beginning of an actual conversation, 3J hoped.

"I'm not sure," 3J responded.

"Wayne got a big bonus for the Franklin portion of the loan to Paxton—it was a $28 million loan. I'm guessing he got more than a hundred-thousand-dollar bonus. But there was another borrower, Greg McCoy's client. Somehow, Wayne figured out a way to originate a loan to the other borrower to buy the same land Paxton wanted. He'd have to shut down the Paxton loan to do that. Two bonuses."

"You're saying Shumaker got paid twice?"

Thomason nodded. Then she closed her eyes. "It was three dips, not two."

"*Dips?*"

"I called all of Wayne's scheming at the bank 'dips.' If he got paid more than once on a loan, I called it double-dipping. Paxton was the first loan I knew of where he'd get paid three times. The triple-dip."

"How was it a triple-dip?"

"That other borrower was Greg McCoy's brother-in-law, Martin Fillmore. To put this whole—I'll call it a transaction, but scheme or ruse might be better to describe it—together, Wayne was going to get an override on the oil and gas produced from Fillmore's drilling. Do you know what an override is, Ms. Jones?"

3J shook her head.

"It's a percentage of the proceeds generated from oil production, calculated before considering production expenses. Trust me, it's a pretty good chunk of change. That's the third dip. A percentage of the gross revenue received from the oil sold at the wellhead. It's a pretty valuable interest in oil and gas. One of the best interests to have."

Leah looked at her hand to count out the dips. She made a fist, and as she identified each dip, she opened a finger, her palm facing upward. "The Paxton bonus." She opened her pointer. "The Fillmore bonus." She opened her middle finger. "And the override." She opened her ring finger.

There might be no coming back tomorrow, 3J realized. Something about this topic must have hit a nerve, and Leah Belle Thomason was not just commenting. She was singing.

"You seem to know quite a bit about oil and gas production."

"It's all Wayne did at the bank. I guess you could say the master broke me in under his lash."

3J found her description surprising. Lash? It suggested more was going on.

Thomason explained, "He worked other angles, too. He made borrowers give him an interest in their company, like a venture capital firm might take, only he didn't invest. The interest was given in exchange for Wayne pushing the loan through the committee.

"He made borrowers pay him cash under the table in exchange for getting the loan approved. He considered filling out false papers to draw on a borrower's line of credit for his benefit. I never saw him follow through and do that. But his need for money grew, and with it, so did the chances he would take. He continued to branch out and look for other ways to extract money from the bank, or borrowers, or both."

"But how did you learn about the different dips?"

"I listened. Wayne talked. Not just at work. We were… companions… I guess that would be the best way to describe our relationship."

"I see."

"And I was responsible for filing Wayne's papers, and Wayne kept a ledger. At least that's what he liked to call it."

"A ledger?"

"Right. His version of a little black book. It had notes on his deals, his bonuses, and some of his dips at the bank."

"There were others?"

"Yes, but I'm most familiar with Paxton because it was by far and away the most complicated hustle he orchestrated. The more complicated things got for Wayne, the more he wrote in the ledger to make sure he could keep it all straight."

"Why did you and he split up?"

"There was no 'you and he.' And 'split up' sounds so mutual. Amicable. There was none of that. I left him. I found him in bed, *my* bed, with another woman. We understood we weren't exclusively tied to each other, but we—I—had a hard and fast rule. There'd be no fooling around with others in my bed. Extracurricular activities occurred outside the house. The house was ours and for us."

"Do you want to take a break or keep talking?" 3J asked.

"This is fine." Thomason replied.

"How did the two of you meet?" 3J inquired.

"In a bar. I picked him up. Awful forward of me, but he liked it, and, at least at first, he seemed to respect me. Plenty of men see me, and respect isn't the first thing on their minds."

She smiled, but her eyes betrayed her sadness. "I sit at a bar, and the men all figure I'm their favorite target to sidle over to and use whatever pickup line they've been practicing all week. I try to give them the side-eye before they get to my table, and it usually works to ward them off.

"One night, I saw Wayne sitting alone at the bar nursing

a whiskey on the rocks, and he wasn't scanning the bar for women. He was staring at his drink, deep in thought. I don't know why, but I decided I'd be bold, go over to him, and pick him up. It worked."

3J smiled. She liked Leah Belle Thomason. Honest and to the point and with just the right amount of self-awareness. At least in the story, she was a confident, strong woman.

Thomason continued, "Then he hired me as his administrative assistant at the bank. It was a good job. To start, I liked the bank. As a result, he got to see me all the time—at work, at home, and when we went out—and I guess he liked what he saw. He also liked that when we went out, other people looked at us. We made a good-looking couple." She had a wistful look on her face.

People were probably looking at Thomason, not Shumaker, 3J thought. They were probably thinking that Shumaker was a lucky fellow.

"Our relationship was great for a while," Thomason explained. "I moved in with him right off the bat. He has this remarkable house built at the turn of the century. I loved that house." She smiled.

"At some point, we tired of the full-blown relationship, but we stayed together and worked out our arrangement. Even with that, when we were together, it was still good, I mean, other than when he hit me and pushed me around. He did that more and more at home. I was used to it. My father had forced himself on me when I was just a kid, and my mother banished him. That's me. I shouldn't have, but I stayed with Wayne and remained his admin. It was a good job."

"Thanks for all the background on your relationship. It's very helpful," 3J said softly.

"No problem at all. It's therapeutic to talk about it. Do you want a drink? Water? Diet Coke?"

"Water would be great. Thank you."

Thomason left the room and returned with a tall glass of water for 3J and a Diet Coke for herself. She took a sip.

"From the first time I met him, Wayne needed money," Thomason continued. "He has expensive tastes. The house, me, the other women, fancy wine and cigars, parties, too many nights at the bar, nice suits, designer ties, A BMW in the garage. He dabbled in the crypto market and lost money, and he maxed out on his credit cards with interest running over 20 percent. He had mortgages on the house that used up all his equity, and of course, he had to service large mortgage payments.

"He spent a ton of money. More than a banker, even an executive vice president, might spend if he were being prudent.

"And then the time came when he started trying to figure out ways to get more money without working harder. His little 'dark designs,' as he called them. They made me uncomfortable, but I was just his assistant. I kept track of what was going on, and I kept my mouth shut. I had no say in what he was doing. We didn't talk about it."

Thomason paused, looked at 3J for a long moment, sipped some more from her soda can, and said, "His dark designs," she repeated quietly, "like Paxton Energy."

Thinking back to what Thomason told her about the Paxton loan, 3J recapped, "Are you saying Wayne Shumaker had the bank buy into the Paxton loan and then shut it down to clear the way for someone else to get a loan from the bank to buy the same land Paxton wanted to buy?"

"That's what I'm saying. I'm saying it because it's true."

"Before you left, had you heard about the video the bank group used to try to shut Paxton Energy down?"

"It's all in the ledger."

"When you say all… ?"

"All of it. Who made the video for Wayne and who authenticated it for him. How Wayne got ahold of it. It's all in the ledger."

"I deposed Wayne. He was supposed to bring any documents related to the video. Sounds like that would be the ledger?"

"Of course. But he didn't bring the ledger, did he?" Thomason asked.

"He did not."

"He told you there were no documents related to the video, right?"

"Right."

It was as if Leah Belle Thomason were in the room while Shumaker testified and lied under oath.

"You're saying Wayne lied?" 3J asked.

Thomason shook her head, smiling. "Excuse my sarcasm. I'm stunned." But she wasn't stunned, and 3J got the message loud and clear.

"Now that I know about the ledger, I can't subpoena Wayne to testify in court. He's too far from the courthouse, more than a hundred miles. If I reopen the deposition and demand that he bring the ledger, he'll just say there is none. He lied once. I guess once you open the door, the darkness decides how far you go."

"Hmm. I didn't know about the hundred-mile rule." She paused. "Ms. Jones. It's challenging to deal with Wayne. I understand. Believe me. No one appreciates that more than I do. Now it's your problem as well, and I apologize for that." Thomason smiled wistfully.

"You're smiling. Why?"

"I'm tired. We've gone far enough tonight. It's been a pleasure. I need to wind down now. I'll call you tomorrow. Here's my cell phone number if you need it." She handed 3J a piece of paper.

They shook hands, and Thomason showed 3J to the door.

On her drive downtown, 3J had mixed feelings about her meeting. She had found her mole who could take down Shumaker and break through his wall of lies. That was a significant positive. But for it to work, Leah Belle Thomason would have to testify and open up wounds that were fresh and hadn't had time to heal. That was a significant negative, but 3J saw no way around the pain Leah would feel on the stand.

Thomason had obviously gone through a flood of emotions to tell her story. 3J hoped that the flood would subside and Thomason could be of help in court. That's what was needed to put this case in the win column.

Chapter 36

THE BELFRY

IT WAS LATE in the day as 3J returned to the office. Pascale had already left. She packed up her things and went home at a reasonable hour, defined by the small amount of sunlight remaining in the sky.

She and Steele decided to walk several blocks to their favorite downtown restaurant—The Belfry, owned and operated by Celina Tio, 3J's friend and a James Beard chef. It was close to 3J's condo, and they always walked.

They shared the Mega Dope Chorizo appetizer—Manchego cheese sauce, sherry marinated onions, and house chorizo—and for their main dishes, they each had seared scallops, sunchoke purée, crispy Brussels sprouts, and pickled apple gremolata.

Chef Tio was short-staffed and only had time for a quick "hi" and "how's it going?" before she had to race back to the kitchen. The restaurant and bar business was one of the most challenging around. But Tio pulled it off without ever appearing harried.

Over dinner, 3J described her meeting with Thomason. "She took me right to the precipice and then left me hanging until tomorrow. But it's clear she knows everything."

"Glad I could help find her. This person Shumaker sounds like a real dime-store novel bad guy to me," Steele commented.

"He is, and he has the ledger. I just can't get my hands on it." She shook her head.

They finished eating without talking. Her mind was drifting. As they finished, Steele said, "Y'know, the idea to look for a scorned lover and work colleague was genius."

"Thanks." She didn't want to tell him over dinner that Robbie McFadden helped her figure out she should find a mole to take down Shumaker.

"I'm surprised somebody like Shumaker could rise to the executive VP level at a big bank while pulling all this shady stuff," Steele mused. "Poison dressed up and ready to roll."

"He's poison, all right. And he likes to sound like a noble banker well above the fray. I just have to pull him down into the fracas and see what happens. Thomason's key in doing this. I'm nervous, but all I can do is reach out to her tomorrow and hope she finishes the story and then agrees to testify. I have my work cut out for me."

They walked back to 3J's condo and turned on some jazz, the Mary Lou Williams recording, "Messin' Round in Montmartre." Kansas City piano jazz supreme. Williams was yet another gift Kansas City gave to the world. It had been a tough couple of weeks for 3J. She nodded off on Steele's shoulder, and he carried her into bed still asleep.

This would be the first night in a while she didn't dream about bad things that might happen in the Paxton Energy case.

She was too tired to dream. She'd have plenty of time tomorrow to remind herself of how things can go wrong in litigation at the drop of a hat.

Chapter 37

WHEN THE MORNING COMES

THE NEXT MORNING, 3J sat in Pascale's office explaining her encounter with Thomason. He was encouraged; Thomason could be the breakthrough they needed to crack open Shumaker's story and expose him.

3J returned to her office and called Thomason. It went right to voicemail, and the mailbox was full. Then she phoned Jane Thomason and asked to speak to her daughter.

"I'm sorry, Ms. Jones. That won't be possible."

Panic started to set in. "May I come by and see her?"

"She's not here. Leah left at the crack of dawn this morning."

"Heading where?"

"Wichita. She said something about heading at least a hundred miles from the courthouse. I am afraid I didn't understand what that meant."

3J thanked Jane for the information and hung up. *Not again. Another runner.* But this time, she didn't have the luxury of days to find and serve Thomason with a deposition subpoena. There was no time to get ahold of Little, have him find and serve Thomason, drive to Wichita again, and depose Shumaker's recalcitrant ex.

3J tried Thomason's mobile number again, worried. Would she even answer?

"Leah Thomason."

"Leah. This is 3J. Josephina Jillian Jones. Where are you?"

"Let's see. The last sign I passed said I was ninety miles from Wichita. That means I'm somewhere on I-35, 109 miles from Kansas City."

3J closed her eyes. The hundred miles from the courthouse she mentioned to Thomason yesterday. *Damn!* She remembered a line from a thriller movie she and Pascale saw years ago, which Pascale adopted and modified for the practice of law: "In any case you handle, there are a hundred ways to screw it up. If I were a genius and lucky, I might identify fifty of them. And I'm no genius."

Apparently, me neither. And I should never have mentioned the hundred-mile rule to Leah.

"Why are you driving to Wichita?"

"I just need to decide whether I'm going to be your star witness on the stand, taking Wayne down. That's what you want, isn't it? That's why you came over yesterday to talk, isn't it?"

"You didn't need to drive all the way to Wichita, Leah."

"I felt like I did. I didn't want you to serve me with a subpoena while I was still at my mother's house, sorting all this out."

3J inhaled deeply and let her breath out slowly. "There are many things I want to ask you. Need to ask you. I guess I'll just hold my water until I hear from you. Can I at least text you the information about the next hearing—you know, the date, time, and place?"

"Of course. That's fine. I might need it if I decide at three in the morning the day of the hearing."

"Call me anytime, day or night, if you have questions."

"I will. I appreciate your professionalism."

✄

"Jesus, Pascale. Now what?"

3J had just explained that Leah Belle Thomason was in the wind and beyond the subpoena power for the upcoming trustee hearing. "I can't believe I babbled about Rules 45 and 9016. Can't compel a witness to be dragged across the country to testify. I get it, but I should have kept my big mouth shut." 3J rubbed her forehead and shook her head in disgust.

"Ease up. You were gaining her trust and having a conversation. You got her talking. She opened up to you. You don't know—she may have already known about the rules," Pascale said, trying to offer a more soothing outlook.

3J doubted it. "Without Leah, we may lose this case."

"We may. You can't worry your way into winning, but you might very well be able to worry your way into losing. Call her again; leave a voicemail; ask her to call you. Ask her to come. Promise her dinner at The Belfry if you'd like.

"Then please put her out of your mind, and let's prepare the rest of the case to try before Judge Robertson. At this point, we've done all we can for the client, and we're at the point when we need to be ready to roll the dice and finalize the rest of our case preparation. Whatever happens, happens.

If it'll make you happy, prepare an examination of Leah, and if she shows up, you're ready. But remember, we've done all we can."

"Including losing?"

"Yep. Paxton gets our best effort. Nothing more. And certainly not a guarantee of a win."

Chapter 38
THE BANKRUPTCY SHOP

Jennifer Cuello had pulled the evidence authentication articles Judge Robertson requested, and the two of them boned up on the evolving era of fake videos. They learned of the growing movement to use caution when admitting videos into evidence to make sure they were authentic.

"In the not-so-distant past, I'd usually allow evidence in and figure out how relevant it was later," Judge Robertson reminded Cuello. "I don't have jury trials, and like most bankruptcy judges, I would just let everything in and weigh how useful it was once I got back to chambers after the trial was over.

"Now, I may need to be a bit more cautious and guard the gate of admissibility more carefully. If it's not real, I shouldn't let it into evidence in the first place. But figuring out whether it's real or not is like black magic. It seems a bit like the days of the alchemists of old, who said they could change lead into gold or command a hidden flame. Could they really? Who could tell? Was the gold bar really gold or a subterfuge?"

He paused to gather his thoughts, took a deep breath and exhaled, then continued.

"Today, I've got a video that may be gold or just lead, trying to fool me into believing it's gold. I shouldn't allow the bar into evidence with such ease until someone shows me it's really gold and not just black magic performed by a computer alchemist. And how will they do that?"

"It's very messy, Judge. I guess you'll have to listen to both experts and figure out who you believe."

"You're assuming Ms. Jones shows back in court with an expert of her own, right?"

"She has to, doesn't she?"

"I suppose so. Two experts. Hmm. And if it's a tie? If both of them are convincing, then what am I supposed to do?"

"You'll use your alchemist powers and divine the correct result?" Jennifer asked playfully. After working for him for two years, she had a license to add levity to a case.

"That's me. The alchemist with the magic gavel and elixir to help divine the unknown," the judge said sarcastically. "Jennifer, were you able to find anything else on this topic? The legal one, not the alchemy one."

"Not really. I get the sense it has the judiciary on edge, just like you're feeling. Judges are concerned they don't have the skill or the training today to decide what's real and what's not."

"We don't, but I guess I will still have to decide." He shook his head slowly. "Whatever happens next, happens. At least we'll have good seats for the show. Thanks, Jennifer."

As she left his office, he turned to read the pile of papers on his desk. More orders to review and sign. More motions and oppositions to absorb. More claims of emergency and a need for an instant ruling. *Job security. Still… a break in the endless queue of papers every once in a while wouldn't be a bad thing.*

❧

That night, Judge Robertson left the office for the drive home. As he drove south on Main, he passed the newly completed construction of the north-south light rail extension to the Plaza. It was getting closer to his house but was not quite far enough south. He hoped someday it would extend all the way to his neighborhood, Romanelli Gardens, and its 1920s Tudor homes just off Ward Parkway. He would enjoy not driving to work every day.

Usually, the drive was relaxing. A time to unwind. But all he could think about was his upcoming "video trial," as he called it, for only Jennifer Cuello's ears. But he wasn't relaxed at all. When he got home and went inside, his wife of almost forty years could see it on his face.

"You okay?" she asked.

"Oh, just another day at the bankruptcy shop," he replied with a weak and unconvincing smile.

"You know I don't believe that at all."

"I know. You are a wise one."

"I know, and don't you ever forget it," she said as they hugged.

Chapter 39

THE PATIO

THEY SAT ON Pascale's stone patio in his Loose Park home's backyard, just across from the ground where Union troops under General Samuel Ryan Curtis drove back Confederate forces during the Battle of Westport more than 150 years before. Curtis had positioned artillery north of Brush Creek, firing up at the Confederate line on the bluffs that now form the park's northern edge.

Now, not far from those bluffs was Loose Park's Laura Conyers Smith Municipal Rose Garden—one of 3J's favorite places in the city—where the roses and other cultivated flora grow in soil once watered with the blood of fallen Confederate soldiers.

On the patio, Pascale and 3J talked about the Paxton case and the upcoming trial. They had done all they could do and were ready to put on their case for Judge Robertson. The trial would start the day after tomorrow.

They had divided the case between them. Pascale would examine Knoll and handle any surprise witnesses the banks would call. 3J would take on the experts: Elkin and Wilson. She would also admit the depositions of Fillmore and Shumaker, and if they came to testify live, she'd take care of that as well. Pascale would put Remmy on the stand if necessary. Finally, 3J would handle Bearfoot Stockton and Leah Belle Thomason if he followed through on his promise to testify and if she returned to Kansas City for the trial.

It was a lot of work for 3J and Pascale to prepare. But they were as ready as they could be and found a small respite from Paxton Energy in Pascale's backyard.

"What's up with you and that guitar of yours?" 3J asked.

"Still playing. But now I play *with* a band, not *in* a band."

"I don't follow."

"Anyone with a guitar and a little nerve can step onto a stage for three minutes in the spotlight, whether fame or infamy," Pascale explained. "That was my thing, but not anymore. We had three in the band, and one moved to San Francisco and a new job. When he moved, no more band. Honestly, the world may be a better place without me on stage."

3J smiled. She had heard Pascale and his band play several times. He was much better than his self-deprecating comments let on.

"But I can still play. Anyone with a computer can find a backing track with a professional band playing, practice along, and even record the lead guitar while the band plays. No more need to walk into Sun Records Studio and lay down tracks. I've gone from a small band to a completely solitary gig in whatever size band I choose and whatever genre I pick that day. And I like it. That's why I say, *with* the band, not *in* it."

"Ah. Now I get it."

"I'll always love playing as long as my fingers will let me. How about you?"

"Not much in the way of hobbies. I guess Ronnie is my primary hobby."

"And a good one at that. Have things quieted down between you two?"

"Maybe, but it's tenuous at best. We love each other but I know if I utter the word Robbie, I'll never get to say the word McFadden, and Ronnie and I will be battling again."

"Maybe. You never know. He might surprise you."

3J nodded then slowly shook her head. She decided to change the topic. "I'm wondering, Bill, any ideas for the next act?"

"You mean when I pack it in?"

"Exactly."

"Trying to slide me out of the firm?" he asked teasingly.

"Of course not. Just wondering."

He took a sip of wine before answering. He had gone over the question more times in his mind than he could count but without a suitable response. "Not yet. Taking the first step. Trying to give myself permission to have a new life. Maybe one where I measure success differently. I've been trying to live by something I heard Clint Eastwood say. Getting up every day and trying not to let the old man in. But that old guy… He's certainly been knocking on the door louder and louder. Soon enough, the door will open, and he'll ask me to follow him out. But not quite yet."

Pascale spoke without looking at 3J, his attention directed to the horizon.

"It's important for me to belong to something," he continued, "to stay engaged." He turned his gaze back to 3J and said, "For now, that's the firm until something else comes to mind. It's challenging to make new friends as you get older and even harder as friends around you die. But no one wants to die a lonely old man. It's important to stay connected to something."

3J had always taken mental notes when she talked to Pascale about getting older and moving on from practicing law. Someday, she'd be in the same place. Everyone gets there. There was no avoiding it unless you planned to die at your desk.

"I had one of those talks with Bob Swanson the other day," Pascale observed. Swanson was the managing partner of Greene Madison. "He wanted to make sure I understood there was no expiration date on my career at the firm. I smiled."

"Well, that's comforting to know."

"It is. No expiration date at the firm, but I know there's a shelf life for me. I just need to figure out what that is."

He sighed. "It's a new world. I take less time to walk out my door and head for work. I have many fewer hairs to comb. I don't have to tie a tie. I get my coffee from a barista instead of my coffee pot. Progress, right?"

She smiled.

"Someday, maybe I'll even have a car that drives me to work. Who knows?"

They sat and watched the sky darken over the park. Peaceful. Every once in a while, two bankruptcy attorneys could use a little peace.

"What about you, 3J?" Pascale asked. "Is everything okay with you at the firm?"

"I suppose so."

"A resounding meh."

"Really, everything's good. When I got here all those many years ago, I went into meetings as a question mark. A Black woman in a White man's firm. Both new to the idea of lawyers from different backgrounds joining together in one place. I'm still learning to be my own advocate, and the firm is still learning to hear me when I speak up for myself. We're both getting a little better at it. Little by little, right?"

"But do you like what you do?"

3J pondered for a moment. Pascale continued, "I know it's hard to say you like everything you do every day of the week. What attorney could say that? But on balance, do you like what you do?"

"Why ask me this after all these years?"

"I got you into this line of work. It's on me. Or at least I feel it is occasionally."

"Then, sure, I like what I do."

He nodded as he stood up, satisfied with the brief answer but not sure whether he believed it 100 percent.

As he rose, she asked, "And what about you?"

"You mean do I like what I do?"

"Exactly."

"I used to do the things I didn't really want to do as the price to continue to do the things I wanted to do. Now I can do whatever I want. I just need to figure out what that looks like." He walked over to the grill. "Time to put the steaks on. Here," he said, passing his wine glass to 3J. "Refill, please, while I cook."

"Lots of evidence to present," Pascale said, switching gears to the upcoming trial.

"And lots of uncertainty," 3J added. "Will Shumaker and Fillmore come and testify? Will Bearfoot Stockton come? Will Leah Belle Thomason?"

"We have to be ready to examine each of them as if they were coming," Pascale said.

"Of course. That's why we still have a good amount of work ahead of us. Outcome prediction, Bill?"

"On this one, no idea. We still don't know if we'll need to put Remmy on the stand or even if we should. It's a game-time decision."

⌇

Dinner with Pascale was just what she needed. He could be fatherly without being a substitute father. Who would've ever believed she'd have a White Kansas City father figure in her life? Maybe after losing his wife and daughter in a car crash, he needed a surrogate daughter to fill the void. She must have seemed like his worst nightmare—a Black teenage wild child for a daughter, one who took on danger without considering the risks. *Poor Pascale,* she told herself. *I'm sure he could have found a more manageable woman to adopt.*

After dinner, they hugged, and she headed home. As she drove and pondered the father-daughter notion, her phone rang. Another blocked ID. She knew it had to be Robbie McFadden.

No pleasantries. He came right to the point.

"What's the update, Counselor?"

3J gave him the view from 20,000 feet but didn't mention Leah Belle Thomason.

He wasn't asking about the whole case. "I meant Leah," McFadden explained. "Where does that stand? Is everything okay?"

"Yes and no."

"How can it be both?"

"We live in a nuanced world, Mr. McFadden, where I find

myself speaking to you all the time to help me in my case."
She sighed. "Sorry, long few days. If I had to pick one, I would
have to say it was just no."

"Continue," McFadden directed.

"I mean… I met her at her mom's house. She started off
talkative, then cut off the discussion, and now it seems she's
back in Wichita to get away from me, beyond the subpoena
power. On purpose. As it sits, the good: I decided she'd make
a significant witness and might even be the pivotal witness
to get us a win. The bad: she's gone, and as far as I can tell,
won't testify, and I have no way to make her. We start putting
on evidence the day after tomorrow. Without her, our case is
much weaker. We may lose."

McFadden sighed. "Jesus. What a fuckin' world." He
sighed again. "Okay. Let me see what I can do."

"Do you have some kind of sway over her?"

McFadden didn't respond.

"What's with you and Leah?" 3J probed.

"Leah Belle Thomason. Hmm. I met her at a bar—the
Phoenix—on a jazz night. Ever hear of the club?"

"Of course."

"The boys and me go there every once in a while. We sit
in the back near the emergency exit. Always good to have an
emergency exit plan. Leah was a regular. The club has quite
a history. It's on a corner in the Garment District that was
originally part of the Phoenix Hotel, built in 1888. It passed
through a lot of hands: Frank Valerious, whose name is still on
the stained glass and still watches over the club, and Madame
Linna Laws, who may have rented out rooms upstairs by the
hour, if you catch my drift. It's always been associated with
saloons and nightlife."

There he goes again. At least this time, it had a jazz theme to it. She could imagine a young Ben Webster playing a secret after-hours set there. But right now, she didn't need a sweet, late-night saxophone. She needed McFadden to stick to the facts.

"Anyway, Leah was a real looker who needed work. I put her to work running numbers for me. You know about running numbers?"

"I have to admit I've heard about it only in passing."

"Well, I've brought it back. Jesus, here I am talking to an officer of the court about one of my divisions. I'm going to need an attorney-client privilege with you if this keeps up."

3J was quiet, but his comment concerned her. Was that the payback? She would have to be one of his lawyers?

McFadden continued, "Being that it's kinda like a lottery, bettors pick a number sequence, put money down, and bet that the sequence will be a winner. My runner folks pick up the sequence from each bettor with their bet and bring it back to my accountants. That was Leah Belle. One of my runners. I publish the winning sequence, pay the winners, keep the losers' money, and start over. It's cash-heavy, which I like. Better odds of winning than the state-sponsored lottery, which the clients like. Works just like the old days, but now it's slicker and more efficient.

"When some of the boys got one look at her, they said she should be working in a different division, doing 'favors' for clients. I said absolutely not.

"You may have noticed there wasn't a dad at the home. Before her mom booted her husband out, when Leah was twelve, he started to take advantage of her.

"This guy was a genuine piece of work. He worked, came home, and relieved his tension using the daughter he had brought into this world. I met her mother one day down in the Bottoms. She talked to me about a service. I won't bore you with the details. But I will say this: Mr. Thomason is no longer with us, and I found his departure from planet Earth particularly satisfying.

"I set the boys straight about Leah Belle. She was running numbers for me, and that was all. She did good work. Reliable, good at math. Then one day, she tells me she's off to Wichita to make it on her own. Kind of a Mary Tyler Moore flair to it. She had grown wings, and she was ready to fly.

"Off she went. Until I found out she took up with this Wayne Shumaker guy. He also had an abusive strain in his personality. He gave her a job at the bank. She was even better at math by then. But he didn't treat her nice. You've seen her. She could have most any guy she wanted, and yet she was attracted to guys who had no respect for her. Shumaker started popping her, and she stayed with him. Jesus.

"That's when I started checking out this Shumaker guy. The whole thing about him was creepy. Almost like Leah Belle's father had died and come back as Wayne freakin' Shumaker, destined to hook up with her. Reincarnation gone bad." McFadden paused. He had now explained more about why he had an interest in 3J's case, and there was more to come.

"I've stayed in touch with her, and she finds me when she needs me," he continued. "You might say that I've provided, let's call it, 'guardian angel' services for her.

"That's why I'm helping you. I want to see Shumaker go away. Let Leah Belle figure out a better way to live her life and find a better guy to share it with. Maybe Shumaker's exit will be like how Daddy Thomason got gone one night. There could be a similar outcome. It might be that he'll just go to jail. But he's out of Leah's life, and the chapter has closed. Right now, that's all I care about."

"Sounds like you're considering a hit on him," 3J stated, concern in her voice. "You've got me involved to make it easier for you to kill him?" There was concern in 3J's voice.

"Not at all. Wayne doesn't have to die to go away. A simple trip to Leavenworth will do the trick. If he died, it would be too easy a way out for him. Leavenworth would be a better outcome. Shumaker in prison among some of society's worst of the worst doing real penance and fearing for his life every day. Much more satisfying."

"Oh. I see." *A bad guy helping to send a worse guy away. What a nuanced world we live in.*

McFadden continued, "I had hoped Leah Belle would follow through without me having to intervene. But she's got wings now, and I need to talk to her. I'm not saying Leah has now found religion. But she wants out of the life of being around abusive men. And I want that to happen for her. Which means I have to talk to her."

"You're helping me to help her?"

"Among other reasons, Counselor. Among others."

3J got to her garage, parked, and walked to the elevator up to her condo and Ronnie Steele. She wondered about Leah Belle. *Are you coming to the trial, Leah?* 3J wondered. *I just need you to testify. We can solve the world's problems after that.* "Without you, I'm going to be screwed," 3J muttered.

Chapter 40

THE ODYSSEY BACK

AFTER SHE GOT to Wichita, Leah Belle talked to her mother until just after 2 a.m. Her mother said she should take a stand by taking the stand.

Wayne was a bad man. He was no good for her, no good for borrowers, and no good for Franklin.

Leah was unsure what she should do. Then, at 3 a.m., he called. She always took his calls. He wasn't like the other men. He respected her, looked out for her, and came to her aid when she needed it. She enjoyed it when they spoke. It wasn't too often anymore; not like the old days, when she worked for him.

This time, it wasn't a long talk. But it was a talk she needed to have. He left it up to her... sort of. He told her that if she would just return to Kansas City to testify, she would find it one of those liberating moments that come along only once or twice. He left her with one observation: don't be someone who, for the rest of your life, says, "Look at me now. If only I had..."

She spent the next twenty-four hours pondering and slept

little. She thought he might call back one more time, but he didn't. By 3 a.m., it was just Thomason and her thoughts. She knew the trial would start in the morning at 9. 3J had texted Thomason where to be and when.

Finally, she made a decision.

She got dressed conservatively but with style to make sure people would notice, got in her Honda Civic, and at 4:30 a.m., headed north on I-35 bound for Kansas City. She hadn't called 3J; she didn't want to talk to her and was still embarrassed she had left 3J in the lurch. The return to Kansas City would right that wrong.

The sun ticked upward on the horizon, and the pink and purple sunrise was dazzling. The sunlight shone on the Flinthills' sandstone, making it come alive with an electrifying shade of red. It was quite a sight. *Who said Kansas is ugly?*

Somewhere around the entrance to Highway 99 and Matfield Green, about 120 miles from the courthouse, there was a blast under the right front side of her car like a grenade had exploded. It was a tire blowout. She fought the steering wheel, took her foot off the accelerator, gained control of the car, and navigated to the shoulder.

She had made it all of fifty miles out of Wichita. She couldn't believe her bad luck. And maybe she was about to share some of it with 3J because, if she couldn't get back on the road soon, she'd never be able to testify.

She got out and saw the shredded tire. She called the 800 number for Triple A, but she was smack-dab in the middle of nowhere Kansas, and it was early. The dispatcher said it would be at least an hour before he could get a truck there.

She looked in her trunk. She had a spare. She could change

the tire even though it would make her look like a mess on the witness stand. But she needed a jack, and there was none.

Twenty minutes later, she looked south on I-35 and saw an eighteen-wheeler in the distance barreling north, the first vehicle to approach her since getting her flat.

One way or another, I've got to get to Kansas City in time to testify.

Out of options, she decided to flag down the truck driver. She worried he would be just like Wayne Shumaker and her father. Once again, she was stepping into danger and the risk of putting herself into an abusive situation with a man. But her whole life, she was somehow able to take care of herself even through the abuse. She'd just have to hope she could do it this time as well.

The truck pulled over, and the driver reached across the cab and opened the door. "Need a lift, ma'am?" a female voice asked. The driver was a redheaded woman, maybe fifty, and, at five foot three, she cast more presence than shadow.

"Yes, please. I need to get to the federal courthouse in Kansas City to testify at a trial."

"Well, it's your lucky day. I'm on I-35 to I-70 in KC, and that'll take me right by the courthouse. Lock your car, get your things, and hop up into the cab. What time do you have to be there, honey?"

"Nine. Maybe a little after."

"It'll be close, but we should make it."

Leah got her things from the car, locked it, and with the driver's help, hoisted herself into the cab.

In a moment, they were off.

Chapter 41

IN MY OPINION...

THE DAY OF the next trustee hearing had arrived. 3J had worked out the particulars with the court clerks and the court's tech department to make sure Darius Wilson's PowerPoint would be displayed on all the screens. That way, everyone in the courtroom could see the deck as Wilson went through it, and the attorneys could see it on their table screens.

The stage was set.

"Good morning, everyone. Are the parties ready to proceed?" Judge Robertson asked.

Everyone was.

"Ms. Jones, I believe we left off pending your cross-examination of Mr. Elkin and his expert opinion that the video was genuine."

Remmy Paxton was seated next to 3J and Pascale at counsel's table. Chet Drucker sat next to Frank Davis at the other table. Now that his bank had voted no to Paxton's loan requests, he was all-in on winning the hearing. While he didn't personally agree, he was a good soldier who understood his bank's reputation was on the line.

In the front row of the pews, the judge could see Linda Knoll, Paul Elkin, and Bree Paxton. No Shumaker. No Fillmore. 3J and Pascale figured they wouldn't come, that it was not in their best interests to appear and testify.

Moreover, no Leah Belle Thomason. This was not a shock to 3J. She had hoped Thomason would reach out. But when she heard nothing from Thomason, she knew she would be forced to try the case without her star witness. It did not make for a winning hand.

❦

At a table in front of the bench where the judge presided sat Jennifer Cuello. From her vantage point, she could see everything and was close enough to pass notes to Judge Robertson.

As the proceedings began, three men entered the courtroom and sat in the last row of pews nearest to the exit. One was a redhead with a closely cropped beard dressed impeccably. It had been a long time since Robbie McFadden had stepped into a federal courtroom. It wasn't something someone in his line of work did very frequently. But he didn't want to miss this one. He was sure that Thomason would show. He didn't share 3J's view that the Paxton team had a losing hand. Maybe 3J didn't hold four aces, but maybe two pairs were enough to win the hand.

"Very well, Ms. Jones. Please proceed."

"Thank you, Your Honor. If it pleases the court, we ask for your indulgence and allow us to call Mr. Darius Wilson to the stand before I cross-examine Paul Elkin. Mr. Wilson is our expert, and I believe it would be better if Mr. Elkin

241

heard Mr. Wilson's opinion before I cross-examine Mr. Elkin. Otherwise, I'll just have to recall Mr. Elkin to the stand after Mr. Wilson's testimony. We'd also like the court to direct Mr. Elkin to remain in the courtroom while Mr. Wilson testifies."

"Highly unusual, Ms. Jones. Mr. Davis. Comments?"

"It is unusual, but I have no objection. I hope Ms. Jones remembers my position on this one in case I also need an accommodation as this trial proceeds."

"Well, Counsel, one issue at a time," Judge Robertson replied. "If you have no objection to Ms. Jones's suggestion, then I'll allow it. Let's proceed."

"Thank you, Your Honor and Counsel," 3J said, nodding at Davis. "The debtors call Darius Wilson to the stand."

McFadden leaned forward and rested his elbows on the back of the pew in front of him, then rested his chin on his forearms. This was the first time he would listen to Wilson testify and he wanted to make sure not to miss a single word.

᪣

Thomason learned the driver's name was Abigail Naughton. Abby. After her divorce, she went back to school and got the necessary training and certifications to drive big rigs. She was an indie, taking jobs and handling her calendar. Hauling for whomever and whenever she wanted. She owned the cab. "Or at least my bank does and lets me use it." She laughed.

The two talked as Naughton pushed the big rig to seventy-five miles per hour and beyond on the downhill stretches.

"What's your story, honey?" Naughton asked.

Thomason didn't want to be rude; the woman was doing

her a massive favor. But she wondered how much of her story to share. She started slowly to see how Naughton reacted. Thomason couldn't help glancing at her watch. Not making the deadline was extremely worrisome. But Naughton seemed calm and in control, confident they would make it in time.

∽

3J had Darius Wilson explain his background and experience to establish he was an expert in the field of fake videos. As he spoke, Judge Robertson leaned forward. It was fascinating testimony, as it skirted an admission that Wilson may have violated the law.

"Have you also developed a system to analyze whether a video is real or fake?"

"I have."

"Is that system one that anyone can acquire?"

"No. It's proprietary."

"Where do you work now?"

"I work for Systems Analysis. It's a Missouri-based limited liability company."

"Are you an owner?"

"Yes."

"As part of its business, does Systems Analysis determine if videos are fake?"

"Yes."

"Are you the person at Systems Analysis who analyzes videos to determine if they are fake?"

"I am."

"How does the work flow in general?"

"Clients bring us a video. Often, they claim it is a fake.

For example, sometimes, there is a video posted that might be embarrassing, revealing, or damaging. The client might have been contacted by someone seeking to blackmail them."

"How would the blackmail work?"

"Here is a typical scenario: The blackmailer shares the video with the client and tells them they have forty-eight hours to pay a fee, or the blackmailer will post the video on social media. The client hires SA to determine whether the video is fake or not. If it's fake, my conclusion provides the client with the ammunition to avoid paying the blackmailer."

"Are all the videos you analyze fake?"

"Not at all. Some are, and some are not."

"How many videos have you analyzed?"

"Hundreds. A sign of our times, I am afraid."

"You're telling me that this former boyfriend of yours beat on you regularly and also stole money from his bank?" Naughton asked as she and Thomason thundered along I-35 at near full tilt.

"In a nutshell," Thomason replied.

"And you're on your way to testify against him?"

"I am."

"Wow. Takes plenty of guts."

"Maybe. But it's time. It has to be done. I'll get it all off my chest and move on. Maybe I'll feel freer, and maybe I won't. But I need to do it."

"What will happen to him?"

"Not my problem. I'm hoping his new zip code will be at a correctional facility in Leavenworth, Kansas."

"Damn straight!" Naughton replied. "And you're sure you know enough to take him down?"

"Pretty sure, but I guess we'll find out soon enough."

"Just your word against his?"

"Oh, I have some backup for what I'll say." Leah glanced at her shoulder bag and clutched it tighter.

"Geez. This sounds like good late-night television stuff. I may just park the rig and come in with you to watch."

If you do, I'm sure you won't be the only redhead in the room, Thomason thought as she looked out the passenger window and allowed herself a small, quiet smile.

Frank Davis had raised a weak objection, claiming Wilson was not an expert. The judge overruled it and directed 3J to proceed. Time for the Darius Wilson show.

"Mr. Wilson, have you analyzed the video, Banks Exhibit 1?"

"I have."

"How long did that take?"

"To do my usual thorough and all-encompassing examination, it took me three full days. That's pretty typical for this length of video."

3J turned to the court. "Your Honor, Mr. Wilson has prepared a PowerPoint deck to take us all through what he did to examine the video and what he found. With the court's permission, may Mr. Wilson leave the stand with his clicker and take us through his analysis? Of course, I will continue to ask questions."

"I have no problem with that, Ms. Jones. Please proceed," Judge Robertson directed.

"Thank you. Mr. Wilson, do you have the Banks Exhibit 1 video loaded on the deck?"

"I do." Wilson stepped down from the witness stand and onto the courtroom floor, PowerPoint clicker in his hand.

"Can you play it at normal speed, please?"

There it was again for the judge and the audience to see. Damning as ever, but 3J knew the judge would withhold judgment until he heard everything Wilson had to say.

Wilson played it at normal speed, and then as he had at Greene Madison, he played it slowly and then even slower, directing the judge to focus on the various anomalies: the jagged cheek, the shimmering light, the absence of shadows, the lack of blinking and facial emotion, and the quavering voice. Wilson sounded like a PhD scholar lecturing a roomful of students, and the students—in this case, the judge, Jennifer Cuello, Frank Davis, Chet Drucker, and, indeed, Paul Elkin—listened. Elkin had put his phone away and was focused on Wilson's testimony.

Wilson then explained he had compared the Exhibit 1 video to other company marketing videos that also showed Paxton speaking to an audience. He showed some corporate footage in another slide. The difference was stark. In the corporate footage, Paxton blinked, showed facial emotion, and had no quaver in his voice.

As Wilson explained the analysis, Elkin fidgeted more and more. On several occasions, he leaned over and whispered in Davis's ear. Davis listened the first time. After that, Davis waved him off as the lawyer tried to hear every word Wilson said. Davis would have to create an effective cross-examination of Wilson on the fly, and he whispered a stern, hoarse response to Elkin that he needed to keep his attention on the witness, not on Elkin's growing sense of anxiety. 3J and Pascale heard him.

"Mr. Wilson, based on the anomalies you saw when you slowed the video down, could you draw a conclusion as to whether the video is real or a deepfake?"

"Yes."

"What is that opinion?"

"To the highest degree of certainty I can offer, it is fake. That is not Remmy Paxton in the banks' video."

"When you say, 'to the highest degree of certainty I can offer,' what do you mean?"

"I am 100 percent certain. It is a fake."

"Did you reach any other conclusions about the video?"

"Yes. While on first blush it looks well-made and therefore real, when I dug in and found the anomalies, it was clear someone made the video in a hurry."

"How did you reach that conclusion?"

"On one level, whoever made the video knew what they were doing. If I accept that premise, then the only explanation for the anomalies is that the video creator didn't have enough time to clean up the quavering voice, smooth out the jagged cheeks, reintroduce more natural blinking, add shadows by the lamps, and eliminate the wiggly light through the curtains."

"Did you discover anything else as you took a deep dive into Exhibit 1?"

"Yes. Many computer files contain what we call tags that are like file labels or markers. Like a sticky note used to mark a page in a book. Think of them like a note that says, 'From Mom,' or 'Read this.' They don't change the file itself. The software can use tags to sort the file, identify the file, or provide information about the file."

"Did you find any tags in the banks' video file?"

"Yes. One in particular. Someone encrypted one of the video file tags. Meaning, the creator didn't want an outsider—someone like me—to read what the tag said."

"Were you able to crack the encryption?"

"Yes, the encryption was quite robust, leaving me with the impression that someone wanted the information to stay private. But I managed to get through the encryption and read the tag."

"What does it say?"

Wilson advanced to his slide that showed the tag. "It says 'Elkin: Fillmore: McCoy.'"

"In your experience, do people who create deepfake videos tag them with their name and the names of their clients?"

"Very common. Most deepfake creators are proud of their products and want people in the industry to know they created a good one."

"Any other conclusions you reached?"

"Yes. I found it reasonable to assume that the 'Elkin' referred to Paul Elkin, who's already testified that the video was real, not fake. My conclusion is that Mr. Elkin didn't analyze the video to determine if it was real or not. He created it and therefore knew it was fake all along."

Davis had stopped taking notes. As any good lawyer would, he tried to remove all emotion from his face. Here, however, his efforts failed. All at once, he looked pained, angry, confused, and unhappy that he was about to have to cross-examine Wilson. He now understood why 3J wanted Wilson to testify first.

As the Wilson testimony unfolded, Davis also realized he was going to have to deal with Elkin's false testimony. But he had no idea how he would do that. According to Wilson, Elkin lied under oath in a federal court. Not something he could just walk back or explain in a word or two.

Judge Robertson had been leaning forward. Understanding the gravity of Wilson's statement, he leaned back in his chair, clasped his hands, and raised an eyebrow. Jennifer Cuello stared at Elkin, then passed the judge a note. He read it, then they glanced at each other. Silent communication. They were on the same page.

"Mr. Wilson, have you prepared a written report setting out your analysis and conclusions as you've testified today?"

"I have."

"I hand you what's been marked as Exhibit A. Is that your report?"

"It is."

"Your Honor, we offer Exhibit A into evidence."

Davis had no objection, and the judge admitted the report.

"We also offer Mr. Wilson's PowerPoint into evidence as Exhibit B."

"Objection, Your Honor. The PowerPoint adds nothing to the written report and is duplicative."

"Maybe so, Counselor, but we have no jury and I see no harm in the duplication. Exhibit B is admitted into evidence."

"No further questions, Your Honor," 3J stated.

"We'll take a ten-minute break." Judge Robertson and Jennifer left the courtroom.

⋘

"Fascinating," Judge Robertson said.

"Never count a talented lawyer out," Jennifer replied.

"Talented?" the judge repeated. "That would be Ms. Jones right now and Mr. Davis next. He'll have his chance soon. I felt it was fair to give him another ten to sort this out, if he can."

"Not sure if he will be able to."

"Well, we'll see. He's pretty good. Let's get back to our front-row seats and what happens next."

❧

During the break, Davis, Drucker, and Elkin went to the room off the courtroom. They closed the door. 3J and Pascale leaned on the wall outside the courtroom, stretching their legs. Muffled yelling emanated from the closed-door room, but 3J and Pascale couldn't tell who was yelling or what they were saying.

❧

McFadden and his bodyguards stayed in the courtroom during the break. He scrolled through his emails. Without looking up, he said, "Yep. I'll be adding that one to my Rolodex. Ya never know, boys, when I might need a good bankruptcy lawyer."

❧

"I know you drive a truck. But what's your story?" Thomason inquired.

"My story? Nothing special. Had a kid. Had a husband. Had a house. Even had a dog. Plus a great job. I was an engineer at a tech company. My husband left. No idea where he is. The kid went off the rails. No idea where she is. I outlived the dog. Lost the house to the finance company and the job to a reduction in force.

"This little cab we're in? I've got this. This is where I live. I've got everything I need, except I wouldn't mind getting a small pup to keep me company. I will at some point. I've got my belief in myself. I keep my nose clean. I hope my kid has also learned that lesson. I've got a purpose. I don't care where my ex is or what he's doing. He was a mistake.

"In a nutshell, I've got my belief and my hope."

Thomason listened. She had no words. Naughton didn't flinch in telling her story, condensed as it was.

"Land of opportunity, I guess," Thomason said after a few moments of silence.

"Damn straight, honey. And you've got yours. Make sure you grab it and don't let it go. Make the most of it."

They were still thirty minutes from the Western District Courthouse.

Chapter 42

BUT YOU WORK
FOR THE MOB

THE HEARING RESUMED, and Davis had his chance to cross-examine Wilson.

"Mr. Wilson, who else owns Systems Analysis besides you?"

"Another LLC."

"Who owns that?"

"Not sure, to be honest."

"Mr. Wilson, isn't it true that a gentleman named Robbie McFadden controls these other companies?"

"That might be correct."

"Don't you work for Robbie McFadden?"

"I don't have a manager per se. And I'd like to expand Systems Analysis, and that would mean there would be other employees who would work for me."

"My question was about Mr. McFadden."

"I consider him my boss if that's what you mean."

Judge Robertson looked up from his notepad and furrowed

his brow. He then looked over to 3J and made eye contact. His facial expression looked like he was sarcastically saying *Really?*

"Thank you," Davis said. "What is Mr. McFadden's avocation here in Kansas City?"

"He runs an organization. I don't know all the details."

Davis turned to the judge. "Your Honor, it's common knowledge that Mr. McFadden is the head of a mob organization based here in Kansas City. I would like the court to take judicial notice of this fact."

3J stood to object, but Judge Robertson put his hand out slowly, palm down, and nodded as if to say, "I've got this."

She sat back in her chair. "Mr. Davis, courts may take judicial notice of facts that are beyond dispute. Such as that the American flag is red, white, and blue. Or the address of this courthouse.

"I've seen an article or two every so often in the *Kansas City Star* about Kansas City's rich mobster history, and one or two of those *Star* articles may have mentioned the mobsters today that are still among us. One article may have even mentioned Mr. McFadden by name. But my feeling is that the mention of Mr. McFadden in an article hardly constitutes a fact that is beyond dispute. You don't know what he looks like. I don't know what he looks like. You don't know what business he conducts. I don't know what business he conducts."

Without knowing that McFadden was in the courtroom, the judge added, "He's not here to explain himself. I understand why you're asking for this relief, but it's not appropriate in this situation. I'm denying your request. It would continue to make for interesting reading, but it won't qualify as a fact beyond dispute or something of common knowledge. Do you have further cross of this witness?"

"I do, Your Honor," Davis asserted. "Mr. Wilson, in your role at SA, you said you create deepfake videos."

"Correct."

"Is that a crime—to make fake videos?"

"It may be in some states in some very limited situations."

"Are you telling us you're a felon?"

"I don't do porn. I don't do explicit. I don't do children. Am I a felon? I don't know. I'm not sure that what I do is a crime. And I don't look at myself that way. No one has ever charged me, and no one has ever convicted me of any crimes in my life. Videos or otherwise."

"It sounds like you're telling the court that you commit crimes for your boss, Robbie McFadden, but you're an upstanding citizen?"

3J leaped to her feet. "Objection, Your Honor." She was about to explain that Davis had misstated the witness's testimony when Judge Robertson gestured for her to sit.

"Counsel," Judge Robertson said, addressing Davis. "That's not what the witness said. If you have a federal or Missouri statute you want to share with me criminalizing deepfakes that aren't porn and aren't explicit, please do so. But more to the point of today's hearing, Rule 404 prohibits you from eliciting testimony of the witness's prior crimes to show his character and that on a particular occasion the person acted in accordance with the character. It is only admissible to show motive, opportunity, intent, preparation, plan, knowledge, identity, absence of mistake, or lack of accident," the judge said, reading from his evidence rule book. "Even if what Mr. Wilson does for a living is a crime, your questions fall within the 'bad character' part of the rule, and the rule prohibits the question.

"Also, there's no jury here. You know that. I get it, though.

I understand Mr. Wilson may be in, let's call it, an edgy line of work. I get that his boss is Robbie McFadden. I sustain Ms. Jones's objection. Please move on."

Davis nodded at the judge and returned to questioning Wilson. "For whom do you create these videos?"

"For whoever hires me to perform that task."

"Why do these people want you to make deepfakes for them?"

"You'd have to ask the clients. I don't know, and it's my practice not to ask them."

"Isn't it true your clients, as you call them, use them, for example, for blackmail or to discredit a competitor? Or to destroy a political career?"

"Or maybe for a funny birthday party joke. As I said. I don't know, and I don't ask."

"You're telling us you don't know the reason they ask you to create them?"

"Correct. I do not. I offer a service."

"Mr. Wilson, is it fair to say that we live in a world where our confidence in what's real is fading at an ever-increasing speed?"

"I suppose that's true."

"You add to the problem when you create deepfakes, don't you?"

"Like I said, I provide a service. What the client does with the video isn't my concern."

"Where did you work before Systems Analysis?"

"I was an independent contractor."

"Creating deepfakes?"

"Yes."

"Did you use the dark web to market yourself?"

"Yes."

"Do you still use the dark web to market Systems Analysis?"

"Periodically."

"Do you know Paul Elkin?"

"No."

"You've testified about a tag that was encrypted in the video file?"

"Correct."

"You said it likely meant that the video Mr. Elkin created was for a Mr. Fillmore and a Mr. McCoy?"

"Correct. That is my opinion."

"Could the tag legend mean anything else?"

"I doubt it. I don't see how it could."

"But anyone can get ahold of a video file and add a tag, can't they?"

"Yes and no."

"How could the answer be both yes and no?"

"Yes, they'd have to possess the MP4 file and the skill to access the file's codes and the skill to add a tag and the skill to encrypt the tag, and they'd have to have at their disposal the names Elkin, Fillmore, and McCoy. I'm sure you can see, numerous things would have to come together for someone else to add the tag. Bottom line? In my view, is it remotely possible someone besides Mr. Elkin could add the tag? Very remotely. Too remote to be credible."

Wilson paused, but before Davis could ask another question, Wilson continued.

"Also, as I understand it, the only people who had the video in their possession were Mr. Shumaker, who brought it to the bank meeting; Mr. McCoy, who interacted with Mr. Elkin and maybe Mr. Fillmore; and, of course, Mr. Elkin. I've heard nothing to suggest that Mr. Shumaker or Mr. McCoy or Mr. Fillmore had the technical skill to add the tag."

This was a long answer, and there was nothing that Davis could do to shut down the witness. Davis opened the door, and Wilson took the opportunity to stride right through it and tell the judge what he thought. All that Davis had was the follow-up question, "But you don't know for certain, Mr. Wilson, do you?"

"Nothing is for certain in today's world, Mr. Davis. But the facts fully support my belief that Mr. Elkin created the video for Mr. Fillmore and Mr. McCoy."

"But you haven't said it is a certainty, have you?"

"I've given you my best answer."

Davis flipped through his pad as if he had more questions, but it was all for show. He was finished. He had no technical questions to ask Wilson. Nothing about Wilson's proprietary software. He would rather not open the door for Wilson to tout how advanced his systems were. All he had was an attempt to question Wilson's veracity and plant the seeds that the things Wilson said were not a certainty.

He dropped his right hand that held the pad to his side and his shoulders slumped. He took a deep breath, turned to the judge and said, "Your Honor, no further questions at this time,"

As he returned to his seat at counsel's table, he fixed Paul Elkin with a cold, withering stare that could have frozen the air between them. No one else in the courtroom could see the stare, but it was so intense that Elkin was forced to raise his head and scan the ceiling. Anything to break the eye contact with Davis.

The judge gathered his papers as he announced, "Okay, let's take a short break, people." the judge announced.

As the judge and Cuello left the courtroom, Elkin was still looking at the ceiling. The ceiling, however, would provide him no respite. He knew he would be back on the stand shortly answering 3J's questions and trying to explain away his lie.

Chapter 43

THE ANSWER IS NO

OUT IN THE hallway, 3J whispered to Pascale, "What's your impression?"

"Still unclear. I saw the judge's reaction when Davis made the point that Wilson worked for the mob."

"Yes. Me too. There was an ugly look on his face." Pascale smiled.

"Bill, this isn't funny stuff," 3J chastised him.

"As my grandmother would say, 'What should I do? Cry?' You know how this goes. We make choices in any trial. At times, we choose the lesser of two evils. Now and again, we pick the only evil available. We didn't have the luxury of time. We had a single option to choose from. That was it. Choice made, Wilson hired. Now we play this out. That's all we can do."

"I know." 3J's hazel eyes were clouded with concern.

"It went about as we expected. Wilson was great, but he has warts. He makes deepfakes. His clients use them for bad reasons. A mobster signs his paychecks and owns part of his company. There's nothing we can do to clean that pig up. Still a sow's ear no matter how much we try to make it into a silk purse."

3J nodded. "Davis did what he needed to do. I guess we'll have to see how Judge Robertson sorts it all out." After a moment, she sighed and added, "We've done what we can do. We put on our big boy pants, sucked it in, and played the game. That's the job."

Pascale nodded as he pondered whether to share his thoughts with 3J. After a moment, he said, "If we had a case about a hack and we hired a professional hacker to testify and explain it, the judge would probably say, 'Who cares if this gentleman is a hacker? He knows what he's doing. He's an expert.' We're kind of in the same boat."

"Understood. It's a weird boat. It takes on water here and there. I just hope it's able to stay afloat until the ruling."

Naughton was making good time until she got past the I-35 Mission Road exit not too far south of downtown Kansas City, Missouri. Then there was a problem. She needed to get to the edge of downtown on I-35 and follow the signs to merge onto I-70 as the highway wrapped around to the east and skirted downtown. It was a straightforward journey. But there was road construction ahead, and there were no viable alternatives for an eighteen-wheeler to get downtown.

Naughton and Thomason needed to get to the courthouse. But Naughton couldn't put the pedal to the metal in the bumper-to-bumper traffic. All she could do now was ride the brake and curse.

"Dammit. Dammit! Why now?" Naughton begged no one.

"Roads have to be fixed."

"But not now. Not here," Naughton replied in a helpless tone.

"Look up ahead. It looks like traffic is moving."

And it was, at a snail's pace. It would take a few minutes for the break in the logjam to reach them.

They had precious few minutes left. Time was ticking, and the second hand seemed to move much faster than normal.

❦

Pascale returned to counsel's table, and 3J remained in the hallway to stretch. She saw Chet Drucker, on his mobile phone, turn to face the wall. She couldn't hear him because she wasn't close enough, but she could see he was animated. When the call ended, Drucker muttered under his breath. It sounded like he said, "Fuckin' Shumaker. My mess? Yeah, bullshit. He should get his ass up here and fix this."

❦

When the trial resumed, 3J recalled Paul Elkin to the stand.

Her cross was blistering, but Elkin held his ground. He denied creating the video for Fillmore or McCoy. He denied that jiggly curtain light, jagged edges on a face, unnatural blinking, and a quavering voice meant the video was a fake. He dug in his heels and held his ground. To every question 3J asked, his answer was a firm "No." He never looked comfortable, but he always said no.

He also offered no explanation for the anomalies.

"Did you make the video?" 3J asked.

"No," Elkin answered as he gazed off into the distance.

3J had no further questions for him, and he stepped down from the stand.

Frank Davis then approached the podium. "Your Honor, the banks have no further witnesses."

"Ms. Jones, are you ready to put on your case in addition to Mr. Wilson?" Judge Robertson inquired.

"Yes, Your Honor. To start our presentation of evidence, I offer the depositions of Wayne Shumaker and Martin Fillmore into evidence in lieu of live testimony. As you will see in the deposition transcripts, Shumaker is a bank officer at Franklin Trust, one of the banks in the bank group and the one with the largest share of the loan. Fillmore is an oil and gas producer and a customer of the bank. As the deposition reveals, he was also the brother-in-law of Greg McCoy, another officer at Franklin. Mr. McCoy is deceased, Your Honor, and did not provide testimony before he died.

"I deposed Mr. Shumaker in Wichita, where he lives, and Mr. Fillmore in Liberal, Kansas, where we found him and served him. Both are beyond the subpoena power for this trial since they are more than a hundred miles from the courthouse. I asked Mr. Davis to produce both for trial, and he could not."

"Mr. Davis, any objections?"

"None, Your Honor."

"The deposition transcripts are admitted as Debtors' Exhibits C and D."

Chapter 44

LINDA KNOLL

"What's next, Ms. Jones?" the judge asked.

"The debtors call Linda Knoll to the stand. Mr. Pascale will examine her."

"Very well. Ms. Knoll. Please come forward, raise your right hand for the oath, take the stand right there, and state your name for the record," Judge Robertson directed.

Pascale began by asking Knoll to establish her background, place of employment, position at Paxton Energy, and expertise. Pascale then had Knoll explain her role. She testified that, for each prospective project, the geologists and engineers provided her with the extent of the total reserves and of the reserves in each category—possible, probable, and proven undeveloped.

According to Knoll, Remmy Paxton, her boss, reviewed the work of the engineers and geologists, signed off on it, and then she began her work. Based on the reserves, she created the valuations. She explained her methods and said that when she finished her valuations, she delivered them to Remmy and then moved on to the next project.

"What did Mr. Paxton do with your work product?"

"He reviewed it, asked me questions he might have about my conclusions, and made whatever adjustments to the numbers he felt were appropriate."

"Was it unusual for Mr. Paxton to make adjustments?"

"I would say it was his prerogative. It's his family name on the letterhead, and he certainly knows oil and gas, maybe better than anyone in these parts."

"Did you ever check Mr. Paxton's adjustments to see if you agreed with them?"

"No. That wasn't my job, and I had no reason to question them. If I doubted him for a minute, I would have left the company before that minute was up."

"Ms. Knoll, let me hand you what's been marked as Debtors' Exhibit E. Please identify it."

"This is a spreadsheet I created to analyze my valuations against the adjustments Remmy made over the past five years."

"How did you pick five years to look at?"

"It was a good representative sample of our drilling projects. It also coincided with three renewals of the bank line of credit, and as a result, it would show exactly what information we shared with the banks to support loan renewal and draws on the line of credit."

"What does the spreadsheet show?"

"In short, there were few, if any, adjustments Remmy made to my numbers, and I can support the few he made."

"Can you explain that answer?"

"Sure, in oil and gas valuation, there are ranges. For example, how long it will take to extract depends on whether we run into drilling problems we didn't foresee. Another example is that oil prices fluctuate. There's a risk they may be lower in the future than we predicted."

She paused for a drink of water from the pitcher on the witness stand and continued.

"Do we try to be as precise in predicting the path to extraction and cash receipts? Of course. Are we perfect? Unfortunately, we are not. No one in this business is. Another example: since we will pull oil out of the ground over a long period, we will also sell it over a long period. Therefore, we will have a stream of income we receive over time. We are valuing the stream of income. In its simplest form, how much is a dollar worth when we receive it in one year? In five years? Et cetera. To calculate that, we have to apply what is called a discount rate. An interest rate to reflect the receipt of money later, considering the risk of whether we will receive that money. Banks do this all the time. They know full well that the proper interest rate is the subject of disagreement and debate.

"A higher rate means it is riskier, and the value in today's dollars will be less. A lower rate means the value will be higher. Minds greater than mine disagree all the time about the proper rate.

"My spreadsheet shows instances where Remmy adjusted the rate upward—meaning a lower value—and other instances where he adjusted the rate slightly downward—meaning a higher value. On balance, there was very little change to my numbers and the values that we then presented to the banks.

"Plain and simple. When the banks wrote in their court papers that Remmy Paxton inflated the values, they were dead wrong. And if any values had been inflated, it would have been my handiwork, and I did none of that."

As Pascale continued to elicit testimony from Linda Knoll, Abby Naughton navigated the eighteen-wheeler through the traffic logjam, around the I-35 bend to I-70, then exited the highway and pulled the truck up against the curb a block from the courthouse entrance on Oak Street. Ever since the Oklahoma City bombing, no one could park next to the courthouse, and likewise, the marshals prohibited drop-offs. As they parked next to the park that ran from the courthouse to City Hall, Naughton hustled to Thomason's side of the truck and helped her down.

They hugged, and Naughton whispered in Thomason's ear, "You got this, girl. You're Superwoman. No one has any kryptonite inside there, and no one can hurt you anymore. You won't let them."

Thomason knew she needed to get into the courthouse and that would mean running as fast as she could in her high heels. But before she turned to run, she listened to Naughton, began to cry, and hurriedly said. "Abby, I'm so glad we had the chance to meet. You're remarkable. Can we keep in touch?"

Naughton handed Thomason her card with her mobile number and said, "Text me yours when you finish up here."

Leah Belle Thomason, clutching her shoulder bag, turned and sprinted toward the courthouse to her appointment with freedom from Wayne Shumaker, her father, and all the Waynes in the world she hadn't yet met. She suddenly stopped and turned to Naughton, who was heading back to the driver's side of her cab.

"Abby, what should I do about my car?"

"Not to worry, honey. I'll get a service to change the tire and tow it to the Matfield Green rest stop. I'll text you. When you're done, all you'll need is a ride back to Matfield Green. Sorry, that won't be me. I'm heading east to St. Louis."

Thomason waved and ran up the steps to the atrium and the marshal's metal detector security checkpoint.

She dropped her shoulder bag in a container to run through the X-ray machine and breezed through the metal detector, then grabbed her bag and took the elevator up to Judge Robertson's courtroom. She took a seat alone in the middle pew of the courtroom. Robbie McFadden saw her enter and looked down to his lap to make sure no one would see him smile. 3J heard the courtroom door close and turned to the pews and saw Thomason. She nodded. Thomason nodded back. 3J mouthed the words "Thank you" and nodded again.

3J smiled. *Game on.* She was ready to ask the questions and wondered what Leah Belle Thomason would say on the stand.

Pascale was continuing his questioning of Linda Knoll.

"Ms. Knoll, did you inflate the values presented to the banks?"

"One hundred percent never, absolutely not. I would never do that."

"Did any bank ever call you to challenge your values?"

"Again, never. Every six months like clockwork, the banks sent in their auditors—my counterparts, if you will. They scoured our books. They asked me questions. They never challenged or disagreed with our assumptions about drilling costs, timing of production, when we would receive the payments, the predicted price of a barrel of oil, or the proper discount rate to use. I find it shocking to read in their papers that now they believe we—correction, I—have been scamming them for years. To the contrary, for years, the banks have had full access to my data, and for years, after detailed analysis, they agreed with my numbers."

"No further questions, Your Honor." Pascale returned to his seat.

❧

In the middle of a trial, sometimes things speed up. The heart races and respiration comes in quick bursts. When that happened to 3J, she always tried to remember something her father instructed: "Just keep doing the things you're supposed to do. Remember the box breathing technique I taught you. Take a slow, deep breath for a count of four. Hold it for a count of four. Exhale for a count of four. Don't breathe for a count of four. Repeat. Slow your mind. Slow your heart. If you do, it'll all come clear, and good things will happen." Her father had learned the technique as an Army Ranger.

3J did box breathing several times, just like Papa had taught her. She was counting down to whatever happened next. She was in whatever zone lawyers get in just before examining an important witness. She was ready.

McFadden looked on. He was as well.

❧

As Pascale finished with Linda Knoll and took his seat, Davis rose to cross-examine her. She had left the day-to-day communications with bank officers to Remmy Paxton, and Chet Drucker didn't know her. As a result, he hadn't provided Davis with information about her.

Davis was brief. He didn't question her qualifications or

her work. But he ended his examination by making a point for the judge to remember.

"Ms. Knoll, isn't it true that Remmy Paxton at any time could have changed the numbers and changed the data and presented the altered information to the banks?"

"I suppose that's true. Like I said, it's his name on the letterhead."

"And if he did, you might not know about the alterations?"

"I might not, but I would expect that the banks and their auditors would have had ample opportunity to discover any alterations, as you call them. The banks didn't, and I believe that was because there were none."

"But he could have?"

"I answered that already, Mr. Davis. If you have any alterations for me to look at, I'm happy to."

The judge looked down and smiled. Her answer caught Davis off guard with no bullets in his cross-examination gun.

"No further questions, Your Honor."

Chapter 45

LEAH BELLE AND THE LEDGER

"CALL YOUR NEXT witness, Ms. Jones," the judge directed.

"Your Honor. The debtors call Leah Belle Thomason to the stand."

Thomason strode to the stand, raised her hand, took the oath, and took her seat. All eyes were on her, but this time, in court, for a different reason than when she was in a bar.

"Ms. Thomason. We've met once before, correct?"

"Yes."

"Have you ever testified before?"

"No."

"Understood. To the best you can, just try to relax and answer the questions I will ask you. If you don't understand what I'm asking, please let us know."

"Okay."

"Tell us a little about your background."

"I was born at St. Luke's Hospital here in Kansas City and grew up with my mother, Jane, and my father, Victor, in

Brookside on 60th Terrace. At some point, my father left, and my mother raised me. I went to Lincoln College High School, and when I graduated, I went to Johnson County Community College for two years, studying accounting and bookkeeping."

"Why did your father leave?"

Leah looked down at her lap. "My mother told him to go. I've always guessed she kicked him out."

"Leah, why did your mother tell him to leave?"

"My mother discovered that my father was abusing me, starting when I was about twelve. It started out every once in a while. Then it was almost every night. At first, my mother didn't know it was going on, and I was too embarrassed to tell her. But she figured it out and then kicked him out. Since then, he has not been in my life. I heard he died."

"Thank you. I know that must have been very hard for you to say."

Leah nodded. Judge Robertson and Jennifer Cuello leaned forward to listen to her. This was not the kind of testimony usually elicited in a bankruptcy court. Most witnesses talked about matter relating to business disputes. This was different, and the judge and his law clerk's posture revealed just how much.

"After community college, what did you do?"

"I moved to Wichita and met a man in a bar there. Wayne Shumaker."

"Where did he work?"

"He was an executive vice president of Franklin Trust, a Wichita bank."

"What happened next between you and Mr. Shumaker?"

"I moved in with him, and we lived together for several years. He also hired me to be his administrative assistant at the bank."

"Do you still live with him?"

"No."

"Why not?"

"I moved out. For a while, the relationship was good, but he got handsy with me. Hitting me. Pushing me. Forcing himself on me, like my father. Then, I caught him in my bed—sorry, our bed—with another woman, and I told him we were done. I quit the bank job, moved out, and came back to Kansas City to live with my mother in the same house I grew up in. I needed time to sort all of it out."

"How many years did you work for Mr. Shumaker at the bank?"

"About four years."

"Did he have any lending specialties?"

"Yes. He was the head of the oil and gas lending group at the bank."

"What were your job duties?"

"Whatever Mr. Shumaker asked me to do. I kept track of his appointments, the details of loans he originated, and the bonuses the bank owed him because of the originations. He made numerous loans, and there was a lot to keep track of. I took messages. I typed letters. Made his appointments. If he went out of town, I worked on his travel accommodations. I would say the usual things an AA does for the boss."

"Was he ever abusive to you at work?"

"I would say no."

"I'm sure he was a very busy man. How did he keep track of everything?"

"Well, of course, he had me. I was good at organization. And he kept a ledger."

"What was in the ledger?"

"Pretty much everything. It was his personal business diary. He used to say it helped him keep everything straight in his mind. Names, loan amounts, due dates, and contacts. Loan prospects. Kind of like a Day-Timer."

"Where did he keep the ledger?"

"With me. He used to say that way he wouldn't lose it."

"Did you have access to the ledger?"

"Yes. I kept it for him. I had physical possession."

"At some point, did Mr. Shumaker start to play the lending game outside the lines?"

"Objection, Your Honor," Davis said in a raised voice as he stood. "The phrase 'outside the lines' is too colloquial to know what it means, and we haven't established this witness is an expert on what is inside and what is outside the lines at a bank."

"Ms. Jones, I will sustain the objection. Rephrase the question, please."

"Ms. Thomason, at some point, did Mr. Shumaker begin to take payments from borrowers to originate loans for them?"

"Objection," Davis said again.

"Overruled," the judge said. "She's just testifying as to facts. You'll have your chance to cross-examine her when the time comes. Please answer the question, Ms. Thomason."

"Yes."

"Did Mr. Shumaker ever tell you he was calling an oil and gas loan the borrower would use to buy property so he could make another loan to a different borrower to buy the same property?"

"Yes."

"That would be two loans for the same property?"

"Yes."

"And two origination bonuses for Mr. Shumaker on the same property?"

"Yes."

"How do you remember this?"

"Two reasons. It started to make me nervous when Wayne—sorry—Mr. Shumaker started to do these things. And second, it was all written down in detail in the ledger. I guess as things got more complicated, like these practices I called 'double-dipping,' he had to write it all down to keep track of it."

"Objection, Your Honor. She's testifying about what's in the alleged ledger, but we don't have the ledger here to know whether it's true or not. Her testimony is hearsay."

"Ms. Jones, I tend to agree with Mr. Davis. Without the ledger here in court—"

"Your Honor, excuse me," Thomason interrupted. The judge stopped mid-sentence, surprised, and nodded to Thomason to continue. "I have it here with me. Or at least a copy of it I made." She reached into her shoulder bag and pulled out a several-hundred-page document.

The photocopy of Shumaker's ledger.

"I see," Judge Robertson said with a tone of intrigue in his voice. "Ms. Jones. Let's lay a little foundation about the ledger and the copy, then we can circle back to the double-dip testimony, and I can rule on Mr. Davis's objection."

Davis sat down. It was more of a slump down than a straight-back sit. The judge was giving 3J the roadmap to allow testimony about the contents of the ledger. Never a good sign for the objecting party.

Davis looked worried. No more poker face. Chet Drucker, sitting next to him, looked worried too.

3J took Thomason through the questions necessary to authenticate the copy of the ledger. Where was it kept? In whose handwriting were the entries? What control did Thomason have over the ledger?

"Ms. Thomason, when did you make a copy of the ledger?"

"The day before, I had planned to leave Mr. Shumaker, both professionally and personally."

"Where did you copy it?"

"At one of the copier machines in the bank."

"Was Mr. Shumaker there when you made a copy?"

"I don't believe so. He was with a customer that day."

"Have you done anything to alter the information contained in the ledger or in the copy you made?"

"No. The copy I have here is an exact replica of the ledger."

"Has the copy been in your possession the entire time since you made it?"

"Yes."

"No one else has had it?"

"Correct. No one else."

3J turned to Judge Robertson. "Your Honor. We believe Ms. Thomason's testimony establishes the document as an authentic copy of the Shumaker ledger. As such, we offer it as Debtors' Exhibit F."

"Mr. Davis? Comments?" Judge Robertson's tone suggested he expected no objections.

Davis stood up reluctantly. "None, Your Honor, and no objection."

"The ledger is admitted into evidence as Debtors' Exhibit F. Ms. Jones, please continue."

3J asked Thomason to find the pages that showed the times Shumaker required a borrower to pay him a fee under the table in exchange for him pushing a loan through the committee. There were four such loans in the past year. Leah read each entry. They were all similar.

"In each of those instances, Ms. Thomason, Mr. Shumaker received a bonus from the bank and a payment under the table from the borrower?"

"Correct. A double-dip."

"Did the under-the-table payment go to Mr. Shumaker rather than the bank?"

"Correct."

"How do you know the payment Mr. Shumaker took in didn't go to the bank?"

"Each time he received a double-dip fee, he took me out for a nice dinner to celebrate. Champagne. The whole works. On this last loan, for example, at dinner, he raised his wine-glass and said, 'We can thank the borrower for this dinner, Leah Belle. He paid me, and dinner's on him.'"

Davis half rose, both hands on the table to push his reluctant body up and out of the chair. "Objection, hearsay."

"Overruled. It's a statement from a representative of one of the banks, the movants here. Your clients, Mr. Davis. That's not hearsay. And Mr. Shumaker could have been here to tell his story and refute Ms. Thomason's testimony and the words in his ledger but chose not to come. Perhaps we're all beginning to see why."

"Can you find the entries where Mr. Shumaker took an interest in the debtors' oil and gas holdings as a condition to pushing the loan for approval before the loan committee?" 3J continued.

Thomason complied and read the entries. Davis said nothing. He stared at his pad. Drucker knew what was happening.

It was unraveling for the banks in slow motion. As Thomason read the entries, Drucker leaned over and whispered to Davis in a voice loud enough for 3J to hear, "Frank, I had a feeling about Shumaker the first time I met him. He'd never make it in banking in Western Kansas. It was just a feeling then. Now I know why I felt that way."

Davis nodded. It was all he could think to do.

"Okay, Ms. Thomason. Do you recall the Paxton Energy loan?"

"Of course. It was the biggest loan at Franklin after we bought into the existing bank group's loan."

"Did Mr. Shumaker get a bonus for placing that loan for Franklin?"

"Yes." She read the entries in the ledger. "A large one because it was a $28 million loan."

"Then came the video, correct?"

"Yes."

"Can you find the video entries?"

"Yes."

"Are there any entries about creating the video?"

"Yes."

"Read those, please."

Paul Elkin had remained in the courtroom to observe the trial after his cross examination. He listened to Darius Wilson testify, but nothing in the trial interested him, and he spent most of the time looking at his phone. But now, he put it down to listen.

From Elkin's side of the courtroom, it was like watching a train approach in slow motion while he was tied to the rails.

Thomason read Shumaker's journal entries about his discussion with McCoy. The plan was for McCoy to get someone to make the deepfake video. The next entry said McCoy had hired someone named Elkin to make the video. Thomason read other entries that "Paul Elkin" had finished the video, and McCoy left it on Shumaker's desk. Then, she read another entry that said once Paxton was out of the picture, Shumaker and McCoy could move forward to get the bank to approve a loan for McCoy's brother-in-law, Martin Fillmore, to buy the same land Paxton hoped to purchase but that the banks had blocked.

Elkin closed his eyes and shook his head almost imperceptibly. Drucker, eyes wide open, just shook his head in disbelief. Davis turned his head slowly and shot a look at Elkin again reprising the icy glare he reserved for witnesses who had committed perjury.

⁊

A limousine pulled up near the courthouse. Two men assisted an elderly man out of the limo and up the courthouse steps. He was almost six feet tall and deeply wrinkled, but his dark brown eyes sparkled. He used a cane, which he held in his left hand, a workingman's hand that was gnarled from decades of manual labor. But while parts of his body had begun to fail, the eyes told the real story. As alive and vibrant as when he was twenty.

The man and his assistants cleared security. They asked for directions to the bankruptcy court where the trial was going on and made their way up the elevator to Judge Robertson's courtroom.

He stumbled as he entered the courtroom, and his two assistants caught him under his arms and steadied him. It

wasn't the first time they had prevented a fall. The small com-
motion caught everyone's attention, and 3J, Pascale, Davis,
Drucker, and McFadden turned around.

3J smiled. She had never met Bearfoot Stockton, but she
knew it was him the minute she saw him. She was relieved he
was okay.

He took his seat in the pews and waited his turn. He
would be the final act and curtain call on 3J's case. He knew
it. And he would just tell the truth. Everyone knew he always
just told the truth. There was never another option. Honor
was so important.

Remmy turned around and saw Stockton. No nod. They
locked eyes for a moment—a silent *Thank you* from Remmy
and a look from Stockton that said *Of course*.

"Are there any other entries about the creation of the video,
Ms. Thomason?"

"Just two more that I can see."

"What does the first one say?"

"'Remind McCoy to pay Elkin for the video.'"

"And the second one?"

"'Told McCoy to get Elkin to say the video is genuine.
Not a fake.'"

"Are you aware that Mr. Shumaker took the video to the
Paxton Energy bank group meeting and played it?"

"Yes. I knew he was planning to do that."

"When did you quit in relation to the bank group
meeting?"

"Days later. He wanted to go out and celebrate all the

money he would make off his dealings on the Paxton Energy loan, and I said no. He hit me pretty hard that night, and afterward, I didn't sleep with him in his house. The next morning, I came back for a change of clothes and found him in my bed with another woman. And Ms. Jones, I want to point out that Paxton was a triple-dip, not a double."

"How is that?"

"Wayne made a bonus on Franklin's $28 million share of the Paxton Energy loan. He was about to make a bonus on the Fillmore loan, also substantial. And he would get an override on the Fillmore oil and gas production. Mr. Shumaker told me the override would be substantial. Three payments. Three dips." She counted each dip off on her fingers as she testified, just as she had done in her mother's house.

3J had Thomason explain to the court what an override was in the oil business.

"Ms. Thomason, just one more question. Why are you here today testifying?"

"I've just reached that point in my life when I need to do the right thing. Plain and simple. No more being the victim. No more covering up someone else's bad acts."

"Thank you, Ms. Thomason. No more questions."

Davis rose to cross-examine Leah Belle Thomason. Try as he might, he got nowhere with her. Each time he tried to discredit her, there was the ledger and the entries in it screaming the truth. His efforts to discredit her looked like they backfired in the judge's eyes. Each time Davis tried to make the point that Thomason was nothing more than an angry, jilted lover on the stand for revenge, the judge's eyes narrowed. He didn't like the line of questions.

3J decided not to object to Davis's attempt to discredit

Thomason. She felt Thomason more than held her own, and it was clear the questions were getting nowhere with Judge Robertson. Davis looked dejected and gave up, telling the judge he had no more questions.

Chapter 46

THE FIFTH AND KIOWA HONOR

THE JUDGE TOOK one more brief break. When he returned, 3J informed him there would be just two more witnesses.

During the break, 3J and Pascale had noticed that Paul Elkin was still sitting in the courtroom. They weren't sure why he had stayed, but they decided it was an acceptable calculated risk to call him back to the stand to testify. When 3J announced that she was calling Elkin back to the stand he looked panicked. Davis had surmised the Paxton team might recall Elkin. He looked down at his pad and pretended to write something.

No one would help Elkin, and he reluctantly took the stand again. Judge Robertson admonished him he was still under oath with a tone that suggested the judge knew the oath was of no moment for Paul Elkin.

"Mr. Elkin, you've heard Ms. Thomason's testimony?"

"Yes."

"And you understand you're still under oath?"

"Yes."

"Do you wish to change any of your testimony?"

"Ms. Jones, I decline to testify under the Fifth Amendment on the grounds it may tend to incriminate me."

Davis covered his eyes with his hands and rubbed hard. It was all he could do.

⚜

"You may step down, Mr. Elkin." The judge had a hint of a scowl on his face. "Last witness, Ms. Jones?"

"Yes, Your Honor. We call Bearfoot Stockton to the stand."

Stockton rose unsteadily. His assistants helped him get to the bar gate separating the pews from the front of the courtroom. From there, one of the marshals helped him to the witness stand and into the chair.

3J had Stockton explain who he was, his military service, and the land he owned in Kiowa County. Then she asked, "Mr. Stockton, did you meet with Mr. Fillmore about your oil and gas land in Kiowa County that you had agreed to sell to Paxton Energy?"

"Yes. He came to my house once."

"What happened?"

"He made me an offer to buy the same land I was selling to Remmy Paxton's company. I told him no and that I was already under contract to Paxton. He got angry and offered more. He had all kinds of conditions and bells and whistles in his offer. And it was a big project, so I wasn't sure his little company could perform. But he seemed to know what Remmy was paying. I told him 'no' and that 'no meant no.' I told him to leave. He got angry and said something like it was one

Kiowa Indian taking care of another. Mr. Paxton and I are both of Kiowa descent."

"Were you offended?"

"In my line of work, it's nothing I hadn't heard before. But I've lived an honorable life, and I'm eighty now, and I wish I didn't have to listen to that kind of stuff at my age. It's just the way it is with some folks." He smiled, but it was not a smile of happiness; it was one of weariness. "As Fillmore started to leave, I muttered that I thought he was just another stupid White man. I think he heard me. I was fine with that."

The judge smiled at Stockton's observation. Jennifer tried to repress her smile.

"Did he say anything else?"

"He said he wasn't through with me yet."

"What happened next?"

"He filed some kind of document called a *lis pendens* against my land in the county records. A notice to warn the world he had an interest in my land, but he didn't. It was full of crazy talk. It said I agreed to sell it to him, that he had first dibs on it. Probably didn't say 'dibs,' but I can't remember the exact words he used."

"Is this a recorded copy of the document he filed?" 3J asked, handing him the *lis pendens* from the real estate records marked "Debtors' Exhibit G."

"Yes. That's it."

"We offer it into evidence, Your Honor."

"Any objections, Mr. Davis?"

"None, Your Honor."

"Mr. Stockton, the *lis pendens* states you agreed. Had you agreed?"

"I had not. I turned him down."

"Was there a written agreement you both signed?"

"No."

"Did you sign the *lis pendens*?"

"Never."

"Do you do oral or handshake deals?"

"I do not. I learned early on that, in the oil patch, it ain't a deal till the lawyers write the contract up and everyone signs. I never asked my lawyers to write up an agreement with Fillmore because I never had a deal with him."

3J paused and looked up to the court. "No further questions."

This time, rather than flounder with the witness, Davis said, "No questions, Judge." He didn't rise.

"Counsel for both parties. Any other witnesses or exhibits?"

3J and Pascale took a moment to huddle with Remmy Paxton and told him they didn't think he needed to or should testify. He agreed with no pushback.

Both attorneys said they had nothing further.

"Okay, folks. It's late, and I need to read the Shumaker and Fillmore depositions. Here's what I'd like to do. You'll each have ten days to submit final arguments in writing, pointing to any law you want me to consider and any evidence you want me to focus on. Your submissions will be simultaneous. There will be no rebuttals, so say whatever is on your mind in the submissions. I'll review those and rule as soon as I can. Questions?"

3J rose to speak. "And the examiner, Your Honor?"

The judge nodded. He understood what 3J wanted. But until he ruled, he had no choice; the examiner had to remain in place. "Ms. Jones, Mr. Williamson remains in place, charged with examining and investigating. I'll address what happens next in my ruling."

Not what Remmy, 3J, or Pascale wanted to hear, but Judge Robertson was tired and wasn't looking for a discussion. He had decided the examiner would remain in place for the moment. Period.

As 3J and Pascale packed up, Remmy thanked them and said he, Bree, and Linda would like to walk back to the office with them. 3J turned to the pews and saw Thomason who waved to 3J, mouthing *We'll talk*, and headed for the back of the courtroom and the exit. 3J expected Thomason to leave. Instead, she stopped to talk to a smiling McFadden. 3J sure wished she could be a fly on the wall for that conversation.

∽

Back at the office, it was time to debrief.

"What's your best guess of what the judge will do?" Remmy asked 3J and Pascale.

The lawyers looked at each other. It was Pascale's client, and it was his job to handle the answer.

"We just don't know with any certainty, Remmy. We put on all the evidence to get a favorable ruling. But it can go either way. We're hopeful the ledger will carry the day. It was a smoking gun no one expected. It was good smoke for us." Bree nodded. She understood it had gone as well as it could.

They stood in the twenty-ninth-floor reception area and then sat down on the couches behind the front desk. The couches faced west. The sun was almost done setting. It was one of the better views in Kansas City.

"No matter how this comes out, Bree and I are grateful for the effort. We're in good hands," Remmy said as he and Bree gathered up their things to leave.

Chapter 47

IMPRESSIONS

AFTER THE HEARING, Jennifer and Judge Robertson returned to his office. As he removed his black robe and hung it on the coat rack, he asked, "What are your impressions, Jennifer?"

"I wasn't sure what to expect. Ms. Jones and Mr. Pascale certainly put together a robust defense in a short time. Quite the range of witnesses. I found Ms. Thomason and Mr. Stockton to be very solid. I guess Mr. Davis must have felt the same way. He didn't have much of a cross-examination planned for them."

Judge Robertson nodded.

"But Judge, I'm still not sure what to make of Mr. Wilson. I mean, he works for a criminal organization."

"That he does. He was, however, a good witness. An excellent one."

"Yes, I'll concede he was knowledgeable and polished. But when he talked, I imagined hearing Al Capone testify as an expert witness about how to avoid paying income taxes."

Judge Robertson laughed. "I could see that as a quandary."

"What's your view, Judge?"

"I would like to see the closing arguments and read those two depositions, of course. But as to Wilson, I'm a little less bothered than you about his employer. You know, when the government prosecutes someone for racketeering charges, the government's star witness against the defendant is often another criminal the government granted immunity to. Maybe, for the sake of argument, this star witness is someone who murdered five people. He might take the stand and give stellar testimony for the government, implicating the defendant in murder plots over and over again. On cross-examination, defense counsel homes in on the witness's credibility by pointing out he is a felon, and a killer at that. A cold-blooded murderer who cut a deal for immunity, who would say anything to help the prosecutor. The defense argues that the jury should not trust the witness. The jury listens closely, and at the close of evidence, they leave the courtroom and deliberate. Five hours later, they hand down their verdict and convict the defendant on all counts. How? They accepted the star witness's testimony. Why? Sure, he's a killer. Sure, he testified because the government gave him a deal. But he also had firsthand knowledge. He was there at the time of the murders. He was there for the conspiracy. Like your Al Capone example, he is an expert. Who better than the star felonious witness could there be to testify?"

"Judge, you're saying that just because Wilson is doing bad things and works for a mob organization doing bad things, he's still knowledgeable?"

"Right, and I don't see any ax he has to grind. Unlike the murderer in my example, Wilson didn't testify in exchange for immunity or anything else. He didn't know any of the bankers. He didn't know Fillmore or Elkin. And he didn't know Remmy

Paxton. Seems like he was just there giving his honest opinion and backing it up. And I must say, his backup was impressive. A real lesson in deepfakes."

"That it was, Judge."

"Let's read over and summarize the two depositions while we wait for the closing arguments. Okay?"

"That's a plan, Judge."

Chapter 48

HE WON'T FIND ANYTHING

THE TEN DAYS went by quickly as 3J and Pascale researched, wrote, and rewrote their closing argument. They hammered home the contrasts between Shumaker and Fillmore's deposition testimony on the one hand and Thomason's testimony and the ledger on the other. At every opportunity, they drove home the point that Shumaker and Fillmore had lied, plain and simple.

They concluded by addressing the expert opinions and testimony and underscored that, when caught red-handed in a lie, Elkin took the Fifth.

They felt satisfied with the closing argument, and their paralegal filed the papers for them at 5 p.m. on the tenth day. Within moments, Davis filed his closing argument. They read over Davis's filing. He stressed that Wilson worked for the mob but seemed to be oblivious to Thomason's testimony and the ledger.

It seemed like a pleading that pounded the table, not the law or the facts. 3J and Pascale viewed Thomason and the ledger as unassailable. Davis must have also, as he elected to gloss over both.

Now the lawyers and the clients had to enter a holding pattern. 3J knew that Remmy Paxton would have to ride it out while the examiner dug deeper into the Paxton Energy records, but there was nothing anyone could do except hunker down.

3J had a notion to call Davis and ask for another meeting between the banks and the debtors. In light of the testimony, she wondered if it would now be a good use of the banks' time to meet. She called Paxton. He must have found great satisfaction in saying, "We'll have time for that. Let's just wait to see how the judge rules."

"And the examiner?" 3J asked.

"Yeah. He's here. He's examining. I hate it. But I'm learning to live through the long, cold watch. We've waited this long. Let him look. Keeps him busy and out of my hair. He won't find anything."

There was that phrase again: "He won't find anything."

Does it mean he won't find anything because there's nothing to find or because it's buried too deep to be found? 3J wondered.

Chapter 49

THE RIGHT CROSS

Several days later, 3J received a call from Thomason, who was sobbing.

"3J, Wayne Shumaker called me. He was furious. He screamed over and over that I would never take him down."

"Jesus, Leah. Are you okay?"

Thomason ignored the question. "Then, last night, he parked his car a few doors down from my mother's house. His black BMW sat right outside my mother's house. He must've driven all the way from Wichita just to sit outside the house here. I couldn't sleep, and I sat on the couch in the front room, peering through the blinds. 3J, he sat in his car almost all night. He left only as the sun rose."

3J said nothing. Attorneys sometimes get a feeling and use it to develop a case strategy. She had one of those feelings, except this time, it was a feeling anyone would have after hearing Thomason's story: it was like Shumaker was trying to figure out if he had the guts to do one more beating, or worse.

"Leah, I'm going to get an investigator to sit in a car outside your house for a few nights. Look at it as protection for you and a deterrent that Shumaker will notice. Is that okay?"

"Of course. Thank you." 3J described Ronnie Steele and his car to Thomason so she would recognize him when he parked out front to protect her.

3J called Steele, and he agreed to stake out the Thomason house. "And, Ronnie, if needed, you're there to take action, not just to watch and report."

"Action is my middle name, remember?"

3J was unaware that Thomason had also called McFadden, who sent one of his contractors to stake out the house as well. On the first night of the watch, at one in the morning, Shumaker pulled up. The car was a real looker. A late-model BMW. Sleek, fast, eye-catching. On the long drive from Wichita, he had decided what he would do.

When he pulled up, he took no time to exit the car. He looked like he hadn't shaved in days. He looked menacing. But he was too late to preserve the fraudulent empire he had built at the bank because Leah had already testified. He knew that. He was there to cross a line and take revenge.

But Thomason's deed had already been done. The judge would rule regardless of what Shumaker did to her. He knew that. There was nothing left to preserve.

As Shumaker's feet hit the ground, Ronnie Steele exited his car, and the McFadden muscle exited his. The three converged. Steele recognized McFadden's man, and without speaking, the two collaborated to grab Shumaker, spin him around to face them, and then they both punched him.

Shumaker yelled out, "Who the fuck are you guys?" They answered with their fists. One worked the midriff; one worked the face. Shumaker went down with a thud and groaned, gasping for air from the body blows but finding none. As he lay on the ground in the fetal position, Steele and McFadden's man kicked the banker in the ribs for good measure. With each kick, Shumaker grunted and tried to move his body out of harm's way and cover up. But he couldn't hide. There was no way to avoid the beating.

McFadden's man spoke first. "Boy, this is the one warning you'll get from me. Mr. McFadden was feeling generous tonight, and only tonight. Get up off your butt, get back in your car, head back to Wichita to your sorry-ass life, and never come back here or any other place Leah Belle Thomason is. I don't want you in the same zip code as her. You're out of her life or you'll suffer the extreme consequences. Next time, I'll make sure our meeting is your last on this planet."

The McFadden storm came without warning, and Steele didn't expect he would have an impromptu collaboration with a beat-down expert in McFadden's employ. He also couldn't have predicted he would so willingly take part in roughing up Shumaker. But 3J wanted action. Still, when McFadden's man finished, all Steele could say was, "What he said," as he leaned over Shumaker and flexed his fists.

Shumaker struggled up to his knees, then to his feet, and, at last, to his car, shaken by the beating he took. Every step looked painful.

Steele got back in his car as soon as Shumaker drove off. McFadden's man and Steele said nothing to each other.

What Steele didn't know was that sitting in the back seat of his collaborator's car was Robbie McFadden, who had a ringside seat and watched the events unfold.

When his man got back in the car, McFadden said, "Well done. Did Steele say anything to you?"

"No, boss. His eyes got wide when he saw me, and then they narrowed. Then we took care of that guy for you."

"Did he say anything to Shumaker?"

"He agreed with what I said. When the beating started, he got a nice right cross in as well. Heavy punch. That one took the banker down."

McFadden chuckled. "I knew he could. I knew he would."

Shumaker arrived back at his house at 5:30 in the morning. He was sore: ribs, jaw, the places they hit him, and his ego. School and work had trained him in numbers. Home life had trained him to hit women and dole out pain. He was a banker. Nothing trained him to absorb physical pain.

He took off his shirt and pants and sat on the edge of his bed in his underwear. His big, empty bed. Across from the bed was a double closet with two mirrors on runners serving as the closet doors. He looked at the two mirrors and saw two reflections, both of himself. Both bruised and battered. Even though there were two reflections, he was alone.

It was his own doing. Alone at work and alone at home.

Traveling the road was rough. Traveling it alone was nearly impossible.

He had spent years making money his false idol. He obsessed over it. He had spent his life chasing a pot of gold at the end of a rainbow. He didn't see a rainbow anymore, but he had made progress. He realized he was no longer broke, but broken.

The thing is, when you're broke, you try to find ways to make money. But when you're broken, you have to find ways to survive. Every day. One day at a time. One foot in front of the other. Stumbling onward. Numb. Until you feel you're just walking on fumes. Until you can't anymore and just give up.

He closed his eyes and fell back onto the bed. In the end, you don't get to outlast or outlive. You take nothing with you. You leave it all behind.

It had been a long time in the making. He was getting ready to take the next step. He didn't need to look around his room. He wasn't planning on taking anything with him.

Chapter 50

A LEMON DROP

It had been more than two weeks since Pascale and 3J had filed their closing argument. She was confident the judge was hard at work writing his ruling. But it was difficult to wait for the judge's decision. It always was, no matter how many trials she had.

During the wait, Leah Belle Thomason called 3J, her first call since the one about Shumaker stalking her. Thomason sounded upbeat, but 3J wasn't sure why. 3J agreed to meet for cocktails and suggested Cafe 333, a brand-new jazz club.

A few days later, 3J arrived at the restaurant and got a table. Thomason got there a few minutes later. She wore jeans and a tattered blue Levi's work shirt with white pearl snap buttons and modest accessories—small post earrings, a simple bracelet, and a silver ring on her right pointer finger. Thomason looked good in it. As she made her way to the table, 3J noted she wasn't sashaying her way there. No more Ann-Margret stroll. It was the new Leah Belle Thomason walk.

They ordered drinks: red wine for 3J and a Lemon Drop

for Thomason, who lifted her glass and thanked 3J for every-thing she did.

"Of course. It's kind of my job," 3J replied.

Thomason talked about getting to the courthouse the morning of the trial. She apologized for fleeing to Wichita. "I shouldn't have done that. The list of things I shouldn't have done is long."

3J still wasn't sure why Thomason had asked for the meeting and decided to be bold. "After you testified, I saw you stop to speak with Robbie McFadden at the back of the courtroom. What is your relationship with him?"

Thomason smiled and closed her eyes for a moment. Then she looked at 3J and explained, "He's kind of my godfather, or at least he acts that way. I ran the numbers for him. When I did, all was good. No beatings. No bullies. No one would disrespect me because Robbie was looking over my shoulder. Protecting me, I suppose you could say. Then I left for Wichita to make it on my own. Didn't work out so hot. I met Wayne, but there was no Robbie there to keep Wayne in line or guide me away from Wayne in the first place."

She took a sip of the Lemon Drop. "Robbie's the one who convinced me to come back and testify. I'm not sure I told him about the copy I had of the ledger. I think he kind of liked that part of the trial."

3J smiled. She did too.

"But I'm back here in KC, I hope for good, and I've told Robbie I won't come back and work for him. No running numbers. No helping him with whatever books he keeps. Nothing. I need to start my life because I don't feel like I ever did. My first and second launches were unsuccessful. Now I've asked him not to watch over me. 'Please let me do this myself,'

I said to him. He said he wouldn't watch over me, but honestly, I don't believe him. He and his wife have boys. No girls. I'm like his adopted daughter, I guess."

3J found the story interesting, but she was still in the dark about why it was important for Thomason to share this with her.

"I just wanted you to know more of the background. The Robbie part. I also wanted you to know that Robbie's not a bad person. He's in a bad line of work. Some of his colleagues do bad things in that line of work. And I know he does bad things as well. But he's not bad. I know that sounds impossible, given what his organization does in this city. But he was there to help me. And as I understand the story, he was there to help you. Maybe you'll be his next project and he'll protect you. Who knows?"

This surprised 3J. She stumbled as she tried to come up with an appropriate response. All she could muster was, "Leah, I appreciate you reaching out to me. I don't need someone to adopt me. And I don't want someone to protect me. I pass no judgment on Robbie McFadden, but he is what he is. And I'm not what he is, and I'm not in that world. I would rather not be."

"I understand. Well, that's all I had to say. Stay in touch, will you?"

Thomason stood, bent down to hug 3J, then turned and left. No sway in her walk. No looking over her shoulder. Moving forward and hoping for a better life.

Chapter 51

THE RULING

TWENTY DAYS AFTER the submission of the final arguments, Judge Robertson was ready to rule. Jennifer Cuello had drafted a ruling for the judge to edit, covering all the issues he asked for. Where appropriate, she inserted citations from cases and law review articles.

It only took an eight-page order for the judge to destroy the banks' case and deny the request for a trustee.

The judge ruled the video was fake, accepted all of Leah Belle Thomason's testimony as believable, and ruled the ledger was genuine and the video was the work product of Paul Elkin. He recounted the many things Shumaker had done at the expense of borrowers and his employer, Franklin Trust, and said, in a word, they were despicable. Jennifer had added a footnote that it would have been satisfying to see Shumaker live in the courtroom, testifying. But the revelation of the ledger helped explain why Shumaker stayed away. The judge deleted the footnote. While true, he didn't see the relevance in offering that insight into how he felt. The word "despicable" covered it.

He devoted a paragraph to Darius Wilson. He explained

that he found making deepfakes for a living to be unsavory, and now even more so since he joined the mob. But Wilson was still an expert with no motive other than to opine on the video, and his expertise was all Judge Robertson was interested in for the trial.

He also accepted Linda Knoll's testimony and rejected Frank Davis's argument that the judge should ignore her testimony because she worked for Paxton. Instead, the judge ruled her testimony was credible and wrote:

> There is no evidence that Remmy Paxton improperly adjusted the company's numbers presented to the banks. The numbers presented to the banks came to almost the same value conclusion each year as Ms. Knoll's yearly analysis. Sometimes the Paxton conclusion was somewhat higher, and sometimes it was somewhat lower. But never did the two differ in any meaningful way. Therefore, the banks never lent to Paxton Energy based on a false analysis of value by either Ms. Knoll or Mr. Paxton.

Based on the ruling, he asked the United States Trustee to reconsider its request to appoint an examiner and to withdraw the motion promptly. It took the trustee's office several days, but it withdrew the motion to appoint an examiner, and within hours, the judge dismissed Asher Williamson, thanking him for his service.

Williamson did not linger at the Paxton Energy offices when he read the order dismissing him from his examiner duties. He packed and, for the first time during his appointment, straightened his tie. But he would never win a tie-knotting contest.

On the way out, he wanted to see Remmy Paxton one last time. Paxton saw him coming down the hallway, closed his door, and feigned a call on his desk phone, the same one he was reluctant to use during the examiner's reign.

Days later, the examiner filed his final report. It was a short one. He explained what he had reviewed and whom he had interviewed. He found nothing out of the ordinary. Later that day, he delivered his bill to Remmy Paxton for payment for "services rendered." The invoice stated it was due upon receipt and requested that Paxton inform Williamson when the check was ready, and Williamson would come by to pick it up.

The invoice was large—$30,000. *Services rendered?* Remmy wondered. *To whom?* he questioned. "Not to Paxton Energy," he muttered. He had his assistant draft a check, reluctantly signed it, and had it mailed to Williamson.

He then asked his assistant to let the examiner know the check was in the mail. He never wanted to see Asher Williamson in the corporate offices again.

⋈

3J was in Pascale's office after they both had read the ruling. Neither had gotten much done in the weeks since they had filed their closing argument. The trial was exhausting. Pascale had once observed, "Life is a marathon, not a sprint. Cases, however, are a sprint to the finish line." The Paxton sprint had been draining, but at least the victory would be restorative. Still, the clients troubled 3J, and the feeling lingered.

"Do you believe Knoll and Paxton were telling us the truth, Bill?"

"We have no evidence they lied to us. My old boss once

told me, 'The absence of evidence is not evidence of its absence.' The truth is, we will never know. And as I've gotten on in years, I've come to assume debtors won't tell us everything. The questions are, have they told us everything we need to know to give them good representation, and is what they told us the truth? I believe Paxton told us what we needed to know. I can only hope it was truthful. I'm confident we gave them the best we had."

3J nodded. Pascale hadn't answered the question. But then again, maybe he had. It was like Buck O'Neill had said once at the end of his speech: "Listen to old people—they might teach you something."

Chapter 52

MISSING FROM THE BOX

When Davis read the ruling, he wasn't surprised. He knew he had lost as soon as Darius Wilson opened his mouth on the witness stand. The other witnesses and evidence were just icing on the cake for 3J and Pascale. And then there was the ledger. The dagger he never saw coming. He wondered if 3J and Pascale knew about it, or if Leah Belle Thomason surprised them as much as she surprised him when she pulled it out of her bag. Davis tipped his imaginary hat to the Greene Madison duo. They put on a great case.

But like a colleague once told him, invoking Nelson Mandela, he never really lost. He either won or he learned. In this case, Davis learned. As he read the opinion, he went over the engagement in his mind. Not his favorite client nor his favorite case.

He felt strongly that the case should have settled. The bank group, however, wouldn't even permit settlement discussions. Franklin dominated the group with its large share of the loan, and Davis assumed it was Shumaker who blocked the discussions. A settlement would have interfered with his nefarious plans and the triple-dip, as Leah Belle Thomason called it.

But now that he had lost, there were things about the case that bothered him. He had been handcuffed by his clients in other ways. They would rather not pay "big-city fees," as Chet Drucker had explained.

To control the costs, the banks didn't let Davis act like he normally would in a case. No meeting with 3J. No attending out-of-area depositions. No deposition preparation for Shumaker. Davis chuckled, knowing Shumaker would have benefited from a little practice before testifying and perjuring himself.

At his request, the banks had delivered a box of documents with many of the audits they had conducted of Paxton Energy over the years. But as Drucker defined the scope of Davis's engagement, he was to focus only on the video and Paul Elkin, not the documents.

As a result, at trial, Davis had only a single exhibit: the video. Not ideal.

Davis met with Elkin and watched the video. He was unimpressed with Elkin, and the video was short and to the point.

In a brief meeting Davis had with Shumaker just before the deposition, Davis recalled hearing the names Fillmore and McCoy, but he didn't know enough to piece their part of the story together.

It was an easy trial to prepare for, especially given the banks' handcuffs. There was very little for him to do: put Elkin on the stand and introduce the video. The trial became more difficult when Wilson, Thomason, and Stockton appeared and testified, and Shumaker's ledger left the banks' case in ruins.

He sighed. The trial was over. Judge Robertson had ruled.

But Shumaker had the banks' box of records. Just as Drucker had ordered him, he had never gone over the records because the banks told him they wouldn't pay for it. It would only duplicate what the banks had already done.

He wasn't supposed to charge the banks to look at the records, but now that he had lost, if he rummaged through the box, it wouldn't be in furtherance of the trial. It would be on his own account. He was curious. He had a degree in finance before he went back to law school. He could peruse the records on his own time and see what he could see.

He decided to look.

Sure, he reasoned, *the video turned out to be a fake.* He never felt good about Paul Elkin. 3J had solid witnesses; the banks sent in auditors. He imagined them laughing it up and drinking coffee around the coffee machine with Remmy and his staff, exchanging pleasantries.

But now that he was looking at the records on his own time, something just didn't feel right. He understood there weren't significant changes made by Remmy Paxton to Knoll's numbers, but as he flipped through the lengthy documents, he had two questions: Where was the banks' analysis of the oil and gas *reserves*? And where were the banks' geology audits? Paxton Energy had done its own geology and engineering work. How did the banks verify that work? Or did they even bother to?

He wasn't sure what to do with his suspicions. He couldn't call Drucker to ask questions. He'd just tell Davis the case was over and ask him to send back the box.

After the ruling, Drucker had called and told him that, if Franklin would just be reasonable, the banks were content to go back to lending Paxton the money he wanted. They had always made money on Paxton's drilling operations, and he expected they would again. Perhaps, it was a case of all's well that ends well, even though a sophisticated oil and gas company can always try to massage the extent of its reserves. Did Paxton massage them? Did Knoll? Did anyone, or were they spot-on estimates with no adjustments? He didn't know, but he was pretty sure the banks didn't know either.

He returned the records to the box, carried it to his assistant's desk, and asked her to overnight the box back to Chet Drucker. Davis wasn't a geologist. He was just a bankruptcy lawyer with a curious streak and a suspicious mind.

He went back to his desk and chalked it up to a loss. He had lost before. Just not quite this way.

Clients paid him to do their bidding, even if ill-conceived, and he had tried bankruptcy cases for years, whether the outcome was boom or bust. It's what he did.

Alfred, Lord Tennyson, wrote, "'Tis better to have loved and lost than never to have loved at all." No such corollary in the practice of law. No one ever said, "'Tis better to have tried a case and lost than never to have tried a case at all."

This was one in his loss column that never should have been tried. It should have settled. Period.

Chapter 53

THE HYPOTHETICAL

REMMY AND BREE sat around the kitchen table in his childhood home in Ulysses. Their second home away from home. They had both read Judge Robertson's ruling.

"All in all, that went pretty well," Bree said.

"Could have taken a few bad turns for sure," Remmy replied. "I never expected we'd be helped out by such a shady banker as Shumaker. You can plan and plan, and then something happens you never planned for."

"For sure."

Bree smiled at Remmy, her jewel-like blue eyes even bluer and brighter than usual. "In the end, no one ever figured out what you have been doing for years. Linda was quite good on the stand. She looked right at the judge and used her testimony to make everyone believe her. And they did. They never figured out the massaging you did to get the loans."

"Not too bad for a Western Kansas hick, eh?"

$\backsim$

Remmy Paxton had arranged to drive to Kansas City to take Pascale and 3J to lunch at Pierpont's in Union Station to thank them. Pascale had a prior appointment, and that meant it was just Paxton and 3J.

3J took the light rail to the station. As she rode, she pondered how deeply she had come to rely on McFadden. She shuddered, knowing she'd entered the mob world.

At one time, Union Station was called The Gateway to the West, bustling with passengers making travel connections. It replaced the Union Depot in The Bottoms upon completion. Its design was one of monumental scale, symmetry, and classical detailing, opening in 1914 and boasting 850,000 square feet.

3J got off at the Union Station stop and walked past the Old Post Office Building, where bullet holes on its east façade remained, marking the infamous 1933 Union Station Massacre. In the massacre, mobsters ambushed the FBI but failed in their attempt to free Frank "Jelly" Nash from FBI custody as the agents escorted him back to Leavenworth prison. Some suggested the ambushers were "Pretty Boy" Floyd and others. But different accounts sprang up. Some had boss man Tom Pendergast or bank robbers opening fire. Nash and FBI agents died in the crossfire, and they never reached Leavenworth.

She knew the story well. Jazz and mobsters in the Kansas City version of the 1930s... and now they were still a fact of life today. *Some things never change.*

She found Pierpont's, walked over to Paxton, and sat across from him.

He thanked her again for the good job she and Pascale did. As they finished lunch, he said, "You know, even if we did some cooking to get the loans, it was no harm, no foul. The banks have never lost a dime."

3J was taken aback. "Jesus, Remmy. We told the court you and Linda were saints. Perfect citizens. She took the stand and testified. She was rock solid. Are you telling me it was a lie?"

"No. No. She testified about her final numbers compared to my minor adjustments. Nothing else. Everything she said was true. Everything I've said to you is true."

"Then, I'm confused. What are you saying here?"

"Not to worry, Counselor. You won. We'll hope the banks allow the draw to buy Bearfoot's land. We've told the banks how many hydrocarbons are in the ground on that land. They accepted the geology. End of story."

3J was still confused. "Are you saying you massaged the geological conclusions?"

Paxton smiled. "I'm saying no one has ever challenged that. I'm saying that, to save money, the banks used our estimates. Relied on our expertise, accepted our geology. Period. All I'm saying is, if we were massaging anything, oil and gas underground would be the way to go. Much harder to contest. Much pricier for the banks to examine. And anyway, you're my attorney. It's privileged, right? But I'm just speaking hypothetically. It's a big 'if we did,' not 'we did.'"

3J could feel her face get warm. Had Paxton scammed her?

"Did you?" 3J asked firmly, breaking the attorney's rule of never asking the client if they committed the crime.

"All hypothetical, Counselor."

⚜

The lunch ended with little left to say. There was a cloud of tension. They shook hands, but 3J's heart was not in it.

On the light rail back downtown, she stood and took stock of the Paxton case and Remmy Paxton. It was a case of roadkill scattered like dead armadillos lying face up on the shoulder. She tallied up the casualties as the railcar passed Southwest Boulevard heading north to downtown. A dead banker, a fraudster banker, a fraudster deepfaker, an old Kiowa about to get in bed with an oil and gas company run by a possible fraudster, a mobster and his staff, deepfakers who seemed to be everywhere, an attorney who may now owe the mobster favors, a boyfriend (at least most of the time) whom she needed to find a gentle way to agree to disagree with and find lasting peace, an aging mentor working on his next act, and a woman who may have finally found a way to rise out of all this rubble and claw her way back to normalcy.

3J got back to her desk but was unproductive. Remmy Paxton and oil and gas reserves dominated her thoughts. She tried to move on, but the more she did, the angrier she became.

Pascale was back from his meeting as well. 3J popped her head into his office and asked if he wanted to meet up at O'Brien's, and he did.

She took a deep breath and practiced her box breathing. *Just another day at the ranch*, she noted.

The next morning, the *Star* reported that the vice squad had arrested Robbie McFadden on suspicion of trying to bribe a local politician. At the arraignment hearing, the judge had the deputies release McFadden on his own recognizance. On the courthouse steps, he stopped to give the media some sound bites as he denied the charges.

"It wasn't a bribe. It was a campaign contribution. All legal."

McFadden slid into his waiting car. On the drive away from the courthouse, he said to his driver and bodyguards, "People would do well to remember the legacy of old Tom Pendergast. He was good for the city. He was good for most of the citizens here. I am too."

3J read the article with interest. She needed to be more careful when she met with McFadden. Law enforcement was watching all the time.

Chapter 54

THAT FIRST STEP

There's a new bank building in downtown Wichita—glass and metal, sleek and modern. An architectural designer's spire at the top. Wichita's nod to the next century. When construction was over, a skyscraper crane made its way downtown to lower a sign onto the top that read, "Franklin Trust." Ever since, people had called the building the Franklin Building. They dropped the name "Trust." The new tallest building in downtown. Onward and upward.

When the banker told people where he worked, he said, "Franklin." He also dropped the "Trust."

Late at night, long after hours, the banker, dressed in his usual suit and tie, parked his BMW in his reserved spot in the underground garage and took the elevator to the building's elegant lobby.

"Hi Jerry," he called out, waving to the night guard in the lobby. The night guard waved back.

The banker headed to the cluster of elevators near the far corner of the lobby. He walked slowly on the polished granite floor. From a distance, he looked thoughtful. Up close, he would have looked full of purpose.

He had a glass-enclosed corner office in the suite of executive offices on the twentieth floor. A brass plate announced his name and position—head of oil and gas. But he didn't press the twentieth-floor button when he entered the elevator.

He wasn't heading to his office. His destination was the top floor. Floor 25. It housed one of the bank's many arrays of computer servers. He exited the elevator, but he had no intention of entering the server rooms. Instead, he headed to the north side of the floor and a locked door with a sign that said, "Roof. Do Not Enter."

He was a senior executive. He had a key to the roof door. He unlocked the door and walked up fifteen concrete steps to a locked steel door with a sign that said, "Roof Access." He used his same key to unlock it, swung the heavy door open, and stepped over a steel threshold to the building's roof. The sky was dark and the clouds masked the stars and the moon.

He continued his trek under the "Franklin" sign, which was illuminated in LED lights and held in place by substantial steel girders. Architects had designed the sign and the building to flex in high winds and withstand most tornadoes. It was Wichita, after all.

He cleared the sign and made his way to the west side of the roof.

The wind had kicked up that evening. The roof was even windier than the street-level sidewalks below. Swirling gusts blew between tall downtown buildings, gaining speed, And then whistled through the Franklin sign girders. A line of thunderstorms had passed through downtown earlier and left winds in its wake. He had been to the roof before. Sometimes to contemplate. Sometimes to catch a smoke since there was no smoking anywhere inside the building. Sometimes just to take in the view.

This night, he wasn't contemplating or smoking or looking. He stood for a few minutes, shaking his head. His mind ran through the list he had created before. His personal reckoning list: No kids. Check. No spouse. Check. No remaining family. Check. No Leah Belle. Check. A dead colleague. Check. Perhaps no job in the coming days. Hmm. Likely, check. Not enough money. Check. Nowhere to turn. Check. The ledger in evidence for all to read. Check. A federal judge who documented his dips and called him despicable. Check.

He had been through parts of the list before, but one more run-through couldn't hurt just to make sure he hadn't missed anything.

There was nothing he missed.

He was calm and steady. He was ready. Too ready.

Some experts say that a person who jumps to their death from a high-rise building loses consciousness before their journey ends at the street level. That may not be true. At least not with a Franklin-sized building. The time it would take to fall from the top floor of the Franklin Building, roughly three hundred feet, would be three or four seconds, traveling in a free fall at about 9.8 meters per second. Not long enough for oxygen deprivation or g-forces to cause him to black out.

He had figured all of that out beforehand.

He wanted to remain conscious for the entire ride down. Caught between awake and oblivion and…aware for the last few seconds of his life. He wasn't sure why, but he just knew he did. He was well beyond the ability to hit the personal reset button. Instead, on his way down, he hoped he would have one last chance to take stock, albeit a brief chance.

He had planned everything. He figured he would fall straight down. That might have been his one planning error. Because it was windy. You can't always plan for mother nature.

He looked at his watch. He knew it worked, but the hands seemed frozen. He didn't need a watch. He didn't need to know the time. All he needed to know was that it was time. He seized the moment before he changed his mind, moving forward with an air of inevitability to the edge of the building.

He stood there paused, his center of gravity evenly balanced in all directions. He raised his arms to shoulder height out to his sides as if they were wings Then he stepped confidently and decisively into the evening air, left foot first, disturbing his center of gravity and tipping forward into the darkness.

His last journey still began with the first step.

As he stepped off the building's roof, the wind came up. Between the sixteenth and fifteenth floors, a blast of wind drove him off course and he bounced off the building's façade, his head smashing into a window, knocking him unconscious. The window withstood the crash, but the impact made a violent thud when his head struck the glass. It was late enough that no one was there to hear the sound.

Did he survive the encounter with the window? No one would ever know.

His last wish—to be awake the whole way down—likely unfulfilled.

Alive or not, he had set his plan in motion and, as he had hoped, seconds after he started his descent, he slammed into the front windshield of a parked car on the street, shattering it. Just like he planned. The car alarm sounded its ear-splitting siren, and the shrill noise bounced off the walls of the downtown buildings and echoed. Just like he planned. At that hour, downtown was empty except for the homeless. The siren didn't seem to bother them. Maybe nothing did. They'd heard worse.

The police arrived shortly after impact and mopped up the mess as usual. They set up a perimeter with their yellow tape while they surveyed the scene and collected evidence. Blood everywhere. Shards of safety glass scattered all over the scene. Impossibly twisted limbs partially inside the front seat of the car. Nasty. One of the cops at the scene called it "another evening cleanup on aisle four."

In the morning, the newspapers reported a senior banker had jumped to his death last night. Some reported, inaccurately, that he worked for Franklin Bank, leaving off the "Trust" part of its name.

To his horror, Judge Robertson read about it in the *Kansas City Star*. He pulled out his ruling to reread the parts about Wayne Shumaker. He called Jennifer into his office and showed her the article. They said nothing to each other. He put his hands deep in his pocket and walked over to his favorite window and gazed out. He hadn't been harsh in describing Shumaker. Just honest and truthful. Every so often, the truth can be mercilessly candid. Had Shumaker read the ruling? There was no way to know. He saw what he always saw at the window. Two rivers moving on. That was their message for him.

Robbie McFadden saw it on the news. "Good riddance," he said to no one in particular. It wasn't as ideal for the mobster as imprisonment in Leavenworth would have been, but Shumaker was gone, and for McFadden, that would do.

3J heard about it from Pascale. She couldn't believe the news. She wasn't distraught, just surprised.

Leah Belle Thomason's mother, Jane, told her about it.

Leah just shook her head. No more black BMWs to watch for over her shoulder. Another chance for a new beginning. She only felt relief.

Franklin Trust's senior management had read Judge Robertson's ruling and had set the gears in motion to fire Shumaker. They met the afternoon after Shumaker jumped to announce that they had appointed a new head of the oil and gas lending division. Maybe the new head would call the bank Franklin Trust and restore dignity to the oil and gas group.

Remmy and Bree Paxton learned of the tragedy when they read the *Wichita Eagle Beacon* the morning of the jump. They figured Shumaker was a troubled man on many fronts. He was. The death didn't surprise them.

It didn't surprise Martin Fillmore either. He had heard about the trial from Paul Elkin. Before Shumaker jumped, Fillmore decided he wouldn't be buying the Stockton land in Kiowa Goddamned County, as he called it, and moved on. No payments to bankers. No override for Shumaker. No bonus on a Fillmore loan. No drilling for Fillmore. No oil and gas reserves for Fillmore in Kiowa Goddamned County or deal with Bearfoot. Damn Kiowas.

Chet Drucker had intended to call his counterpart, the president of Franklin Trust, and complain about Wayne Shumaker. After he read the story in the *Hays Daily News*, he changed his mind. He wanted a new vote to approve the Paxton Energy loan requests. After the judge's ruling, the owners of Central Bank were all in favor of approving them. He hoped the new Franklin loan officer assigned to the Paxton Energy loan would be easier to deal with. Now he needed to round up the other banks to vote again.

ᕙ

The death of someone you know affects everyone in different ways. In Wayne Shumaker's case, there wasn't anyone to be found to mourn the loss. No one to say it was a tragedy; no one who believed that Wayne Shumaker was gone too soon.

Maybe he got it right. It was time.

Chapter 55

EACH OTHER

It was midafternoon on Friday. 3J left work early, decided not to go to O'Brien's with Pascale, and drove around the city instead. She needed to think. The more she drove, the less she focused on anything productive.

She intended to use the drive to address Remmy Paxton's lie. To the banks. To the court. To the examiner. To her. But she didn't. Maybe that was for the best.

She drove past the Power & Light Building and the old TWA headquarters onto Southwest Boulevard and past the Roasterie Coffee airplane, a Douglas DC-3 nicknamed Betty at 1204 West 27th Street, then back along Wyandotte and past the Webster House, home of a long-ago shuttered girls' school, and last, the Kauffman Center for the Performing Arts.

She stopped in front of the Center building, a unique architecture that had been described as "a cascade of stainless-steel ribbons unfurling toward the sky." She figured if anything in the city was designed to inspire constructive ideas, it was the Center. But she had nothing, and the Center didn't inspire her. She pulled away and made her way back to her garage.

She didn't want to think big thoughts. She just reviewed the state of affairs. The case was over. She and Pascale had won. She should have felt good, but she didn't. So much so that she avoided Pascale and their traditional meetup at O'Brien's. No exclamation point to end the week or the month. Such a meeting might lead to a discussion she just wasn't ready to have with anyone. Not with Pascale and not afterward with Ronnie Steele.

She hoped that being alone in her car with no one to talk to and nothing she cared to share with the two men she was the closest to would bring her solace. But she found none.

She parked her car and headed home.

We live in a disposable world. Throw-away possessions, relationships, even love. It's just the way things are. It goes hand in hand with the modern problem of trying to figure out what is real and what is fake, like 3J's deepfake video case.

You tell yourself it will get easier, but it never does. She rode the elevator up to her floor. Ronnie Steele was waiting on the other side of the door. She wanted him always to be there.

They hugged, but her body language conveyed that something was off.

"What's wrong, boo?" Steele asked.

"I don't know. I just haven't been feeling great these last few weeks. Every once in a blue moon, I look at myself in the mirror, and I don't seem to have as much emotional real estate anymore. I'm sure it's some form of a defense mechanism."

"I had a one-bedroom apartment on Johnson Drive before moving in here with you. I don't need a lot of real estate to be happy."

She smiled. "You know me. Always a work in progress."

Later, as they relaxed on the couch, 3J asked, "Ronnie, what are we doing?"

"We?"

"Yeah, we."

"We're doing what everyone is doing. Get up. Go to work. Come home to someone you love."

"I suppose that's right. But we seem to disagree on important things."

"What things?"

"Just things." She would rather not share the "things" with him.

He sighed. "3J, all I can do is to quote Barack: 'Even when we don't agree with each other, we find a way to live with each other.'"

Anyone could tell there were things 3J wasn't telling him. It was all over her face. She wasn't at peace. But finding a way to live together was the goal.

"Look, 3J, I know there's stuff going on you're not sharing. Attorney-client privileged stuff, I guess. But whatever. I can't stay mad at you, whatever is going on."

He smiled and hugged her, then whispered in her ear, "Who doesn't love to be loved, right?"

Chapter 56

THOSE CHITS

3J WAS AT her desk at 7:30 a.m. Monday morning. The receptionist called, just like the last time: "A Mr. Robbie McFadden and two gentlemen to see you, Ms. Jones."

She sighed, slumped her shoulders, and went to the twenty-ninth floor again to retrieve the guests. Again, she brought them to the War Room to talk. By now, they knew the way there.

Never any advanced notice or agenda from him. It was the McFadden way.

The Paxton case was now over. She had moved on to new matters. She had no inkling of why McFadden was back in her office.

They sat. She offered coffee or tea, and they declined. "Good job on the Paxton case, Ms. Jones. It came out the way it should have, don't you think?"

She nodded. "Sure. We won. Good result for the client. You helped make it happen. Thank you. I've moved on to the next case. There's always a next case." She smiled.

McFadden studied her. The master of silent moments. He wasn't ready to speak.

"Mr. McFadden, I'm not sure why you're here, but why can't we do this on the phone?"

His presence made her uncomfortable.

"We can, sometimes, but this one needs the personal touch," he answered, smiling. His smile didn't put her at ease, though; it had been curated with care and practice and designed to make someone uncomfortable. It was his own little mind game and he enjoyed that it worked as well as it did on her.

"This was never really about Paxton. I'm sure you figured that out."

She hadn't. "What do you mean?"

"No matter the testimony I heard, I'm not certain that he hasn't been pulling the wool over the eyes of a naïve group of banks for years. There's more going on there than meets the eye. Just a feeling I have. But I suspect you already know that. Not my problem. Not my interest."

She said nothing in response. Paxton had intimated. She had wondered. Pascale had begged off. Now McFadden seemed to know. A few seconds passed, and 3J asked, "Then what was this about?"

"First off, it was all about Leah Belle. She required my help. She worked for a bad man. Now he's moved on. Splattered all over downtown Wichita."

"You didn't have anything to do with his death, did you? Jesus."

"I would've been happy to help him launch from the top of the building, but I can report that I didn't. He was a one-man show. His last flight was a solo sortie."

3J shook her head. He could have just killed Shumaker if he wanted to and freed Thomason, but he didn't. Why not?

"Mr. McFadden, why are you here?"

He ignored her question. He'd tell his story on his own time and in his own way. It was how he did things. She knew that.

"Like I said, this was never about Paxton."

A few seconds of silence passed.

"You saw I was arrested on a bogus bribery charge?"

"I saw the news."

"It'll fade away. Always does. But the latest encounter with the police made me reflect on Boss Tom Pendergast. Remember him in the history books?"

"Yes. I've read about him. I read *Tom's Town*." *What the hell is he getting at?*

"People say I'm in one line of work or another. We don't need to talk about those divisions of my organization. My actual line of work: I own people. I learned that from Boss Tom. After he died, people rewrote history and said they had elected him during the years he was a boss. He held no elected office. But he ran the city from his modest lair at 1908 Main Street. Before his conviction plea, his office was always busy: petitioners, political operatives, business executives, and every-day citizens seeking favors or patronage would queue up and wait to see The Boss."

McFadden nodded as he paused for emphasis. 3J didn't want to be there but she had no choice and she listened.

"They all wanted favors. His operation was based on that and chits. He helped people out, and he owned people when he did it. When Boss Tom needed something, he'd call in the chit."

He stopped again this time to observe 3J's reaction. She knew where this conversation was heading. She took her hands from the tabletop where they rested and moved them to her lap. They were trembling. Maybe McFadden couldn't see them.

"Like you. You could have said no to me, but you didn't. You needed what I had to offer, and you took it. When you have a client to save, you're a 'whatever it takes' kind of gal. Not all lawyers stretch beyond the finish line for their clients. You do. But I'm sure you know this: 'Whatever it takes' is a noble motto, but it comes with consequences."

Ronnie Steele had told her that all the time, and now she was hearing it from McFadden. Was it possible they were ganging up on her? She rejected the notion. Not possible at all.

McFadden continued, "On this one, I was what it took. So… now… Ms. Jones, I own you."

He said these last words slowly and used his finger to point to her and then himself.

She stared at him; maybe it was even a glare. But she said nothing. Her hands trembled more. Part anger, part fear.

"I don't make it a practice to visit people I've helped. I don't need to remind them. I don't need to set it out for them. They know the score. But you? Well, I just wanted to make sure you understood where we stand. In person."

He continued, "Like I said. It was always about Leah Belle. She needed to step up and take her life back. She did. She needed to do it for herself. Not just run away from her guy. But take him down and get him out of her life. She did. That's why I didn't take down Shumaker. She did. She had to know she could do it. He needed to know she would, and she did. I hope that was the last thing to run through his mind when he jumped.

"I'm satisfied with how that part came out, and I thank you for your role in her freedom. But I helped you out, did you favors, and helped you win, and now you're in the book. I'm sure you know this part: once you're in the book, you stay in the book."

He nodded slowly at her. All she could do was watch and listen.

"Clear? Good. First off, this has been about Leah Belle. Second off, it's about you and my book."

She spoke softly, not like an attorney. "I don't know what it means to be in your book. But I do know I won't be able to do anything illegal or unethical for you. That would never happen. No matter the consequences. If you need a favor, find one that's legal and ethical."

McFadden narrowed his eyes and studied her. "Moxy. I like that. But I don't do pre-agreements. No handshake deals. That's not how it works. We'll see what I need from you and when, and then we'll see how it plays out. You have a line. Your morals. I get it. I have needs from time to time. Now, you get it. We'll just wait and see how your line and my needs," he paused, nodded again, and then finished, "align and crystallize."

He smiled. She didn't.

Align and crystallize? How deep have I dug my hole?

Neither spoke for a few moments. Then McFadden broke the silence. "One more thing, Ms. Jones. I know you and Ronnie Steele are a thing, and I know you don't want to talk about that with me. But we're not talking. You're just listening. Here are my thoughts. He's a good man despite his feelings toward me. But the fact is, if it wasn't for me, Ronnie Steele wouldn't have had a good job for twenty-five years and a good pension now. There's no vice squad without someone like me to investigate and harass. It's symbiotic. Cops and mobsters. Favors and chits. Needs and wants. They all make the world go round, right? Whatever it takes."

McFadden nodded one last time. It was his punctuation mark at the end of a meeting, and he stood to leave. "Good meeting, Counselor. I enjoy our talks. We'll be in touch."

He was a risk-taker in a risky business. But 3J was just starting to learn that where there is risk, the house always wins.

She escorted the trio to the elevator. No handshake this time. She returned to her desk. She felt lucky Pascale hadn't come into work early only to find her with McFadden again in the War Room.

Her hands were still trembling with the confirmation that her name was in *the book*. The obligor on numerous chits. A Greene Madison partner in a mobster's book of markers, each one with her name on it.

Ronnie had warned her, but she ignored him. Pascale had silently admonished her, and she shut him out. Now she had to face the facts: it isn't always all right today and won't always be all right tomorrow. No matter what McFadden might do or say, he was no Good Samaritan.

The new normal begins here, she realized. *And what a mess it is going to be.*

Acknowledgments

Thanks and gratitude:

To my family, Loren, Zac, Isabel, and Emily for letting me write it all down.

To my friends. For supporting me, enduring me, commiserating with me, laughing with me, and encouraging me to keep writing. I'm a lucky dude.

To Celina Tio for being the best chef I've ever known—visit *The Belfry*, people.

Resources

All Music for all its content-rich history of jazz

"Five Little Known Historic Mob Locations in Kansas City" by Gina Kaufmann, Sylvia Maria Gross, and Matthew Long-Middleton *https://www.kcur.org/show/central-standard/2015-04-22/5-little-known-historic-mob-locations-in-kansas-city*

Forgotten Tales of Kansas City by Paul Kirkman and Kristen Solecki

"The History of the Kansas City Family" by Allan May *http://crimemagazine.com/history-kansas-city-family*

Kansas City Crime Central: 150 Years of Outlaws, Kidnappers, Mobsters and Their Victims by Monroe Dodd

Kansas City Jazz: A Little Evil Will Do You Good by Con Chapman

Kansas City Jazz: From Ragtime to Bebop – A History by Frank Driggs and Chuck Haddix

Mob Girl: A Woman's Life in the Underworld by Teresa Carpenter

Mobsters in Our Midst – The Kansas City Crime Family by William Ouseley

Storied & Scandalous Kansas City: A History of Corruption, Mischief and a Whole Lot of Booze by Karla Deel

Tom's Town: Kansas City and the Pendergast Legend (Volume 1) by William M. Reddig

Wide-Open Town: Kansas City in the Pendergast Era edited by Diane Mutti Burke, Jason Roe, and John Herron

About the Author

Mark Shaiken lives with his wife, Loren, and their dog, Emily, in Denver, Colorado. He attended Haverford College and Washburn University and practiced commercial bankruptcy law for several decades before moving on in 2019 to write, volunteer, travel, and play music.

In addition to his award-winning memoir (of a not famous lawyer) *And... Just Like That: Essays on a Life Before, During, and After the Law* and his award-winning book of essays on life, love, reinvention, and aging (*It's What Makes Me... Me, A Retired Attorney's Relationship With Life and Times*), he is the author of five books in the award-winning 3J legal thriller series: *Fresh Start, Automatic Stay, Unfair Discrimination, Cram Down,* and this latest, *For Cause.*

Connect with Mark at *http://markshaikenauthor.com.*

Review Request

You would make an author happy if you would please leave a short review of *For Cause* on Amazon, Goodreads, or wherever else you find your reading pleasure.

My Library

The 3J Legal Thriller Series:

Fresh Start

Automatic Stay

Unfair Discrimination

Cram Down

For Cause

Essays:

*And… Just Like That: Essays on a Life
Before, During and After the Law*

*It's What Makes Me… Me… A Retired Attorney's
Relationship With Life and Times*

Legal Treatise:

Automatic Stay Litigation in Bankruptcy
(coauthored with Cindi Woolery)

Learn more about each book at my Amazon Author Page:
*https://www.amazon.com/stores/Mark-A.-Shaiken/author/
B001KDYFCU?*

www.ingramcontent.com/pod-product-compliance
Lightning Source LLC
Chambersburg PA
CBHW032140190626
46814CB00005BA/1775